WALKING IN MY SISTER'S SHADOW

A FICTION DRAMA

BY

Angela Mae Morrison-AKA Darnell

Kindle   direct

Publishing

1

Copyright © Angela Mae Morrison-AKA Darnell

Kindle   Direct

                Publishing

First published 2025

Kindle Direct Publishing (UK Office)

44 Ashbourne Drive

Coxhoe

DH6 4SW

Edited by: C Leckie (USA)

J. Morrison (UK)

ABOUT THE AUTHOR

Angela Mae Morrison, also known as Darnell, is a dedicated registered nurse with a wealth of healthcare experience and a strong passion for storytelling. She earned her nursing qualifications from Wolverhampton University and Birmingham City University and has spent years caring for patients with compassion, professionalism, and dedication. Currently working part-time as a nurse, Angela balances her clinical career with her lifelong love of writing. Inspired by everyday experiences, family life, and the subtle humour and mysteries in ordinary moments, she offers a fresh and heartfelt perspective in her stories.

Angela lives in Birmingham, England, with her husband Roy and their cherished children. A devoted nurse and passionate writer, she draws inspiration from her experiences in both healthcare and home life. Whether she's tending to patients or crafting heartfelt stories, Angela's work reflects her deep compassion and commitment to others. Outside of her professional life, Angela enjoys the simple pleasures, spending time with her family, cooking comforting meals, baking with love, and taking quiet moments to reflect. Her Christian faith is the cornerstone of her journey, grounding her through challenges and inspiring hope in all that she does.

Through her writing, Angela seeks to uplift, encourage, and connect with readers on a meaningful level. Her writing combines warmth, wit, and realism, drawing on her experiences as a nurse and mother. Whether she's solving household mysteries or capturing the emotions of family life, Angela invites readers into stories that feel familiar, yet full of unexpected twists.

DEDICATION

This story is dedicated to anyone who has ever felt overshadowed by a sibling, a friend, expectations, or the weight of someone's light.

To those who have struggled to be seen, to be heard, or to believe they were enough on their own.

May you find the courage to step out of the shadows, to walk your path, and to trust that your voice, your journey, and your light are just as worthy.

You don't have to live in anyone's shadow forever. You were always meant to shine.

INTRODUCTION

Melina's elder sister, Monica, is getting married: a grand event that has the entire town buzzing with excitement. Monica is admired not only for her striking beauty but also for her graceful presence, which naturally draws attention wherever she goes. For as long as Melina can remember, Monica has been the shining star in their family, the one praised by teachers, admired by relatives, and held up by their parents as the ideal. Melina, by contrast, often feels like she exists in her sister's shadow. Her quiet nature and thoughtful demeanour are usually overlooked, and her parents frequently encourage her to be more like Monica.

These constant comparisons leave Melina feeling invisible and unappreciated, breeding a quiet frustration she keeps mostly to herself. As wedding preparations unfold and all eyes turn to Monica, Melina is once again expected to play the supporting role. While she loves her sister deeply, she struggles internally with feelings of being overlooked, wrestling with the desire to be seen and valued for who she truly is, not who others expect her to be. Monica has always possessed a natural charm, an effortless grace that turns heads, wins hearts, and often earns forgiveness without the need for an apology. She has been the golden girl for as long as anyone can remember, radiant, admired, and untouchable. Now, with her wedding day fast approaching, the spotlight is brighter than ever. Meanwhile, her younger sister, Melina, is cast once again in the familiar role of the quiet supporter, the dutiful maid of honour, expected to smile, assist, and stay in line. But when Melina uncovers a deeply buried secret about the family of Monica's fiancé, a secret powerful enough to shatter reputations and cast a long shadow over the perfect day, she is forced to confront an impossible choice. Should she reveal the truth and risk destroying the one relationship she has always tried to protect? Or stay silent and allow the wedding, and the illusion, to go on? Torn between loyalty and integrity, Melina begins to question not just the wedding, but the years of quiet comparison, unspoken resentment, and the pressure of always standing second to someone else's light.

Walking in My Sister's Shadow is a poignant and gripping story of family, identity, and the heavy price of silence. It explores the fragile bonds between sisters, the courage it takes to speak out, and the strength required to step out from behind someone else's brilliance and finally claim your own. Because sometimes, stepping out of the shadows doesn't just change your path, it sets the whole stage alight.

WALKING IN MY SISTER'S SHADOW

PART ONE

THE DRIVE TO THE COUNTRYSIDE.

CHAPTER ONE

The drive to the countryside

The drive to the country was longer than Melina remembered, each mile stretching out like a silent accusation. The highways twisted endlessly ahead of them, and what once felt familiar now seemed eerily distant. The sleepy towns they passed, marked by rusted signs, faded storefronts, and cracked sidewalks, brought with them a heavy nostalgia she didn't ask for. The rolling green fields blurred past her window like ghosts of a childhood she had long since tried to leave behind. Even the old brick buildings, sturdy and unchanged, seemed to whisper fragments of the past she had buried: hushed arguments behind closed doors, forced smiles at family dinners, and Monica always shining just a bit too brightly. Beside her in the back seat, her mother hummed softly to a tune Melina didn't recognize. The sound, meant to soothe, only tightened the knot in her chest. It was too gentle, too rehearsed, like a lullaby for someone else's comfort. Her mother's fingers twisted the edge of her scarf in a nervous rhythm, as though she were trying to hold something in, words, perhaps, or regrets. Up front, her father drove in his usual quiet way, hands steady on the wheel. Now and then, he flicked his gaze to the rearview mirror, as if checking that his passengers were still there, that the words unsaid between them hadn't filled the car to bursting. Melina watched the landscape roll by in streaks of green and gold, her own reflection hovering faintly in the glass, familiar, but somehow distant. She pressed her forehead lightly against the window, feeling the coolness seep into her skin, a grounding sensation she'd craved since the morning. No one spoke for a long stretch of road. The silence was heavy, punctuated only by the quiet thrum of tyres and the gentle rattle of loose coins in the glove box. Melina counted telephone poles, watched clouds drift, and tried not to think about Monica or the secret that now sat between her ribs like a stone. But the thoughts always returned, circling back to her in the hush. He glanced back at Melina through the rearview mirror. His eyes were warm but distant, shadowed with the kind of weariness that came from revisiting a place that felt more like a memory than a home. He looked like a man returning to a version of himself he no longer recognized.

"You're going to be okay," her mother said at last, her voice barely more than a whisper, frayed at the edges. She fidgeted with the end of her scarf, looping it through her fingers again: again, a small, familiar motion that betrayed her unease. The words drifted into the quiet like a fragile offering, spoken more to the stillness than to Melina herself. Melina didn't respond. She couldn't. Her throat was tight, and the ache deep in her chest had settled there like something permanent. *Okay* felt miles away, impossible, almost cruel. How could she be okay, with the weight of the secret pressing down on her ribs, and the wedding looming ahead like a gathering storm she couldn't outrun? Outside, the wind rattled the windows, as if echoing the unrest inside her. Her mother looked at her but didn't press further, and Melina was grateful. Some truths weren't meant to be spoken yet, not here, not now. But the silence between them stretched thin, straining under everything unsaid

"I'm fine," Melina muttered, though she wasn't sure if she was trying to convince her mother or herself. Her sister's engagement should have been a reason for celebration. However, the truth was that Melina felt nothing but dread. Monica, the golden child, the one who had everything, beauty, intelligence, and a life everyone admired, was getting married. And for the first time in Melina's life, it wasn't just the usual unease of living in Monica's shadow. There was a growing, insistent feeling gnawing at her stomach. Something wasn't right. The road narrowed as they turned off the main highway, winding between tall hedgerows and clusters of overgrown trees that cast long shadows across the car. Melina shifted in her seat, hugging her arms around her middle, the countryside pressing in with a strange, heavy quiet. Although she had taken this trip several times, each visit to her grandparents' house felt like years had passed. The creaky front door, the lavender soap in the bathroom, and the chill of the stone kitchen floor were all familiar yet distant memories.

"Nearly there," her father said softly, his voice cutting through the silence like a pebble dropped into still water. He didn't look back this time, just kept his eyes fixed on the road ahead. Melina glanced out the window. The late afternoon light slanted golden across the fields, making the world outside look almost too perfect, like something out of an old photograph. But the beauty only made her feel more restless. This place wasn't hers anymore. Maybe it never had been. Her mother adjusted the radio's volume, letting a low instrumental tune drift through the car. She hadn't said much since they'd left home, except for the occasional small talk and that soft, lingering "You're going to be okay." Melina knew better than to believe it. Things weren't okay. Not with Monica's wedding looming and the secret she now carried like a stone in her pocket.

The narrow road curved sharply, and suddenly the house came into view, tucked between two tall oak trees, its white paint weathered and peeling, the shutters hanging slightly crooked like they always had. A swing still dangled from the old maple in the front yard, swaying gently in the breeze. Melina's chest tightened. So little had changed, and yet she felt like an outsider pulling into someone else's life. When they finally pulled up to the old farmhouse where the rest of the family lived, the sight of it, the ivy creeping up the walls, the front porch that sagged under the weight of too many summers, stirred a deep ache in her heart. She'd spent so many years here, running through these fields, learning to ride bikes on the cracked asphalt driveway. Yet now, it felt more like a place she'd outgrown, a place she didn't belong anymore.

Her father eased the car into the gravel driveway and killed the engine. For a moment, no one moved.

"Ready?" her mother asked, turning around in her seat to face her. Melina gave the smallest nod she could manage. She wasn't ready, not for the house, not for the memories, and certainly not for the questions that would come with the weekend. But she opened the car door, anyway, letting the cool country air wash over her. Somewhere behind the house, a dog barked. A screen door slammed. The weekend had begun. Her aunt May was the first to greet them, her wide smile barely hiding the scrutiny in her eyes as she pulled Melina into an embrace.

"Mel! It's been too long!" May's voice was thick with the country accent Melina had tried so hard to lose over the years.

"Hey, Aunt May," Melina replied, although her smile felt forced. As they stepped into the house, a wave of warm air and louder voices washed over Melina, enveloping her in a strange mix of comfort and discomfort. The living room buzzed with conversation and movement, filled with the familiar scent of wood polish, lavender, and something baking in the kitchen, her grandmother's doing, no doubt. A familiar array of faces greeted her: some she had grown up with, others she only saw at weddings, funerals, and rare holiday gatherings. Their expressions were warm, but their smiles stretched just a little too tight; hugs lingered slightly too long, as if everyone was trying a bit too hard. Her

13

grandmother, smaller than Melina remembered, sat hunched in her favourite chair by the window, knitting needles clicking rhythmically as sunlight pooled around her feet. Her hair, once thick and dark, had turned into a soft cloud of grey, and her eyes lit up briefly when they met Melina's. No words were needed, just a small smile, a nod of recognition, then the needles continued their quiet dance. The younger cousins, a tangle of limbs and energy, lounged across the couch, exchanging jokes and stories with the carefree ease of those unburdened by adult expectations. They barely noticed Melina slipping into the room, their laughter spilling over like soda fizz: sticky and sweet. Her grandfather, still sturdy but slower than before, occupied his usual armchair, engaged in a quiet conversation with an old family friend whose name Melina couldn't recall. His deep voice rumbled low, comforting and steadying, a grounding presence in a room that felt both too full and not full enough at the same time. And then there was Monica.

She stood in the centre of it all, radiant as always, effortlessly commanding attention without even trying. Her laughter rose above the rest, light and golden, enveloping the room like the afternoon sun pouring through the open windows. Her hair was perfectly styled, her dress impeccable, her posture graceful. People turned to her as if by instinct, drawn to her glow. Melina watched as her sister accepted compliments with practiced humility, her smile never faltering. In that moment, Melina felt it again, the invisible distance between them. Monica was the centre of gravity in every room she entered, while Melina hovered at the edge, orbiting quietly, unseen. She lingered near the doorway, unsure whether to step fully into the room or retreat to the kitchen. No one had noticed her yet. And a small part of her liked it that way, to be invisible.

Melina paused in the doorway, the weight of her sister's presence pressing down on her. Monica was flawless, as always.

"We're all here waiting for you all to hear Melina's news. Melina," her father said gently, his voice breaking through her thoughts. Melina turned to him, her heart beating faster. She could feel the eyes of the family on her now, waiting. Monica stood, looking up at her with that same bright smile, oblivious to the storm brewing in Melina's chest. Melina cleared her throat.

"Well, um, we have some exciting news," she began, her voice betraying the nerves she hadn't been able to mask.

"Monica... Monica's getting married." She wanted to say it in a very poised way, but it came out all edgy. The room fell into a hush, the news settling like a weight on everyone's shoulders. Melina could feel their eyes on her: her father, her aunt, her grandmother, even the cousins who had always looked up to Monica, and now would look to her for approval, too. Melina glanced at Monica, who was already beaming, holding up her left hand with the engagement ring gleaming like a promise. It was hard to focus on anything but Monica's laughter, the way it floated above the conversation like it had been trained to. She could do no wrong. And there was Melina, tucked away in the corner, her voice muffled by the weight of her sister's spotlight. Monica had planned to draw attention by asking Melina to make the announcement, putting herself more in the spotlight and staying ahead of Melina.

"So, who's the lucky man?" her cousin Johnny asked, breaking the silence that had settled like dust. His tone was casual, but there was a flicker of curiosity behind his words that made everyone glance up from their cups and half-finished conversations. The question snapped Melina back to the moment. She blinked, adjusting to the present like someone waking from a dream. Monica smiled, her lips curling in that effortless, camera-ready way she'd mastered years ago. Without a word, she reached into her purse and pulled out a photo, pristine and perfectly framed. She didn't hold it up herself. Instead, she handed it to Melina, an unspoken command, as if delegating a task to an assistant rather than a sister.

"Here, show them," Monica said lightly, eyes already scanning the room for the next reaction. Melina took the photo without hesitation. It was always like this. Monica led, and Melina followed. Not out of fear, or resentment, but habit. Family gatherings had long been Monica's stage, and Melina had learned how to navigate the wings, helping her sister shine from just out of the spotlight. She held up the picture for the rest of the family to see, a well-dressed man with a confident smile and arms draped around Monica's shoulders. There were approving nods, a few raised eyebrows, and a knowing hum from Aunt May.

Monica soaked in the attention, her smile brightening with every compliment. Melina didn't mind. Not really. Despite everything. The imbalance, the occasional sting, she still loved her big sister. Still looked up to her, even if from a few steps behind. But as she passed the photo along, something twisted inside her, a quiet reminder that admiration could exist alongside something else. Something heavier. Something she hadn't dared to name yet.

"This is Sylvester Longhorn: as in *the* Longhorns of Longhorn Industries," she said with a proud grin, her voice lifting with barely concealed excitement. "They've got ventures all over the place, even overseas." She paused for effect, eyes twinkling.

"You'll all meet him soon enough." Melina had already had the pleasure, as had Mom and Dad. The rest of you will get your chance tomorrow; he's flying in sometime in the morning. His family owns their own private jet," Monica continued, the pride in her voice unmistakable. "And despite his incredibly demanding schedule, he's carving out time just to meet the rest of my amazing family." She smiled, a soft glow of affection lighting her face. "That's just the kind of man he is: thoughtful, grounded, and genuinely interested in the people I love." She paused for a moment, clearly touched. "It means the world to me that he's making this effort," she said, her voice soft with emotion. "Even though he's a promising cardiothoracic surgeon, on the fast track in his field, he still finds time to support the family business when needed. And this weekend? It's supposed to be his only time off in weeks. He could've chosen to be anywhere, Geneva, New York, Tokyo, but even while technically on-call, he's choosing to be here with us. "She smiled gently, her eyes sweeping the room, as if already imagining him there. "He always says family means more to him than any boardroom, surgery, or business deal. That's just the kind of person he is. dedicated, thoughtful, and grounded." Her voice brightened.

"I really can't wait for you all to meet him. I just know you'll love him as much as I do."

There was a brief silence after Monica finished, the kind that falls when people are still processing something meaningful. Then came the soft murmur of reactions.

"Oh wow," Aunt May said, eyebrows raised. "A heart surgeon *and* a businessman? Sounds like someone straight out of a movie."

"He sounds impressive," Dad said, though his voice held that subtle edge of protective skepticism. "Let's just hope he's not *too* good to be true," Melina smirked. "As long as he's not one of those workaholic types who forget how to laugh." Knowing the family has a big secret hiding, she will have to tell Monica, but how? She would believe I was jealous or something. Melina smirked, trying to keep her tone light. "As long as he's not one of those workaholic types who forget how to laugh." Everyone in the room chuckled, and Monica smiled, but Melina's heart wasn't in it.

Behind the teasing glint in her eyes, a storm was brewing. She knew something; something the rest of the family didn't or perhaps chose not to see. A secret that had been quietly festering beneath the polished surface of the Longhorn name. And whether by accident or fate, she'd stumbled across it. She shifted in her seat, her smirk fading the moment the attention moved elsewhere. *I have to tell her,* she thought, eyes flicking briefly toward Monica, who looked so happy, so sure. *But how?* Would Monica believe her? Or worse, would she think she was just jealous? That thought stung more than Melina expected. She and Monica were sisters, just two years apart, but their lives had always moved in opposite directions. As children, they were inseparable: they shared clothes, toys, inside jokes, and even whispered dreams under the covers during thunderstorms. They'd once played dress-up with their mother's scarves and heels, pretending they were famous actresses walking red carpets.

But somewhere in their late teens, the warmth between them began to thin. Monica naturally stepped into the spotlight, graceful, confident, and endlessly praised. She became the one everyone looked to first, the one who sparkled at family dinners and school events alike. And Melina? She learned how to blend into the background/shadows. Monica never seemed to notice, or maybe she did and didn't care. She'd laugh off Melina's interests, wave off her opinions, and say things like, *"Mel, that's not your style,"* or *"You wouldn't like that kind of thing anyway,"* always with a bright smile that made it seem harmless. But it wasn't. It chipped away at Melina, piece by piece. And the family? They played along, almost unconsciously, reinforcing Monica's throne. She was the golden girl, the one who could do no wrong. The one they protected, celebrated, and excused. Now, with Monica's wedding around the corner and a wealthy, accomplished fiancé in the picture, she seemed more untouchable than ever. Her happiness wrapped itself around Sylvester like a ribbon, tight and glossy. Saying anything that might unravel that, especially now, felt like dropping a grenade into a glasshouse. But Melina knew something she couldn't unknow. A secret. A shadow lurked just behind Sylvester's polished smile. And as much as she wanted to keep the peace, silence was starting to feel like betrayal. Melina folded her arms, quietly battling the rising unease in her chest. The clock was ticking. Tomorrow, he'd arrive. And once that door opened, everything might change, for better... or not. Monica laughed, brushing a lock of hair behind her ear. "He's actually got a great sense of humour, dry, but clever. And no, he's not one of those overly serious types. He knows how to balance things. It's one of the reasons I fell for him."

"How did you two even meet?" Grandma chimed in, leaning forward slightly with interest. Monica's expression softened. "We met during a medical conference in Chicago last year. I was there helping coordinate logistics for a nonprofit health initiative, and he was one of the guest speakers. We kept bumping into each other in the most random ways, elevators, coffee lines, the hotel gym." She smiled at the memory. "It was like the universe kept nudging us together." A few chuckles rippled around the room.

"And here we are," she said, with a breath of gratitude. "Now he's coming here, to meet all of you: my heart and my roots."

"Mel! Could you pass the picture around again? Show them my handsome fiancé," Monica called out, her voice laced with pride and that usual sparkle she reserved for moments when all eyes were on her. "After all, *you're* the one making the big announcement," she added with a grin, as if it were a favour Melina had volunteered for rather than been assigned. Melina reached into her bag, her fingers brushing the edges of the photo. She pulled it out carefully, her gaze catching on it for just a second longer than necessary. There he was again, Monica's fiancé. Charming. Polished. The kind of man who smiled like he knew the world would always tilt in his favour. She had met him a few times, polite dinners, clinking glasses, practiced small talk, but it wasn't him that made her uneasy. It was what she'd heard. Whispers about his family that never made it to the surface of conversations. Stories half-told, abruptly ended. Things people didn't say. And the more Melina thought about it, the more it knotted something in her stomach, tight and unshakable. Still, she stood and passed the photo along the table, forcing a smile as relatives leaned in to look. There were murmurs of approval, a few dramatic sighs from the aunts, and someone joked about wedding bells and babies. Monica beamed from her place at the table, basking in it all, as if this moment had been rehearsed in her mind for years. Melina sat down quietly, her hand brushing her lap to steady herself. She wanted to be happy for her sister. She did. But there was something about that smile in the photo, something behind it that made her wonder if Monica had any idea what she was walking into.

Or worse... if she did.

There was something beneath their polished exterior that unsettled her, an undercurrent she couldn't name but felt all the same. Whispers. Reputations. The kind of things people avoided mentioning in polite company. The fiancé looked perfect on paper: elegant, composed, disarmingly charming. The sort of man who knew exactly when to smile, and how to make people feel like they were the only ones in the room. But Melina had learned not to trust surfaces. She'd seen too many people wear masks so well they forgot they were pretending. And there was something about him, no, about *them*, his family felt too clean, too practiced, like a story edited too many times to be real. What was Monica getting herself into?

A knot of worry tightened in her chest. Her sister had always been drawn to the fairytale version of things, to glittering beginnings and beautiful promises. But Melina knew that sometimes, behind the shimmer, there was rot. She couldn't ignore it, not now. Not with the wedding closing in like a train she couldn't stop. If there was something to uncover, she would have to do it quietly. Carefully. And without Monica suspecting a thing. Because if she were wrong, she'd be accused of jealousy or sabotage. But if she was right... Melina glanced down at the photo again, her fingers cold against its glossy surface. She had to be sure.

CHAPTER TWO

Melina had never been the suspicious type. She preferred books to gossip, solitude to confrontation. But something about Sylvester Longhorn Monica's charming, too-perfect fiancé, made her skin prickle, not in the romantic way Monica claimed it did for her, but in the *something's off* kind of way. She hadn't meant to snoop. All she intended was to drop off a few old family photo albums and a stack of wedding magazines, something their mother had insisted be sorted before the upcoming engagement party in the country. Wanting company for the trip, and because Anna was the only one who drove, Melina had asked her to come along. It also seemed like the perfect opportunity for Anna to meet Sylvester, Monica's elusive and oh-so-impressive fiancé, finally. The Longhorn estate was as grand as Monica had described, with imposing iron gates, perfectly trimmed hedges, and a driveway that curved like it had somewhere important to be. But as Melina stepped out of the car, ready to ring the bell and hand over the bundle, something caught her eye. And just like that, she stopped cold. There, just beyond the hedgerow, where the driveway met the side garden, she saw and overheard something she wasn't supposed to see and hear voices. She beckoned to Anna, A shadow of a figure. A flash of movement. A voice she recognized, too familiar, too intimate. Her heart began to pound. But when they arrived at the Longhorn estate, a sprawling manor nestled behind wrought-iron gates and immaculate hedges, Melina caught sight of something or someone that made her freeze in her tracks. Her breath hitched, and the cheerful words she'd been rehearsing vanished. Whatever she thought she knew about Monica's picture-perfect future unravelled in an instant. In the sunroom, through a crack in the slightly ajar door, Sylvester was arguing with an older man, his father, Melina guessed, or some other family member. Their voices were low but tense.

Melina remembered the second time she met too well. The voices echoed from the kitchen, too close, too familiar. She walked in for a glass of water, but the words were sharp enough to slice through her already frayed nerves. Melina wants to warn Monica, but she knows how her sister is likely to react. Monica's world is perfect, and revealing the secret could shatter everything. Or worse, it could make her feel betrayed. There's the pressure of deciding whether to protect Monica from the truth or finally step out from under her shadow by revealing it. Melina gathers the courage to tell Monica. The conversation could be intense- Monica might react with disbelief or even anger. She could accuse Melina of being jealous or trying to ruin her happiness, or she might be hurt and confused by the revelation. The tension at this moment stems from the long-standing dynamic between them: Melina's deep-seated resentment and Monica's seemingly untouchable position in the family.

"You can't keep pretending, Sylvester. She doesn't know who you are, who **we** are. If this goes public."

"It won't," Sylvester snapped.

"No one's digging. Besides, Monica's blind with love. And remember, I am a promising and prominent young cardiologist. Monica will believe everything I said. Melina stepped back, heart hammering. *Pretending? Go public? What was he talking about?* She slipped out unnoticed, her footsteps light against the creaking floorboards, her breath held as though even the walls might betray her. But once outside, the quiet only amplified the chaos in her mind. Her thoughts raced all the way home, looping back to the same question: *Was it true?* Could Monica be marrying into a lie? Confronting her sister without proof was pointless. Monica would laugh it off or, worse, turn it into another accusation. *"You've always been jealous, Melina." "Why can't you just be happy for me?"* The same tired refrains that Melina had heard too many times before. Words that stuck like splinters, no matter how many times she tried to brush them off. So, she did something she never imagined herself doing, she started digging. Quietly, carefully. She sifted through public records, scanned old newspaper clippings, and trawled through social media accounts, piecing together bits of information like a puzzle that no one else seemed to notice was broken. It was slow, nerve-wracking work. But it gave her a strange sense of control in a world where she had always felt voiceless. Just as her thoughts threatened to spiral again, a sudden noise brought her crashing back to the present: the thud of a door, the creak of a floorboard, and then the familiar rasp of her grandmother's voice floating from the living room.

"Mel," her grandmother called gently, "come here and give your gran a hug." Melina blinked, momentarily disoriented. The past and the present were so tightly tangled in her mind these days that it was hard to tell where one ended, and the other began. She hesitated, then stood, forcing a smile onto her face. Whatever secrets she was chasing, whatever truth she hoped to uncover, it would have to wait. For now, she was just a granddaughter in her grandmother's house, summoned back into a world that felt both comforting and suffocating all at once.

CHAPTER THREE

The living room buzzed with overlapping voices as the family chatted animatedly, each trying to be heard over the other. The charming country house, with its warm wooden beams and cozy furnishings, welcomed the visitors who had driven up for their usual weekend escape, completely unaware of Monica's big news. As soon as she held out her hand, gasps and delighted murmurs filled the room. The engagement ring sparkled under the soft lamplight, and just like that, Monica became the centre of attention, basking in the joy and admiration. In all the excitement, Melina faded quietly into the background, her presence almost forgotten. Still, she smiled, content to watch from the sidelines as laughter echoed and stories spilled into the night. Later, as the evening settled into a gentle calm, Monica smiled at her grandmother, "Gran, could you make your famous hot cocoa like you used to when we were kids?" she asked. Then, turning to her sister, she added with a teasing smile,

"

Do you remember, Mel?" "Yes," Melina replied softly, her smile warm but touched with something quieter, something only she noticed.

"What about me?" asked Eton, the second child. "You never really liked cocoa," stated Monica. "I know," replied Eton,

"But when Gran made it, it just tasted different." "Different?" Monica and Melina said simultaneously.

"You mean it's delicious." Everyone started laughing.

"Okay," said Gran. "Cocoa for everyone".

Moved by the memory, the family agreed. Soon, the familiar scent of cinnamon and chocolate filled the air, bringing with it a comfort only childhood could offer. The room grew quieter, cozier, and for a moment, everyone was simply together, past and present woven into one sweet, shared tradition. As the cocoa simmered in the kitchen, the conversations softened, drifting into stories from years gone by. Laughter erupted when Uncle David reminded everyone of the time Monica tried to "marry" the neighbour's Labrador with a paper ring and a bouquet of dandelions. Monica rolled her eyes, but her laughter was genuine, her cheeks flushed with warmth. Then, without missing a beat, Monica launched into one of her classic interrogations.

"So," she said, tilting her head with exaggerated curiosity, "do you have a boyfriend? When are you going back to university? How's the campus? Do you like it?" I raised a hand to stop the questions.

"No to the first question, yes to the others."

She gave me a playful, knowing look, as if she could read more into my answers than I'd offered. But I knew her too well. The questions were just surface chatter, her way of ticking boxes. I wasn't convinced she was all that interested in my studies; Monica's world tended to revolve around Monica. She had good intentions, but a sense of self-importance often accompanied her. She cared but rarely listened beyond her voice. Still, a part of me hoped she was trying. That underneath the wedding plans and hair trials and endless discussions about flower arrangements, there was a piece of her that genuinely wanted to connect with me, not just as her little sister in a matching dress, but as someone with a life of her own. "You'll be one of the bridesmaids," Monica announced with a teasing grin. "So, no more cakes, young lady, and go easy on the cocoa, or you won't fit into the dress!" I stared at her, stunned.

"I'm not fat, Monica. That was mean." Her smile faltered for a moment, and she reached out, softening her tone. "I didn't mean it like that," she said gently. "You're perfect. I was just teasing. but maybe the dressmaker won't be so forgiving. "I looked away, blinking fast. Jokes had a funny way of cutting deeper when they came from someone you looked up to.

"That's just a silly joke, Mel," she said, her voice gentler now. She reached out and tucked a strand of hair behind my ear, a gesture she'd done since I was little.

"You're perfect, you hear me? I was only teasing…but maybe the dressmaker won't be as forgiving. She's a nightmare about measurements." I looked down at my hands, picking at a chipped nail.

"It didn't sound like a joke."

She sighed and sank into the seat beside me. "I forget sometimes," she said quietly. "Those words can land differently when they come from me. I'm sorry." I shrugged, not ready to let it go but not wanting to fight either. "It's just, I don't want to feel like I have to change to be part of your day."

"You don't," Monica said firmly. "You're my sister. I want you standing next to me just as you are. Cocoa and all."

That made me smile a little. She bumped her shoulder against mine.

"Besides. she added, I'll make sure you come and choose the dress with me, and make sure it is stretchy". I laughed, finally, the tension starting to melt. "Stretchy, huh? Maybe I'll have another slice of cake after all."

Monica grinned, clearly relieved. "Now you're just being rebellious."

"I learned from the best."

She rolled her eyes, but her smile lingered. "You always did know how to twist things around on me." We sat in a comfortable silence for a moment, the kind that only years of shared bedrooms, whispered secrets, and stolen clothes could create. The late afternoon light slanted through the window, catching the dust in the air like gold.

"Remember when you tried to cut your own bangs the night before Aunt May's wedding?" she said suddenly, chuckling. "And I had to fix them with safety scissors and lip balm?" I groaned. "And you told me it looked great, until I saw the photos and realized I had a zigzag fringe like a deranged cartoon character."

"Hey, I was trying to be supportive," Monica said, nudging me. "That's what sisters do."

"Lies and sabotage?"

"Lies and loyalty," she corrected, her voice warm. "And a little sabotage, maybe, but only the kind that builds character."

I leaned against her shoulder, the way I used to when we were younger, and the world felt bigger and scarier than it does now. "Thanks for saying sorry," I murmured.

"You didn't have to".

"No," she said, wrapping an arm around me, "but I wanted to. You matter to me more than dresses or photos or cakes. "I closed my eyes for a second, holding the moment close. Weddings were stressful. Families could be complicated. But Monica and I, we'd always find our way back to this. To understand. To each other. Melina sat quietly at the edge of the couch, cupping her mug with both hands. The cocoa was just as she remembered, creamy, rich, with that little hint of nutmeg Gran always insisted was the secret ingredient. She watched Monica glowing in the centre of the room, surrounded by love and attention, and felt the familiar tug in her chest. She was happy for her sister, truly. But there was something about being back in that house, surrounded by memories, that made the space inside her feel a little emptier. Gran, sensing more than anyone else did, sat beside Melina and gave her knee a gentle pat. "You are doing all right, love?" she asked quietly. Melina nodded.

"Just tired, that's all."

Gran didn't press. She just smiled and leaned in, whispering,

"You've always had the kindest heart. Don't let it go unnoticed forever."

Across the room, Monica was already holding court, her voice animated as she spoke about wedding venues, colour palettes, and floral arrangements. Her eyes sparkled with excitement, her hands dancing through the air as she painted a picture of her perfect day. The others leaned in eagerly, captivated, offering suggestions, reminiscing about their own weddings, and laughing at old family mishaps. The living room seemed to glow with warmth, filled with the soft hum of shared joy and anticipation. Someone passed around a photo album; another reached for a glass of wine; cheeks flushed with laughter. The mood was light, festive, almost magical. For a moment, it was as though time had folded in on itself, suspending them all in a bubble of celebration and storybook dreams. And yet, from where Melina stood, it felt like watching a play from behind a curtain. She could see the happiness, hear the laughter, even recognize the love in the room, but none of it seemed to reach her. Not really. Monica shone effortlessly at the centre of it all, and as always, Melina lingered quietly on the edge, wondering if anyone noticed how far away, she felt.

CHAPTER FOUR

Melina moved to the far end of the room, settling into the edge of the worn loveseat near the fireplace. From there, she could observe without being drawn in, her hands folded neatly in her lap, her expression unreadable. The conversation swirled around her stories of honeymoons, the drama of guest lists, the agony of choosing the right shade of ivory, but none of it touched her. She nodded when expected, smiled faintly at the appropriate moments, but inside, she felt miles away.

It wasn't that she didn't want to be happy for Monica. A part of her did truly: Her sister was radiant, in love, and standing on the cusp of the life she had always dreamed of. But beneath that surface-level pride was something heavier: a quiet ache, a frustration that twisted just beneath her ribs. It wasn't jealousy, not exactly. It was the ache of never being the one people leaned toward when they spoke of dreams or plans or futures. It was the weariness of always being the support beam in someone else's story, never the headline. She glanced at Monica, who was now laughing with their aunts about bridesmaid dresses and colour-coordinated shoes. Everything came easily to her: attention, approval, praise. And now, a picture-perfect wedding to complete the fairytale. Melina's fingers curled slightly against her knee. They were unaware of Monica's fiancé's secrets and the impending collapse of the fragile illusion. She had discovered it accidentally, but now it stuck to her like a second skin. And still, she said nothing. Not yet. Not until she was sure.

The laughter in the room swelled again, warm, full, and golden. Melina stared into the fireplace, the faint embers glowing softly in the grate. A storm was coming, and none of them could see it. Not yet. But she could feel it in her bones. But Melina's thoughts had begun to drift, pulled away from the laughter and warmth like a leaf caught in a quiet current. Maybe it was the familiar comfort of the cocoa, or perhaps Gran's gentle presence beside her, but more than that, it was the memory she had tried so hard to forget. The secret she carried about Monica's fiancé and his family. The things she had overheard during that unplanned visit to Monica's apartment with her friend Anna, fragments of conversation never meant for her ears; truths wrapped in charm but shadowed by something darker. A heaviness settled over her, as if the room had suddenly grown colder despite the fire crackling in the hearth. Her fingers tightened slightly around the mug in her lap. She hadn't told anyone. Not then, not now. She'd convinced herself it wasn't her place, that maybe she'd misunderstood. But even now, those words echoed clearly in her mind, careless, arrogant, and unsettling. Melina felt the weight of it pressing down like a storm cloud tucked beneath her ribs. She glanced around the room, at Monica's radiant smile, the joyful chatter, the deep roots of family and tradition etched into every corner of the home, and wondered if she should say something. But the fear was sharp. What if she was wrong? What if she broke something that couldn't be mended? A part of her longed to speak, to warn Monica before it was too late. But another part, the quieter one that had always kept her tucked away in the background, whispered that some things were better left buried. And so, she smiled faintly, forced the thoughts down once more, and told herself, just one more night. She'd carry the secret a little longer. Upstairs, the old wooden floor creaked beneath Melina's footsteps as she made her way to the guest room. The sounds of laughter and soft music from downstairs had finally faded, replaced by the distant murmur of wind brushing against the windows. She closed the door gently behind her and sank onto the edge of the bed, her phone already in her hand. She hesitated for a moment, her thumb hovering over Anna's name in her call log. Then, with a sigh, she tapped it. The phone rang twice.

"Mel?" Anna's voice came through, quiet and a little groggy. "Everything okay?"

"I didn't wake you, did I?" Melina asked, already curling her legs beneath her.

"No, I was up scrolling. What's going on? You sound weird."

Melina let out a soft, humourless laugh. "Monica announced her engagement tonight. Just... dropped it in the middle of the room like a glitter bomb."

Anna was quiet for a beat. "Wow. So, it's official?"

"Very," Melina said. "The whole family went nuts, passing the ring around, talking venues, drinking Gran's hot cocoa like it was 2008"

"I'm guessing you didn't tell her," Anna said gently.

Melina closed her eyes. "How could I? She's so happy, Anna. Radiant. Like... nothing could go wrong."

"But something could," Anna said softly. "You know it. I know it."

Melina nodded, even though Anna couldn't see her. "I keep thinking about that day. At her apartment. When her fiancé and his brother came in. Remember what they said?"

"I remember," Anna said. "I can still hear it. Something about getting rid of a problem quietly. And not having to worry because, quote, 'the family has it covered.'"

"Yeah," Melina whispered. "And the way they laughed about it, like it wasn't a woman they were talking about. Just... an inconvenience."

There was a pause on the line. Then Anna said, "Do you still think we misunderstood?"

"I don't know," Melina admitted. "I've gone over it a hundred times in my head, and it always feels worse. I don't want to be the reason Monica's heart breaks. But I also don't want her walking into something dangerous." Anna exhaled, the sound soft but full of weight. "You can't carry this alone, Mel. You have to tell her. Or at least get more information, something solid."

"I don't know where to start," Melina said, her voice cracking just a little.

"Start with the truth," Anna replied gently. "Even if it's hard."

Melina stared out the window at the moonlit field beyond. "I'll think about it. Maybe tomorrow, when he gets here."

Anna didn't push. "Okay. I'm here if you need me."

"Thanks," Melina said. "Really."

They hung up quietly, and Melina sat in the dark for a long time, the phone still resting in her palm, her heart heavier than it had been before, but somehow steadier, too. Downstairs, the living room still glowed with the last golden embers of the fire and the soft halo of a standing lamp. Half-empty mugs of cocoa sat abandoned on side tables, and a couple of cozy blankets were draped haphazardly over the arms of the couch. Uncle Buster let out a long sigh, stretching as he stood. "Well, I don't know about the rest of you, but my old bones are calling it a night."

"You say that every night," Aunt May teased, nudging him with her elbow.

"And every night I mean it," he said with a wink, already shuffling toward the hallway. Gran was gathering up a few mugs, moving slowly but with that same graceful rhythm she always had. Monica gently took the tray from her hands.

"I've got it, Gran," she said with a bright smile. "You've done enough tonight."

Gran smiled knowingly. "I always do a little more when there's something to celebrate."

Monica beamed, twirling her hand to flash the ring again. "Still can't believe it's real."

"Oh, it's real, darling," May said, coming over to kiss Monica's cheek. "You've got a good man. We're all so happy for you." Monica nodded, but her smile faltered for the briefest moment.   "Yeah... he's amazing. You'll all see when he gets here tomorrow."

"Looking forward to meeting the man who managed to steal your heart," Uncle Buster called over his shoulder as he disappeared down the hallway. Gran moved to the

bottom of the stairs and called up, "Everyone upstairs!
"You too, grandpa", she said to her husband. "Coming
dear," Lights out in ten minutes! And no midnight fridge
raids!" Laughter rippled through the room as the family
began to disperse. Aunt May gathered a blanket, folding
it over the armchair neatly, while Monica lingered near
the fireplace for a moment longer.

"I'm going to sit here just a little while," she said
quietly. "Feels like the kind of night you want to hold
onto."

Gran paused by the stairs.

"Don't stay up too long, love."

"I won't."

One by one, the others climbed the stairs, murmuring
their goodnights. The house slowly settled into silence,
the kind that only comes in old country homes, gentle
and complete. Monica lingered a little longer, alone in the
living room, her eyes fixed on the gentle dance of firelight
as it played against the stone hearth. The silence felt thick,
comforting, and uneasy all at once. Her fingers found the
ring again, tracing its curve in slow, idle circles, this time
without intention, as if it might offer answers she hadn't
thought to ask. Her thoughts drifted to Melina, how quiet
she'd been tonight, how her smile hadn't quite reached
her eyes. Monica's brow furrowed faintly. Something
about it tugged at her, just out of reach, like a word on
the tip of her tongue. But then she dismissed it with a

small shake of her head. Melina was always a little reserved, especially in unfamiliar company. It was probably just the surprise of the evening. The news. The shift.

Probably.

She let out a soft breath and rose from the couch, the warm weight of the moment settling somewhere in her chest. As she crossed the room, she paused to flick off the lamp, casting the space into shadow. On her way to the stairs, her eyes caught the tray of mugs left by the sink, empty, waiting, forgotten. She stood for a second longer, taking in the quiet stillness, the way the night had folded into itself. It had been almost perfect. But *almost* had a way of lingering. She climbed the stairs slowly, her bare feet soft against the wood, the house creaking faintly around her like it, too, was settling in for the night. On the landing, she paused outside the guest room door. Light filtered out from beneath it.

Melina was still awake. Monica raised her hand to knock, then hesitated. What would she even say? *Are you okay? You seemed... off?* It felt too vague, too intrusive. Melina would only wave it off with that gentle smile of hers, the one that could mean anything or nothing at all. She let her hand fall back to her side. In her room, Monica shut the door behind her and leaned against it for a moment, her eyes adjusting to the moonlight that spilled through the curtains. She wasn't sure why she felt so unsettled. Everything had gone as planned: the announcement, the toasts, the quiet applause from family

trying not to wake the baby sleeping upstairs. And yet…
She crossed to the dresser and set the ring down carefully
beside the small ceramic dish where she kept her earrings.
For a second, she just stared at it, how it caught the
moonlight, how *right* it looked, and how somehow, that
didn't ease the strange little twist in her gut.

It's just nerves, she told herself. *A big change. A new chapter.
That's all.* But even as she pulled back the covers and slid
into bed, that lingering *almost* still clung to the edges of
the night like a shadow she couldn't quite place.
Somewhere down the hall, a floorboard creaked. Monica
turned toward the sound, listening, waiting. But the
silence returned, stretching long and still. And sleep,
when it finally came, was thin and easily broken.

CHAPTER FIVE

The next morning arrived with a golden sweep of light across the countryside, dappling the kitchen windows and warming the hardwood floors. Gran was already up, humming softly as she beat eggs in a ceramic bowl. The smell of frying bacon, fresh coffee, and toasted bread drifted through the house, rousing the family one by one. The smell of coffee came first, earthy and comforting, drifting up the stairs like an old friend. A moment later came the gentle clatter of pans and the low hum of the kitchen radio, barely audible over the sound of eggs being cracked and whisked.

Gran had been up since just after dawn, moving with the practiced rhythm of someone who had cooked breakfast a thousand times without ever needing to think about it. She worked barefoot, her robe cinched at the waist, grey hair tucked back beneath a scarf. The kitchen windows were already open, letting in the cool morning breeze and the smell of damp earth. Outside, Grandpa was making his usual rounds, checking the coop, tossing feed to the chickens, fiddling with the latch on the old shed that never quite stayed shut. From time to time, a faint whistle floated in through the window, followed by the low grumble of his voice as he spoke to the dogs like they were people. Which, in his eyes, they were. The collies barked suddenly, sharp and excited, and then again, closer this time, near the side porch. Upstairs, Monica stirred beneath the quilt, groaning softly as the dogs' chorus echoed through the house. She turned over, the morning light already slicing through the thin curtains.

"Ugh," she murmured, face half-buried in the pillow. "They always know when I'm trying to sleep in."

From the other side of the room, Melina let out a muffled laugh. She was curled beneath her blanket; one arm flung over her eyes.

"Maybe they're trying to tell us we've had enough rest." Monica squinted toward the window, blinking slowly.

"Tell them to come back after breakfast."

Downstairs, the radio crackled as Gran flipped through stations until she landed on one playing old gospel songs. The dogs barked again, this time more insistently, as Grandpa's boots thunked onto the porch.

"You girls planning to sleep all day?" he called up with mock sternness, his voice booming through the floorboards. Melina stretched and sighed. "Looks like we've been caught." Monica smiled, but it was a soft one, still touched by last night's questions. "Could be worse," she said, tossing the quilt aside. "At least we're waking up to bacon and fresh air." Melina nodded, watching her for a moment, something unreadable passing over her face.

"Yeah," she said quietly.   "It's good to be here."

The dogs barked again, wild with joy now that they knew they had everyone's attention. And with that, the day began. Mel lay in bed, the warmth of the sunlight streaming through her window, feeling the gentle pull of sleep. But the barking of the dogs shattered the moment, stirring her mind. What could they be barking at this early? She turned over, pulling the covers closer around her, allowing herself a few more minutes of rest. It was a lazy weekend, a welcome break from the demands of university life. Then, as if on cue, the aroma of freshly baked bread and sizzling bacon filled the room. The smells wafting from the kitchen teased her senses, promising a lovely, cozy day to come. Mel stretched and yawned, her eyes fluttering open. She smiled, her heart light, as she remembered why today was so special: her sister Monica's engagement celebration, which she and the other members of the family are planning. It's going to be a surprise. It was supposed to be a day of celebration, a family gathering to share in the joy. But then, a shadow passed over Mel's smile. The memory of the conversation she overheard before about her sister's fiancé suddenly came rushing back. The information was so shocking, it seemed impossible. But was it true? Unbelievably true. Mel's heart sank. What should she do? The weight of the secret pressed heavily on her chest. She was not a vengeful person; her nature was kind, not one to stir trouble or create conflict. Yet, the truth lingered in her mind, nagging at her. She thought of her friend, Anne, who had also overheard the conversation. They had agreed not to tell anyone, no matter how tempting it was to confide in someone. They both understood the consequences. Mel's family was close-knit, and their reputation in the community was important. It was a delicate situation, and there was so much at stake. The idea of shattering Monica's happiness, or delicate situation, and there was so much at stake, or worse, ripping the family apart, was unbearable. Mel closed her eyes for a moment, trying to calm her thoughts. She had to protect her sister and her family. But how long could she keep this secret? How long could she carry the weight of the truth without letting it slip? The question gnawed at her, but for now, she had no answers.

For the time being, Mel decided to hold onto her silence. She would try to enjoy the day with her family and keep up the façade of celebration, even as her mind raced with doubt and fear for the future. Today was supposed to be about joy, and she would try her best to honour that, even if it meant hiding a painful truth. Melina stood at the edge of the staircase for a moment, listening to the gentle clatter of plates and the laughter drifting in from the kitchen. She had barely slept. Her mind had spiralled all night through the conversation with Anna, through the memory of what she'd overheard. Now, with Monica's fiancé due to arrive any minute, the weight of that knowledge pressed heavier than ever. She padded into the kitchen, accepting a mug of coffee from Gran with a tired smile.

"You look like you've seen a ghost," Gran said, her voice gentle.

"Just didn't sleep well," Melina replied, wrapping both hands around her mug. "Too much cocoa."

Gran gave her a knowing look but said nothing more. A few minutes later, Monica burst in from the front hallway, her phone in her hand and her eyes shining.

"He's here! He just pulled up!"

There was a small flurry of movement as everyone gathered in the front room. Coats straightened, hair checked in mirrors, mugs set aside. The excitement was palpable. Monica stood by the door, practically glowing. Then the knock came. As the door opened, a tall and confident young man entered, attired in a crisp wool coat with a polished but slightly reserved smile. His sharp features and meticulously styled hair gave him the appearance of someone who could easily grace the cover of a magazine or a political campaign brochure.

"Everyone," Monica said, unable to contain her excitement, this is Sylvester."

Sylvester offered firm handshakes and charming compliments as he greeted the family one by one. "So wonderful to meet all of you. Monica's told me everything, except how beautiful this place is." He laughed at all the right moments, asked polite questions, and even complimented Gran on the cocoa she'd left warming on the stove. The family has taken to him. Aunt May gave Melina a look that said, *he's even more handsome in person*. Monica stood at his side; her hand loosely wrapped around his arm like it had always belonged there. But Melina watched him closely. She noticed the flicker in his eyes when someone asked about his family, the half-second pause before he spoke. The charm was smooth, but too smooth. She'd seen this performance before, and this time she was watching for the cracks.

"Melina," Sylvester said smoothly, his voice warm but his smile just shy of genuine. "Good to see you again."

She gave a small nod, keeping her expression neutral. "You are, too."

"You know," he added, glancing briefly at Monica, "your sister talks about you all the time. Says you're the only one who keeps her grounded. "Melina let out a quiet breath.

"We've been through a lot together." Sylvester chuckled, just a little too rehearsed. "Well, I hope you'll share some of those stories, at least the ones that won't get me into too much trouble." Melina offered a polite smile, but it didn't reach her eyes.

"I'm sure a few will come up."

Their eyes met and held longer than they should have. In Sylvester's gaze, there was a flicker of something unspoken. Not surprise, not warmth, but a brief, sharp awareness. Like he was trying to gauge whether she remembered. Whether she'd say anything. And Melina did remember every word. Her stomach tightened as the warmth of the room seemed to recede just slightly, like a breeze had slipped in through a crack no one else noticed. Outside, the birds chirped. Inside, the room buzzed with welcome and warmth. But beneath it all, a quiet current had begun to pull, one that only she could feel. Melina excused herself abruptly, muttering something about needing to catch up on sleep that had been interrupted the night before. She turned toward the staircase, avoiding eye contact.

"Seems like you're trying to avoid me, Melina," Sylvester called after her with a half-hearted chuckle, the kind that masked more than it revealed. She paused, one hand resting on the banister. "Why would you say that?" Her voice was quiet, guarded. Sylvester shrugged casually, though there was a flicker of something sharper in his eyes.

"Monica is my fiancée. I'd think her little sister would be a little more... enthusiastic."

Melina forced a small smile that didn't reach her eyes. "I'm just tired, Sylvester. Didn't sleep well. That's all." Without waiting for a response, she turned and made her way upstairs, her footsteps a little too quick, as if she needed the safety of solitude before her expression gave her away. Monica frowned as she watched her younger sister retreat upstairs, disappearing around the bend of the staircase. She had barely exchanged a word with anyone before claiming she needed more sleep. Again. A flicker of frustration crossed Monica's face. Why now? Melina had been acting oddly ever since they all arrived for the weekend. Distant. Jumpy, even. And now she was practically running away. Is she avoiding Sylvester? Monica's chest tightened at the thought. But why would she? She replayed the awkward moment in her mind, the way Melina barely acknowledged him, the tension in her posture, and the way she avoided everyone's eyes. It didn't add up. She glanced over at Sylvester, who was staring up at the staircase with a bemused expression. Monica couldn't tell if he was genuinely confused or if he knew more than he was letting on. The silence stretched, and Monica folded her arms across her chest, the beginnings of unease tugging at her. Something felt off, and it wasn't just Melina's behaviour.

CHAPTER SIX

Melina heard her grandmother calling from downstairs, just as she slipped on her cardigan. The sound of her name echoed through the hallway, sharp with impatience. She winced, remembering she was supposed to go to the village shop early that morning, which had been agreed upon the night before. But after the uncomfortable exchange with Sylvester in the kitchen, she'd gone back to bed, her thoughts too tangled to sleep deeply. By the time she reached the landing, Gran was already waiting at the foot of the stairs, arms folded, and eyes narrowed.

"You're late, Mel," said Gran, her tone clipped with disapproval as she stood at the kitchen counter, peeling potatoes with sharp, practiced strokes.

"Why did you go back to bed? You knew you were supposed to do the shopping this morning." Melina lingered by the doorway, guilt flickering across her face.

"I was just... tired," she mumbled, brushing a hand through her tousled hair. "Didn't sleep much last night." Gran turned to face her, narrowing her eyes. "Are you trying to avoid Monica's fiancé, Sylvester?" Her voice was calm, but probing, laced with that sixth sense grandmothers seem to possess when something isn't quite right. Melina hesitated, her lips parting, then closing again. Finally, she forced a small, strained smile.

"No. Of course not. Just tired, that's all."

Gran didn't respond right away. She studied Melina's face, as if searching for cracks in her carefully placed expression. After a long pause, she sighed and turned back to the potatoes. "Well, tired or not, you've got things to do. The lists on the table, and don't forget the good cheese from Mr. Rodger's, said Gran. Melina nodded silently and crossed the room to grab the list, her fingers brushing the paper with a hint of tremble. As she turned to leave, Gran called after her, not unkindly, "Whatever it is you're not saying, Mel... just remember truth always has a way of catching up."

"I know. I'm sorry," Melina replied, brushing her hair behind her ears. "I overslept again, blame the dogs." Melina paused in the doorway, her back to Gran. For a second, her smile faded completely, replaced by something darker. Then she walked out without a word. Gran didn't laugh. "Go and eat something. I don't know why you went back to bed. Your grandfather's warming up the car. He'll take you into the village."

"Okay," Melina said, relieved. She ducked into the kitchen, grabbed a lukewarm piece of toast and a few sips of tea, then slipped back out with her bag slung over her shoulder. No one questioned her further. Truthfully, the shop run was more than an errand; it was an escape. Ever since Sylvester's arrival, the house had felt just a bit off. Too cheerful. Too forced. And the moment their eyes met in the kitchen, that strange flicker of recognition in his expression… it had unsettled her all over again. Getting away, even for half an hour, felt like coming up for air. As she stepped out into the crisp country morning, the sun coming up through the sky, it's going to be another warm day, so she wore just a light cardigan. The village shop might not have the answers, but at least it offered space to think. And right now, Melina needed space more than anything.

"Gran, can I take the jeep?" Mel called from the hallway, keys already jingling in her hand.

"Not today, dear," Gran replied from the kitchen, not even looking up from her crossword. "You'll need a bit more practice first. It's a big jeep."

Mel folded her arms, leaning against the doorframe. "Gran, I passed my driving test five months ago. Remember?"

"Yes, love," Gran said with a knowing smile, "but passing your test doesn't mean you're ready to tame *the beast*. That jeep's got more attitude than a cat in a bath. Next time, your grandfather or I will ride with you. Preferably with a helmet." Gran said with a chuckle. Mel laughed. "Honestly, I'd rather walk. It's a gorgeous

53

morning, and the shops aren't that far. Besides, the jeep growls at me like it's possessed."

Gran chuckled, finally glancing over her glasses at her granddaughter. "Suit yourself, dear. Take your time and try not to buy out the entire bakery again. Your grandfather still hasn't forgiven you for the cinnamon bun incident." "I make no promises," Mel called as she grabbed her bag and headed for the door.

"I was supporting local business," Mel called back with a grin.

"With twenty-two pastries?"

"They were on special!"

Gran shook her head, still smiling. "Off you go, then. And mind the crossing by the old post office, drivers take that corner like it's the Grand Prix." Mel gave her a quick peck on the cheek and headed out the door, sunlight already warming the porch. As she walked down the gravel drive, a breeze caught her hair, and for a moment, things felt simple again. But only for a moment.

****

Melina Telfer strolled along the gravel path, each step in her beloved black sandals, a birthday gift from her grandmother last June, quiet crunch echoing beneath her. The morning air was crisp and clean, scented faintly with damp earth and the hint of wildflowers beginning to wake in the hedgerows. She tugged her coat tighter around her and let her gaze drift toward the horizon, where the fields met the sky in a soft blur of mist and sunlight. She had always loved this stretch of the slow, familiar walk from the house to the drive, where the world felt suspended for a moment. It was the kind of place that invited thinking, remembering, even hiding a little.

Her thoughts turned to Sylvester. The polite smile. The studied charm. The flicker in his eyes when he saw her again, as if he wasn't entirely surprised to see her here. As if he hadn't quite decided whether she was a threat. Melina exhaled slowly. She hadn't planned on saying anything, not yet. But now that he was here, under the same roof as her sister, every instinct in her body was alert. She didn't want to be suspicious. She wanted to be wrong. And yet, she couldn't ignore what she'd overheard weeks ago. That night still clung to her like smoke. She paused by the old iron gate that led to the drive, resting her hand on its cool frame. Her sandals, already dusted with pale gravel, made her feel momentarily rooted, like she was still herself, still anchored, even as everything around her shifted. *Just get to the village,* she told herself. *Clear your head. Figure out what comes next.* The engine of her grandfather's car rumbled faintly in the distance, waiting. Melina gave one last glance back at the house. Behind those stone walls, her sister was planning a future that Melina wasn't sure was safe. And Melina was running out of reasons not to speak.

CHAPTER SEVEN

The morning sun burned high in a cloudless sky, casting long shadows behind her, while a gentle breeze stirred the air with the bittersweet scent of cut grass and far-off blossoms, like memories drifting just out of reach. But none of it touched her. Not really. A secret pressed heavily on her chest, one she hadn't meant to keep, but couldn't bear to share-not now, not after the way Monica was raging about Sylvester. As she approached the playground, laughter rang out, bright, carefree, and achingly familiar. Children raced between swings and slides, some clinging to their parents' hands, others lost in giggles with their siblings. Melina paused, her gaze lingering on the worn edges of the sandbox and the freshly painted swings.   She vividly recalled her childhood, chasing butterflies, hanging from monkey bars, and her grandmother's evening calls. Despite new benches, brighter colours, and safer ground, the playground still felt like a familiar friend, preserving the warmth and wonder of her youth. The place felt like an old friend, lovingly dressed in new clothes, still offering the same warmth and wonder it always had. Melina continued down the path until she reached the Jonas residence—a quaint cottage tucked behind a row of neatly trimmed rose bushes. Mr. and Mrs. Jonas, her godparents, were warm, generous souls whom she adored. But they had a well-known talent for turning a simple greeting into a half-hour conversation. This morning, with a long to-do list and a mind already cluttered with worry, Melina hoped to pass by unnoticed, no matter how much she cherished them. As she quickened her pace to avoid conversation, a familiar voice called,

"Melina, is that you?"

Caught, Melina turned with a sheepish smile and walked briskly over to the gate. "Good morning, Godmother Jonas," she said warmly. Mrs. Jonas, wearing her signature floral apron and clutching a basket of freshly picked herbs, beamed at her. "Good morning, Mel! How are you, sweetheart? Where are you off to in such a hurry? Shouldn't you be helping your grandmother?"

"Oh, so you consider yourself a city resident now," Mrs. Jonas remarked with a hint of amusement in her eyes. "It seems there is no longer time for individuals like Mr. Jonas and me. The younger generation spends a few months in the city and then appears too preoccupied to engage in conversation with us, more experienced individuals." Melina said,

"I'm going to the shop and taking in the scenery. I arrived last night to spend the weekend with my grandparents," she stated, not mentioning the actual reason for her early errand, a surprise she intended to keep secret for now. Mrs. Jonas narrowed her eyes playfully, as though she could sense there was more to the story. "Mumm-hmm," she said with a knowing smile. "Well, don't let me keep you then. Your grandma told me about Monica's engagement, but you forgot to tell me about it. I am coming over this afternoon, and I will bring Monica's favourite apple scones, and then we can have a proper talk". I've also baked your favourite jam tarts that you loved, don't think I'm going to leave out my favourite Goddaughter?". She said with a chuckle. Melina laughed, her smile wide and genuine, her white teeth catching the morning light. "It's not like that at all, Godmother," she replied playfully. "Gran just asked me to run to the shop quickly." She knew Mrs. Jonas, well, once a conversation started, it could stretch on for ages, drifting from village gossip to long-winded questions about city life and university drama. Her grandmother had warned her gently that morning: *Be polite,*

but don't linger too long. You know how Mrs. Jonas loves a chat."

"I'll come back later and tell you everything," Melina added, stepping backward toward the road with a grin. "Promise!"

Mrs. Jonas raised an eyebrow, clearly unconvinced but not offended, "Alright then, off you go. But I'll be expecting a proper visit before the sun sets!"

"Bye, Mrs. Jonas!" Melina called over her shoulder, already picking up her pace, the gravel crunching beneath her sandals as she continued her way.

Bye, Mrs. Jonas," Melina called over her shoulder, quickening her pace down the lane.

"Don't forget to come and visit me and Mr. Jonas!" her godmother called after her. "We're still your Godparents, child, and we want to hear everything you're doing in that big city!" Melina waved one last time before turning back toward the road, a gentle smile playing on her lips. Her heart swelled with the quiet joy of being home, the kind of warmth that only familiar streets and long-held memories could bring.

The scent of fresh pastries still lingered in the air, a reminder that her godmother hadn't forgotten her favourite treat after all these years, not even Monica, who always claimed to be the favourite, had been remembered so sweetly. It was in these small gestures that love showed itself most clearly, and as she walked on, Melina felt the weight of the world lift just a little. Mel smiled but didn't slow down. She began walking a little faster, half-expecting Mr. Jonas to appear from behind the shed or tractor. He could be even more inquisitive than his wife, and if he caught sight of her, she knew there'd be no escape without a full conversation, complete with advice, a farm update, and a handful of homegrown vegetables.

Still, she couldn't help but feel grateful. The Jonoses had always treated her like one of their own, their warmth and care filling the gaps left when her parents were busy or far away.

They had five children, three daughters and two sons, all of whom had long since flown the nest, chasing careers and opportunities in the city or even abroad. Only one son had stayed behind. *Michael?* she thought, trying to recall the name her grandmother had mentioned over tea one evening. Yes, Michael. He was the second eldest, if she remembered correctly, the dependable one. Gran said he was the one helping Mr. Jonas run the farm now. From what she could gather, Michael was married with three young children of his own and lived in the cottage next door to his parents. Melina had only vague memories of him from her childhood: tall, quiet, with a gentle laugh. They hadn't spoken in years, and she wasn't sure she'd recognize him if they crossed paths. She made a mental note to ask Gran more about him later. For now, though, she focused on the path ahead. The village shop was just around the bend, and the sun had climbed a little higher, casting warm golden light across the hedgerows. Melina felt a subtle thrill of anticipation flutter in her chest. The surprise she was planning was still a secret, but the pieces were slowly falling into place.

As Melina rounded the corner, the Jonas cottage faded behind her, and a soft breeze stirred the wildflowers along the roadside. The village looked almost exactly as she remembered: stone fences lined with moss, old oak trees standing like sentinels, and the faint smell of woodsmoke and fresh bread drifting from somewhere nearby. It was quiet, save for the rustle of leaves and the occasional chirp of a bird. She inhaled deeply, letting the calm of the countryside settle over her. The city was exciting, fast, full of noise and movement, but nothing could replace the peace she felt here. Every corner of the village held a memory: summer picnics in the meadow, rainy afternoons spent baking with Gran, and evenings curled up with a book by the fire.

As she neared the little village shop, its green shutters open and flowerpots blooming on the windowsills, she smiled to herself. It hadn't changed a bit. The bell above the door still jingled the same way she remembered, and she half expected to see old Mr. James behind the counter, humming as he weighed out sweets in paper bags. But today, Melina had a mission, and a secret. She had confided in her grandparents about the surprise engagement party she was planning for Monica and had asked for their thoughts. Their reaction was everything she had hoped for. Her grandparents were thrilled and wholeheartedly embraced the idea.

"We'll try to get the rest of the family involved," her Gran said warmly, her eyes already sparkling with excitement. Melina felt a wave of relief. If everything went according to plan, by evening, Monica would walk into a heartfelt, intimate celebration she never saw coming. She could already imagine the look on her face, surprised, maybe even a little emotional. Monica wasn't one for small gestures; she liked things bold, elegant, and grand. This party, with its modest setting and personal touches, was a world apart from what she was used to. Still, Melina hoped the sincerity behind it would shine through. And when Monica walked in and saw the table set for the celebration, adorned with delicate flowers and handwritten notes, and when her grandmother wiped away quiet tears upon realizing the effort Melina had made, perhaps that would be enough. Enough to remind Monica that sometimes the most meaningful moments come not from lavish displays, but from love, thoughtfulness, and the people who care the most. Melina tried to push the heavy secret from her mind as she continued toward town on the crunching gravel beneath her sandals, the way sunlight filtered through the trees, and the calming scent of rose and earth. If only for a little while, she wanted to forget what she knew, to lose herself in the simple rhythm of shopping lists and the gentle beauty of the day.

Melina followed the dusty path toward the village shop, her grandmother's warning echoing in her mind like a half-whispered caution she couldn't shake. With a quiet breath and a flicker of resolve, she stepped forward and pushed open the shop door. The bell above chimed brightly, a cheerful contrast to the unease stirring just beneath her calm exterior.

"Don't go to Mr. Rodger's shop first. Go to Miss Lola's; she sells almost everything. But be careful, she's sneaky. If she sees you go to his shop before hers, and then come back to her, she won't sell you a thing." It wasn't just a superstition. Melina had experienced it herself. Miss Lola had a sharp eye and an even sharper tongue. If she caught wind that you'd tried Mr. Rodger's first and only came to her out of desperation, she'd throw a fit right there in the doorway, barking at you to leave and waving you off with a scowl. Prideful and possessive, she guarded her shop's reputation like a dragon over treasure. So, this morning, Melina wisely followed her grandmother's instructions and made her way straight to Miss Lola's little store, a cramped, cluttered place stuffed to the rafters with everything from flour and matches to sewing needles and sweets. The bell above the door gave a dull jingle as she stepped inside, and the scent of dried herbs, soap, and something vaguely medicinal met her at once.

"Morning, Miss Lola,"

Melina said politely, pulling the folded shopping list from her pocket and handing it over. Miss Lola, perched behind the counter like a watchful cat, adjusted her glasses and took the list without a word. Miss Lola scanned the list, her lips pursed tightly, eyes flicking back and forth with the precision of someone who'd been doing this for decades. Her wiry grey hair was pulled back into a tidy bun, and she wore a knitted cardigan despite the warming day. Melina stood quietly, resisting the urge to fidget under the woman's piercing gaze.

"Young people these days don't know how to make a proper list," Miss Lola muttered, half to herself, half to Melina. "You've written 'sugar' here, what kind? Brown? White?

Caster? And flour, plain or self-raising? You think I can just guess?"

"I think Gran means plain," Melina replied quickly, trying to sound confident. "And white sugar, please."

"Hmph,"

Miss Lola grunted, scribbling something on the paper and disappearing behind the shelves. The shop was small but packed tight with goods. Glass jars lined the counter, filled with old-fashioned sweets, peppermints, lemon drops, cola cubes, and the shelves creaked under the weight of tinned food, kitchen staples, and the occasional oddity: a pair of garden gloves, a sewing kit, a tin of polish from the 1980s. Dust motes danced in the shafts of light coming through the small front window, and a ticking clock marked the only sound besides Miss Lola's rustling. Melina glanced around, letting her gaze wander to the corkboard near the door, covered in faded notices, church events, lost pets, and a piano lesson flyer that looked like it hadn't been touched in years. Miss Lola reappeared with a paper bag already half full, setting it down on the counter with a soft thud. "You'll need to get the rest from Rodger's. He's got the tea and the washing powder. I don't bother with those anymore, takes up too much space," she said, as though the very idea of stocking such items offended her.

"Thank you, Miss Lola," Melina said, reaching into her bag for the money. Melina loved the little village; her mother grew up in this village, as did she and the rest of her siblings. But she felt like she was struggling every time she visited. She loved to visit her Grandparents, especially during the summer holidays. She appreciates spending time with her grandparents, who are important to her. She notes that the village remains largely unchanged in the 21st century. While this is not necessarily negative, it does not feel suitable for her anymore. Miss Lola's voice interrupted her thoughts, saying,

"Come on, child, what are you thinking about? Your shopping is ready."

Miss Lola nodded curtly, counting out the change with swift, precise movements. Then she paused, looking over the top of her glasses.

"Tell your grandmother I said hello, and that she still owes me her mango chutney recipe. I haven't forgotten." Melina smiled.

"I'll let her know."

As she stepped back out into the sunshine, the bell jingling behind her, she breathed a quiet sigh of relief. One shop down, one to go, and still plenty left to do before the surprise could come together.

Melina adjusted the strap of her tote bag and made her way further down the lane toward Mr. Rodger's shop, her paper bag crinkling softly with every step. Compared to Miss Lola's cramped and fussy store, Mr. Rodger's place was a bit more modern, or at least trying to be. The windows were clean, the door freshly painted, and the shelves were usually better organized. He stocked all the essentials Miss Lola refused to carry and a few things she'd openly sneered at over the years: boxed cereal, shampoo brands from the city, even chocolate biscuits in bulk. As she approached, she saw Mr. Rodger through the window, standing behind the counter, rearranging a stack of canned goods with careful precision. He was a tall man with a gentle stoop, glasses perched on the end of his nose, and sleeves always rolled up to his elbows.

Melina pushed open the door, and the familiar chime rang overhead, this time a cheerful, modern ding rather than Miss Lola's old iron bell.

"Morning, Mr. Rodger," she said brightly, forcing a cheerful tone as she stepped inside. The elderly shopkeeper looked up from behind the counter, adjusting his glasses with a warm smile adjusting his glasses with smile.

"Melina! Look who's back. Thought I saw you pass by earlier. Visiting your grandparents, I suppose?"

"Yes, just for the weekend," Melina replied, brushing a strand of hair behind her ear. "Gran sent me for a few things."

"Of course she did," he chuckled, rubbing his hands together, like a magician about to perform a trick.

"Let me guess: tea, washing powder, and something sweet she doesn't plan to share?" Melina laughed, a genuine sound for the first time that day. "You know her too well."

He leaned down behind the warm oak counter, pulling out a notepad where he kept track of regulars' usual items. "She always wants that special blend of tea, three boxes?"

"Just two this time," Melina said. "She's trying to cut back." Mr. Rodger raised a skeptical eyebrow.

"I'll believe it when I see it. Last time, she said that she would come the next day for another box. "We'll see how long that lasts. And the usual lemon biscuits?"

"Yes, please. Oh, and washing powder, medium size." As he gathered the items, Melina wandered a bit, glancing over the new stock along the shelves: seasonal jam jars, floral-patterned notebooks, even a few plastic toys. A radio played softly from the back room, some old song from the sixties, and the shop smelled faintly of fresh bread and something floral, maybe lavender soap. Mr. Rodger returned with a small box, placing the items neatly inside.

"There we are. Anything else?"

Melina smiled but faded quickly. She looked down at the list in her hand, rubbing absentmindedly at the counter.

"She got the house full this weekend. Monica's here and her fiancé.. Mr Rodger's hands slowed as he reached for the tea. So that's why you look like you've barely slept". Melina blinked, surprised. "Is it that obvious?". He glanced up at her study Only to someone who's known you since you were in nappies." He placed the boxes on the counter gently. "Whatever's weighing on you, just remember keeping it in doesn't make it lighter." She gave a small nod, eyes avoiding his.

"I'll keep that in mind." He moved on, picking out the rest of the items from her list with practiced ease. "Washing powders in the back, and I've got a fresh batch of lemon biscuits that just came in, want to take some for Gran?"

"Better make it two packs," Melina said softly. "One might mysteriously disappear on the way home."

Mr. Rodger grinned. "Now *that's* the Melina I remember". Melina hesitated, then leaned in a little closer. "Do you have any of those small fairy lights? The battery-powered kind?" He raised an eyebrow. "Decorating something?"

"Just a small surprise for my sister Monica. Nothing big." He smiled warmly, stepping toward a side shelf. "I think I've got just the thing." He paused, glancing over his shoulder with a knowing look. "By the way, how's Monica? Still the family princess, I imagine." His tone held a mix of affection and gentle teasing. "But you, child, you've always had the good heart."

"She just got engaged, actually," I said, unable to hide the small smile tugging at my lips. "We're throwing a little engagement party this evening. Nothing extravagant, certainly not on Monica's level."

"Well, give her my congratulations," he said, selecting a small box and handing it over with a wink. "And tell her I'll be waiting for my invitation to the wedding."

CHAPTER EIGHT

Melina stepped out of Mr. Rodger's shop with her purchases neatly packed into a cloth bag. The sun was higher now, casting long shadows from the rooftops and warming the cobbled street. She was just about to turn the corner toward her grandparents' cottage when a familiar voice called out from across the road.

"Melina Telfer? Is that really you?"

She turned, squinting against the light, and then her face lit up.

"Samantha? Ruthie?"

The two girls, now young women, were standing outside the café, drinks in hand, their faces breaking into wide, excited smiles. Melina crossed the road quickly, careful not to jostle her bag.

"Oh my gosh, look at you!" Samantha said, enveloping her in a hug. "You look so grown up!"

"It's been what, two years?" Ruthie added, her eyes sparkling. "Since that summer you came down after the first year?". What brings you to this part of the country?" Ruthie asked humorously. Melina responded with another hug and laughter, extending the same greeting to Samantha. "How is life in the big city treating you?" Samantha inquired. Melina knows that Samantha prefers not to be called Sam, as she perceives it as a boy's name. Samantha likes to be addressed formally, but given their friendship, Melina uses the shorter version

"Probably longer," Melina said, still smiling. "You both look amazing. I can't believe I ran into you like this!"

"Come, sit," Samantha said, tugging a chair from the nearest table. "We were just saying how boring the village is lately. It's like the universe sent you to save us."

Melina laughed and joined them, setting her bags of groceries carefully at her feet. The conversation flowed easily, as though no time had passed. They caught up on everything: university life, old teachers, which classmates had gotten married or moved abroad, and which ones were still stubbornly rooted in the village. Ruthie had started working at a local clinic, and Samantha was freelancing in graphic design while helping her family run the café, and Ruthie helped her out sometimes.

"And you?" Ruthie asked, leaning in. "Still in the city? What's it like?"

"It's… busy," Melina said with a smile. "Loud. Fast. But good. I've learned a lot. Though coming back here makes me realize how much I've missed this place. "They all nodded, a brief silence falling over the table as they sipped their drinks and watched a pair of young children run past, laughing.

"We should do something before you head back," Samantha said suddenly. "Get dinner. Or a walk up the hill like old times."

"Yes!" Ruthie replied. "Sunset at the old tree, where we planned our futures?". Melina laughed. "Tomorrow evening?

"Perfect," they said in unison, then burst into laughter, just like old times, when life was simpler, and their biggest worries were forgotten homework or whether they'd get the top bunk during sleepovers. Their laughter lingered in the air like music, wrapping around them as they sat on the weathered wooden porch, the late afternoon sun painting everything in a soft gold.

"Are you driving back?" Sam asked, glancing sideways at Melina.

Melina shook her head with a resigned smile. "Nope. Gran says the jeep's too big for me. She thinks I need more experience before she'll let me loose on the road with it. She and Grandad promised they'd take me out for a few more practice runs, proper ones, this time."

Sam raised her eyebrows. "You've had your license for how long now?"

"Five months," Mel said defensively, but smiling. "But you know Gran. She's got this idea in her head of how things should be. If it's not done her way, it's not done at all."

"I swear, if she had her way, you'd be riding a bicycle to Uni until you turn thirty," said Ruthie, rolling her eyes dramatically. That got another round of laughter.

"I'm saving up, though," Melina added, her tone turning more hopeful. "I'm hoping to buy a little Fiat, Volkswagen, or something small, reliable. Just enough to get me between the hospital and Uni, at present. Nothing fancy." Ruthie grinned.

"Just wait till you start naming it. Everyone names their first car." Melina laughed. "I already have a few options. I'm thinking something like Daisy or Olive. Something cute." The girls exchanged knowing looks, their amusement gentle and full of pride. They could see how much Melina had grown, quieter maybe, more responsible, but still the same girl who once climbed the orchard fence just to rescue a stray kitten.

"You've really changed, Mel," Sam said after a beat, her voice softening. "In a good way. You seem more... sure of yourself." Melina looked down, a small, shy smile tugging at her lips. "I don't know about that. I still feel like I'm figuring everything out."

"But that's the thing," Ruthie said, nudging Melina playfully with her elbow. "We're *all* figuring things out. You just make it look like you've got a plan."

She smiled, then added more thoughtfully,

"At least you're not constantly stuck in Monica's shadow anymore. You're becoming your own person, Mel." Melina's heart skipped a beat. The mention of her sister's name hit harder than expected. Monica, always the golden girl, always one step ahead. And now, engaged to Sylvester, whose family held a secret that Melina still didn't know what to do with. Her smile faltered, her face drawing into a quiet sadness that didn't go unnoticed.

"Mel?" Ruthie's voice softened. "You, okay? You seemed miles away the second we mentioned Monica."

Ruthie leaned in, concern creasing her brow. "Hey… we were only teasing. Didn't mean to upset you." Melina forced a gentle smile, the kind that tried to convince everyone, including herself, that nothing was wrong. "I'm fine," she said, brushing it off. "Really. Just got lost in thought, that's all." They didn't press, sensing the shift but respecting the boundary. Still, an unspoken worry lingered in the air like the first sign of a coming storm. The three girls settled into a quiet pause; each caught in her own thoughts. The silence wasn't awkward; it was the kind shared by people who knew one another well enough not to fill every gap. Outside, the rhythm of the day carried on. A couple strolled past with bags of groceries from Ms. Lola's corner shop. Two teenage boys darted into Mr. Roger's bakery, lured by the smell of fresh coconut buns. Somewhere down the road, a bell chimed faintly as someone entered the village post office.

The morning light became brighter in the sky, adding a pinkish-gold colour to the area. Although the town was typically calm, Melina noticed a sense of unease during this time. Ruthie leaned back, stretching her legs out in front of her. "You ever think about how weird it is, growing up here?" she asked. "Like, how everything stays the same, even when *we* don't?"

"Yeah," Melina said softly. "And sometimes, it's the sameness that makes the changes feel even heavier. "Neither of the others asked what she meant. They didn't have to. Some things didn't need explaining.

"I started working more shifts at the hospital," Melina offered. "It's hard, but… weirdly, I love it. Even the chaos. Even the late nights. There's this one nurse, Beatrice, who's kind of taken me under her wing. She's tough, but fair. Like Gran, if Gran wore scrubs and carried a clipboard." The girls laughed again.

"She told me something the other day," Melina continued. "She said, '*You don't become a nurse just by-passing exams. You become a nurse the moment you hold someone's hand and realize they trust you completely, even though they don't know you at all.*' That stuck with me."

Sam leaned back, nodding thoughtfully. "Wow. That's… actually really deep."

"She's like that," Mel said. "One moment she's barking orders at everyone, and the next she's sitting beside a patient, holding their hand like they're family." They kept talking about university, awkward professors, annoying group projects, cafeteria disasters, and all the little things that made up their days. The porch light flickered on as dusk crept in, but none of them noticed. Not really. Their conversation stretched on and on, and the time slipped by unnoticed, as though time itself had paused to give them this moment. Melina checked her phone and said, "It's late, Gran needs groceries for dinner, and might get upset if I'm not back soon." As they stood up, stretching limbs that had grown stiff from sitting too long, Sam smiled and said, "This was nice. We should do this more often."

"We always say that," Ruthie teased, "but then life gets in the way."

"Let's not let it this time," Melina said, surprising even herself. "Let's make time."

The other girls nodded. No promises, no overthinking. Just a shared understanding that some things, like friendship, laughter, and long talks at sunset, are worth holding onto.

"It's okay, Mel!" her friends called. Later, she felt a gentle warmth in her chest, like something lost had been returned. The village hadn't changed much, but she realized now that the most important parts of it had been waiting for her all along. Melina felt happy to reunite with her friends Samantha and Ruthie after a long time. She worried she might have talked too much about university and her job, knowing they helped out the family at the nearby cafeteria, because they had not gotten a permanent job yet. Remembering their college days, she began to fear she was becoming like her sister Monica, who rarely let her friends share. Feeling guilty, she planned to invite them to the family surprise she had planned for Monica's engagement party, which she had not told them about. As she thought about her friends, she saw how late it was on her phone.

"Mel has really changed," Samantha remarked to Ruthie. "Yeah," Ruthie agreed. "She's always going on about herself and university these days. "Just like her sister Monica," Ruthie added with a smirk, and the two of them burst into laughter. Melina felt a warm rush of happiness as she reunited with Samantha and Ruthie after so long. But beneath the surface, A flicker of self-consciousness stirred. Had she talked too much about university and her new job? She knew they still worked at the nearby café, and guilt pricked at her. As they chatted, memories of their college days bubbled up, days when laughter came easily and no one kept score. A quiet dread crept in. Was she starting to sound like Monica? Her sister had a way of dominating every conversation, leaving no room for anyone else. The thought unsettled her. Feeling guilty, she planned to visit them later for tea and a catch-up. As she thought about her friends, she saw how late it was on her phone.

"Oh! Gran is going to be very upset, " she said to herself, and picked up the pace to a light trot.

"She had completely forgotten to call her granddad to pick her up. *Great,* she sighed. *One job, Melina. One job.* Still, she tried to spin it positively. *Walking will clear my head, and hey, bonus cardio.* The sun was dipping low, casting long shadows along the familiar street. As she turned the corner, her heart sank. The Jonas's house loomed ahead, all tidy hedges and perfectly aligned flowerpots. She instinctively quickened her pace. *Please don't be outside. Please don't be outside.*

But fate, as always, had other plans. Mr. Jonas was out front in his usual spot, armed with a hose and a suspicious glare, like a suburban sentry.

"Hi, Mr. Jonas, bye, Mr. Jonas!" Melina called out in a rush, barely slowing down as she power-walked past their front gate.

"Jane!" Mr. Jonas barked toward the house, pausing his watering as if she'd personally offended his petunias. "Come here! These young people today have no time and no manners. Melina just flew past like her shoes were on fire!"

Mrs. Jonas looked out the living room window, adjusted her glasses, and tried to see into the afternoon light. She said, "Perhaps she has other commitments, Dear. Young people often have busy schedules."

"Too busy to say a proper hello?" he scoffed. "It's all 'hi-bye' with her lately. I'm going to tell her granddad. She used to stay and chat, ask how my tomatoes were doing. Now she just bolts like I'm chasing her with a broom." Back down the street, Melina could almost feel the commentary following her like an echo. She winced and muttered to herself, "*Next time, take the long way. Or wear a disguise.* "Still, part of her felt guilty.

The Jonas family had known her since she was in pigtails; also, they are her Godparents, and they took that role seriously. But lately, everything felt rushed. Conversations turned into checklists. People became appointments she couldn't fit into her calendar. *Am I really becoming that girl?* she wondered. The one who forgets where she came from? She sighed and kept walking, the pavement under her feet and her thoughts racing just as fast. He muttered, shaking his head, "I'm going to tell her granddad. She used to be such a polite girl." From the window, Mrs. Jonas peeked out, adjusting her glasses. "Maybe she's just busy, dear."

"Too busy for manners?" he huffed. "It's always 'hi-bye' now. No time for a real conversation. "No worries, dear," Mrs. Jonas replied. "I had a chat with her this morning on her way to the shops. And remember, we are invited to Monica's surprise engagement party up at the house. "We'll talk to her directly," said Mr. Jonas, slightly mollified. "Well… alright then." Melina, now half a block away, winced slightly, imagining the conversation playing out behind her. *Next time, take the long way home,* she told herself.

CHAPTER NINE

With her heart full and her bag heavier, Melina made her way back toward her grandparents' cottage. The path felt shorter this time, perhaps because her steps were lighter, buoyed by the unexpected joy of seeing Samantha and Ruthie again. The familiar sights passed by like a living scrapbook: the crooked lamppost by the post box, the old dog that always barked from behind the Lowes' gate, the ivy-covered fence that marked the final stretch home. As she reached the small wooden gate, the scent of rosemary and thyme drifted toward her from the garden beds out front. Her grandmother's handiwork, of course. Everything in the Telfers' home had a touch of care and history, from the herb garden to the peeling paint on the gate that her grandfather insisted gave it "character." She pushed open the gate gently and stepped up the stone path. Before she could knock or call out, the front door swung open.

"There you are," Gran said, hands on her hips, though her eyes were warm with relief. "I was starting to think Miss Lola had kidnapped you." The shops are only ten minutes up the road.

"Why didn't you ring your grandfather to come and get you as planned?

Melina laughed. "Not kidnapped, just cornered for a little while. She did say you still owe her that chutney recipe." Her grandmother waved a dismissive hand.

"That woman's been after that recipe for twenty years. She can wait another twenty."

She understood her grandmother was exaggerating; it is approximately ten to fifteen minutes up the road. Melina replied, "Gran, my Godparents were conversing with me, and you know how they tend to talk for extended periods." This response diverted her grandmother's attention, avoiding mention of her two friends. Melina knew that the moment she mentioned her Godparents, her grandmother would, at least for now, drop the matter. It was a reliable diversion; one she'd used before. Predictably, Gran paused, her expression softening, though not entirely letting go.

"But Mel," her grandmother said gently, "you must make the time to visit them. They've always been so good to you. Such a lovely couple, and they care about you deeply." Melina offered a small nod, careful to keep her tone light.   "Okay, Gran. I'll try to find some time to spend with them while I'm here."

She smiled, but it didn't reach her eyes. The words came easily—too easily. She didn't mean them, not really. They were simply meant to reassure, to smooth the conversation over, to end it without further probing. In truth, she had no intention of making that visit, not because she didn't care, but because everything felt too tangled lately. There was too much on her mind, and too much she wasn't ready to say out loud. Gran didn't press the issue further, but Melina could feel her eyes lingering, watchful, knowing. It was as if she could sense there was more beneath the surface, something unspoken. Still, she let it go, for now, turning her attention back to her recipe book with a sigh. Melina stood quietly, the moment hanging in the air like steam from the kettle. She wondered how long she could keep deflecting before someone finally demanded the truth.

I always enjoy spending time with my godparents; their warmth and quirky stories make every visit memorable. Still, I have to mentally prepare myself for the inevitable round of questions. They'll want updates on my studies, my friends, my weekend plans—sometimes it feels like an informal interview that could go on for hours.

"Mel, did you visit the coffee shop today?" Gran asked with a knowing smile as I stepped into the kitchen.

I froze for a second, then grinned.

"How do you *always* know, Gran?"

She nodded toward the small bakery bag I tried to sneak past her. "You never come back empty-handed, and you *always* bring your grandfather's favourite cheesecake."

I laughed, caught in the act. "I was trying to hide it from you. I didn't want you to see the red velvet cheesecake: I know how he always claims he's watching his sugar."

Gran waved a hand dismissively.

"Don't worry, child. I know he loves that red velvet more than he lets on. He'll 'accidentally' eat half of it by the time the kettle's boiled." We shared a smile, the kind that comes from years of quiet rituals and unspoken understanding. These little moments, filled with teasing and tenderness, are what I treasure most. Even if I have to brace myself for the well-meaning interrogation that's sure to follow. Inside, the cottage was just as cozy as ever, smelling faintly of cinnamon and old books, with doilies on every table and family photos lining the mantel. Grandad was in his usual armchair, half-asleep with the radio murmuring in the background. Melina continued, and I loved the walk; it cleared my head, and I missed that.

"I got everything," Melina said, holding up the bag. "Well, almost everything. Mr. Rodger didn't have the jam you liked."

"He never does," Gran replied with a wry smile, taking the shopping bag from Melina and peering inside.

"But look at you, running errands like a proper granddaughter. I should send you out more often." Melina chuckled and leaned against the kitchen counter.

"Gran, have you noticed that Mr. Rodger's getting... slower? He still remembers everyone's favourite biscuits, but I don't think he should be working alone anymore."

Gran paused, glancing up from the groceries. "Oh, that old goat?" she said fondly. "He's been moving at that pace since the 90s. It's just now you're old enough to notice."

"But seriously," Melina continued, her brow creasing slightly, "he looked tired. He was still cheerful, but... I don't know. I think he needs someone there to help."

Gran nodded thoughtfully as she began unloading the items onto the counter. "His son Sammy lives upstairs, you know, he's around with his wife and those two wild children. You probably didn't see them; they keep to themselves most days. But Sammy's an early riser, just like his dad. He helps when it's needed."

"I didn't realise they lived above the shop," Melina said.

"They've been there for years," Gran replied, waving her hand dismissively. "Mr. Rodger might be slowing down, but don't be fooled, he's a tough old bird. Nothing keeps him down for long. Stubborn as anything, that one." Melina smiled, but her thoughts lingered. She remembered the subtle way Mr. Rodger had paused between tasks, the faint tiredness behind his eyes. He had always seemed timeless to her, as much a fixture of the village as the stone cottages and the ivy-covered church. But now... now he just looked older. Gran gave her a gentle nudge with her elbow. "Don't look so serious. It's just life, darling. People age, things change, but we keep going." Melina nodded, though the weight of that truth settled heavier than expected.

****

Melina rolled her eyes affectionately and followed her into the kitchen.

"I also saw Samantha and Ruthie."

Her grandmother paused at the counter, a smile creeping across her face. "Did you know? That's nice. You girls were thick as thieves once."

"We're meeting up again tomorrow evening," Melina said. "They suggested a walk to the old tree."

"That tree's heard more secrets than a church confessional," her grandmother said with a chuckle. Melina leaned against the kitchen doorway, watching her gran begin to unpack the groceries. The moment felt still and tender, ordinary, yet special in its own way. Her grandmother leaned in and whispered,

"Monica's upstairs. Your mother and the rest of the family are handling the decorations and getting everything ready for the surprise." Mel hesitated, then said,

"I should probably invite Sam and Ruthie. They've always been there for me."

Her grandmother nodded without hesitation, "That's fine with me, sweetheart. Just don't mention it to Monica. You know how particular your sister can be, and this party…" even though it is a surprise. She glanced around the modest room with a faint smile. "Well, it's not exactly up to her usual standards." There was no malice in her voice, just the worn wisdom of someone who had long learned to navigate the delicate balance between sisters.

"Gran, this is just something small for you all up here," Mel said with a soft smile, brushing a stray curl from her cheek. "I'm sure Mom and Dad are already planning the engagement party of the year."

She let out a small laugh, trying to keep it light. *And probably the in-laws too,* she thought. *They'll most likely take over the whole affair, given their social standing; how could they not?* Still, there was no bitterness in her tone, just quiet acceptance. Her grandmother chuckled knowingly, setting a teacup down with a gentle clink. "Don't forget the fiancé," she added, lowering her voice with playful mischief. "I hear his family is absolutely loaded. And with him being a promising young cardiologist, well... I can only imagine the kind of celebration his parents have in mind."

Mel laughed, but it caught slightly in her throat. There was a flicker of something behind her eyes, something quieter, harder to name. Not envy exactly, but a pang of something close. *Distance,* maybe. *Disconnection.* She loved Monica. But lately, it felt like her sister was floating further and further into a different world, one filled with polished dinner parties, high expectations, and people who barely knew them. Would Monica even understand what today meant? Would she see the love behind the folded napkins and home-baked cake, or just see that it wasn't enough? Still, for now, Mel pushed the thought aside. She was glad to be here, back in her grandmother's warm kitchen, wrapped in the scent of cinnamon and old wood polish. The kettle hissed gently in the background, and the familiar creak of the floorboards beneath her feet made her feel, if only for a moment, grounded again. This soft, imperfect gathering was her way of showing love. It might not sparkle, but it was real.

CHAPTER TEN

The small engagement party was nothing like the extravagant celebration Monica had once envisioned. There were no grand venues adorned with crystal chandeliers, no sweeping staircase for a dramatic entrance, and certainly no string quartet playing in the background. Instead, it all unfolded in the same familiar living room where they'd celebrated birthdays, exchanged holiday gifts, and gathered during rainy afternoons with cups of tea in hand.

But what it lacked in glamour, it made up for in warmth. Soft fairy lights were strung across the mantel, casting a gentle glow on the framed family photos that lined the shelves. The scent of homemade food drifted from the kitchen: her aunt's famous lasagna, her dad's signature garlic bread, and mingled with the sweet aroma of roses someone had thoughtfully arranged in a mason jar centrepiece. She took a step back and looked at the finished table. It was simple, but warm. Honest. Love lived in every detail.

Please like it, she thought silently. *Please don't wish it were more.* And later, when Monica walked in, when she saw the candles flickering and her grandmother tearfully covering her mouth in awe of what Melina had done, that was when Melina knew.

It was enough.

It was quieter this time, more intimate, yet no less meaningful. The hum of conversation flowed easily, punctuated by laughter and the gentle clinking of glasses. Monica looked around at the faces she loved, some smiling, some misty-eyed, and realized this was not what she would have planned. Monica had always dreamed of an extravagant engagement party, something out of a magazine spread, with cascading flowers, a live band, and guests dressed in designer gowns. She was used to getting what she wanted.

As the eldest and the favourite, she'd always been spoiled in ways her younger sister, Melina, never was. From childhood dance recitals to university celebrations, Monica's milestones had been met with fanfare, while Melina often lingered quietly on the sidelines. So, this modest surprise gathering, thrown together in the family living room, wasn't exactly her idea of a dream celebration. There were no gold invitations, no event planner, no dramatic reveal of the ring under a spotlight. And if she were being honest, she would've much rather been sipping champagne in a rooftop venue with a skyline view. But she smiled politely, played along, and thanked everyone graciously. She tolerated the whole thing for one reason: their grandparents. They had put so much love and effort into organizing the evening, and Monica couldn't bear the thought of them feeling unappreciated. Despite the flicker of disappointment, she felt every time she looked around the room, she reminded herself that this wasn't just about her; it was about family, and the people who had always been there for her, even when the spotlight wasn't. Melina stood by the open kitchen window, where cool evening air brought the scent of cut grass and wildflowers. Laughter echoed from the living room, but it felt distant.

The front door swung open with a creak, and Dad's voice rang out through the hallway, loud, enthusiastic, and full of that familiar urgency that always meant guests had arrived. "They're here!" he called, barely containing his excitement. Within moments, the house transformed from its usual calm into a whirlwind of noise and energy. Laughter echoed off the walls, overlapping with the rhythm of hurried footsteps and the low hum of overlapping conversations. Aunts, uncles, and cousins began pouring in, some from nearby villages, others from distant towns we only ever heard about in stories. Coats were flung over banisters, cheeks were kissed, and greetings came in a flurry of accents and affection. Some faces I hadn't seen in years, their smiles unchanged, their voices instantly familiar. I offered a wide, welcoming wave and a bright smile, calling out names I remembered while trying to match them to grown-up versions of childhood memories. I was quickly swept into the warm, chaotic current of family, the kind that carries you whether you're ready or not. Gran clapped her hands, her eyes twinkling with joy as she turned toward us.

"Come on now, girls, don't be shy," she said, nudging me and Mel gently forward. "Do you remember your Aunty Jen and Uncle Selvin?"

I glanced at Monica, who gave me a helpless smile. Aunty Jen was already wrapping her arms around us in one of her famously tight hugs, and Uncle Selvin gave a nod and a grin, his glasses slipping down his nose.

"Yes, of course!" I replied, even though I wasn't sure whether my last memory of them involved a wedding or a barbecue. It didn't matter. Tonight, the house was full, alive, and humming with the kind of love that didn't need constant reminders- it simply picked up where it left off. Aunt Jen was unforgettable in the best possible way. She had a gentle presence that lit up a room without trying, and everyone in the family adored her, especially the children. She never missed a birthday or holiday, always arriving with a carefully wrapped gift tied in colourful ribbons, as if she'd stepped out of a storybook. There was something magical about the way she remembered even the smallest details: your favourite candy, the name of your school project, or that book you once mentioned loving in passing. She was soft-spoken but full of warmth, the kind of person who made you feel truly seen. Her hugs lingered just long enough to make you feel safe, and her smile had a way of easing even the most awkward family tension. Aunt May, on the other hand, was a completely different flavour of wonderful. She was loud, opinionated, and famously unfiltered. If Aunt Jen was the gentle breeze, Aunt May was the sudden gust of wind that rearranged everything—and somehow made it better. She spoke her mind without hesitation, and though her words could be blunt, they were always rooted in honesty and love.

I loved them both, Aunt Jen for her kindness and quiet strength, and Aunt May for her fiery spirit and unapologetic boldness. Together, they balanced each other out like two sides of the same coin, and having them in the same room was like watching heart and humour come to life at once. Her perfume was familiar, floral, and sweet, and her embrace was just as warm as I remembered. Uncle Morris followed behind with his usual quiet smile, his arms full of neatly wrapped packages that hinted at more surprises to come. She gently pulled back and wagged a finger at me, her eyes twinkling. "Girl, stop that laughing, and what did I tell you? No 'Auntie Jeanette' nonsense. It's just *Aunt Jen*." All these aunties and cousins, I don't even remember some of their names, I just smiled, and nodded, and when they started

That had been a deliberate slip on my part, and we both knew it. A little mischief between us was part of the tradition, and her playful scolding only made me laugh harder. As the greetings continued, I spotted Uncle Selvin just behind her and hurried over to wrap him in a big hug. He was my dad's younger brother, the second-born, and married to Aunt Jeanette, aunt by title, but never quite as warm as Aunt Jen.

"Well, well!" Uncle Selvin said, holding me at arm's length to get a better look. "How's my little niece doing these days? You've grown a lot since the last time I saw you. What are you up to now, eh? Off causing trouble or making us proud?" His voice still had that rich, lilting tone that always made his jokes land with extra charm, and his eyes crinkled with genuine warmth. The kind of uncle who always remembered your school milestones, always asked the right questions, even if he couldn't always stay long.

"I'm trying to be good," I said, grinning, "but you know how that goes." The room was getting louder with overlapping voices, bursts of laughter, and the clinking of teacups as someone brought out refreshments. The kind of noise that only happened when the whole family was under one roof, and I had almost forgotten how good it felt.

"Are you still planning to pursue nursing?" Uncle Selvin inquired, but before I could respond, he shifted his focus to the activity in the room. With his usual energy, he made a beeline for Monica.

"Ah, there she is, the engagement girl!" he said with a hearty laugh, wrapping her in a big, affectionate hug. His broad smile lit up his face as he held her at arm's length, looking her over like a proud uncle at a graduation.

"Monica," he continued, eyes twinkling, "and where is the lucky fellow? Is he here yet?"

Monica shook her head gently, brushing a loose curl behind her ear as she tried to steady her voice. "He came by this morning," she said, her tone light but slightly uncertain. "But he was called away on something urgent. He's going to try to catch up with us later." Her words hung in the air for a moment, not quite convincing, even to herself.

"He's had a lot of appointments to manage lately," she added quickly, as if that might make it sound more reasonable.

"Busy on a Saturday evening for his engagement party?" Uncle Selvin raised a sceptical eyebrow, a playful smirk tugging at the corner of his mouth. "What kind of work keeps a man running around when he should be with his fiancée?"

"He's a doctor," Monica replied, sitting up a little straighter, her voice filled with pride. "He's always busy. Emergencies don't wait for the weekend, you know. He said there were a few patients he couldn't reschedule."

Aunt May, who had just walked in carrying a tray of fruit punch, gave a pointed look over her glasses.

"Must be some patients missing his engagement party," she said with a teasing huff.

Monica forced a laugh, though her smile faltered for the briefest second. She could feel the weight of their eyes on her, the curiosity, the skepticism, but she wasn't about to let doubt take centre stage. Not tonight.

"I'm sure he'll show up," she said, more to herself than anyone else. "He always keeps his word."

Melina, standing off to the side with a paper plate in her hand, glanced at her sister but said nothing. She noticed the faint crease between Monica's brows—the kind that only appeared when she was trying to sound more confident than she felt.

"A doctor, eh?" Uncle Selvin nodded approvingly. "Alright, I'll let him off for now, but he'd better show up with a firm handshake and a proper smile!" Monica laughed, though there was a hint of nervousness behind it. I caught the brief flicker in her eyes, the kind that only someone close would notice. She was excited, but I could tell she was also hoping everything would go perfectly today. The room continued to buzz with conversation, but Uncle Selvin's voice rose above the rest as he called out, "Well, I can't wait to meet the man stealing our girl". Monica smiled politely, but her fingers fidgeted with the edge of her sleeve, something she always did when she was a little, seemed thrilled, caught up in the excitement of seeing her engaged, but I could see it in her eyes: that flicker of doubt she was trying to keep buried beneath the smiles and small talk.

"I am confident that you will all appreciate his presence," she stated promptly, her voice maintaining a composed demeanour. "He is eager to meet everyone; however, he had to leave due to an emergency."

Aunt Jen, who had been standing nearby listening in, leaned over and gave Monica a quick squeeze. "Don't worry, darling," she said warmly. "If he's as lovely as you say, we'll welcome him with open arms. Just make sure he brings you happiness and treats you right. That's what matters." Monica nodded, but her smile didn't quite reach her eyes. Uncle Selvin, still in high spirits, chuckled as he moved off to grab a slice of cake from the kitchen table.

"He'd better show up with a ring and a story," he called over his shoulder. "And not some flimsy handshake either, I want to see confidence!" The family laughed, and the moment lightened again, but I stayed close to Monica, watching her carefully. I wanted to ask if everything was okay. I wanted to tell her what I had overheard a few days ago, something that still sat heavy in my chest felt like a stone, but the words wouldn't come. Not yet. Not while she was still glowing in everyone else's eyes.

"Are you alright?" I whispered, nudging her gently.

She looked at me for a split second too long before answering. "Yeah. Just a bit tired, that's all."

But I know better.

"Okay, steady on, Uncle Selvin," Monica said with a playful smile. "I'd better make myself comfortable while you launch into your full interrogation. I just hope you go easy on him, this doctor bloke who wants to marry your *favourite* niece."

Uncle Selvin crossed his arms and raised an eyebrow, clearly enjoying the moment. "Hmph. He better *be* worthy," he said in a mock-stern voice. Then, turning dramatically toward the kitchen, he called out, "Chester! We'll have the interrogation room ready when your future son-in-law arrives!" Everyone laughed, but Selvin's eyes still held a hint of seriousness behind the theatrics.

"Selvin," Dad chimed in with a shake of his head and a chuckle, "I don't think we need to go to such extremes. The young man's a doctor, he's supposed to have good credentials, right?"

He paused, his expression softening with pride. "He's in his final year of surgical training. And from what Monica's told me, he's going places. Give it a few more years, and he'll be one of the top surgeons in the country. You'll see." He leaned back, hands on his hips, grinning from ear to ear.   "I'm going to be a very proud in-law. People are going to start calling me when they need a specialist; they'll want the best, and I'll happen to know him personally."

A few chuckles rippled through the room, and Uncle Selvin finally nodded, his stern façade giving way to a knowing smile.

"Alright then," he said, clapping his hands together. "Let's put the champagne on ice. Can't toast to a future top surgeon with warm bubbly.

" Dad laughed. "Now you're talking."

The atmosphere lightened even further, the room now buzzing with playful banter, anticipation, and the clinking of glasses. But as Monica smiled along with the rest of them, a quiet unease fluttered in her chest. She glanced at the clock, then down at her phone. No new messages. No missed calls. He promised he'd be here.

CHAPTER ELEVEN

Melina's mother was talking animatedly with Aunt May by the punch bowl, her father was engaging with their cousins, and Monica, of course, was the star of the show. Dressed in a soft cream-colored sweater and jeans, she looked effortless, her laughter lighting up the room as she spoke about the wedding. Melina, leaning against the counter, couldn't help but notice how her sister seemed to glow. But what stood out the most was that Sylvester Monica had left for an urgent call, saying he would be back later. Monica's fiancé, Sylvester, is always busy.

"I swear, he's the busiest man alive," Monica had said earlier, her voice brimming with affection as she explained why Sylvester couldn't attend the small gathering. "He's a cardiology resident at the hospital, and he has a patient case he needs to follow up on. His schedule is crazy right now." Melina had smiled politely, but something about the excuse didn't sit right with her. She knew the demands of the medical field; hell, she'd heard enough about it from friends who were in med school, but something felt off. *How busy could one man be?* Melina's phone buzzed in her pocket, snapping her out of her thoughts. She pulled it out and saw a message from Monica.

Monica: *"Can you come sit with me for a second?*

Melina glanced around the room. Her sister's smile was wide, but there was something in her eyes, something soft and almost pleading. Without thinking, Melina pocketed the phone and walked into the living room. Monica was sitting on the couch, surrounded by her cousins and a couple of family friends, her hands fidgeting with a napkin in her lap. She looked up when Melina approached, her smile bright but just a little too tight.

"Hey," Melina said, sitting down beside her. "Everything okay?"

Monica nodded quickly, but the tension in her shoulders told another story. "Yeah, yeah, just... It's weird, you know? Having everyone here, but Sylvester is not able to make it. It's like..." She trailed off, her fingers smoothing the napkin one more time. "I mean, this was supposed to be a special moment for the two of us, you know?" Melina bit her lip. She wanted to say something, anything, to ease her sister's mind, but the words stuck in her throat. She didn't know how to explain the creeping suspicion she felt that something about Sylvester's absence felt *intentional.*

"It's fine," Monica continued, her voice lifting slightly, as if trying to convince herself. "He's just so busy right now. He promised he'd make it to the wedding planning next month. And I trust him." "Also, his family will be planning the engagement party of the century," continued Monica. There was a pause, a slight crack in Monica's voice that Melina noticed but chose not to comment on. Instead, she nodded.

"Yeah, I'm sure he's just caught up. You guys are both busy, right?"

Monica smiled at that, though it didn't quite reach her eyes. "Exactly. You know how it is. You and Sylvester are both in your careers, and I get it. I don't want to be one of those brides who nag their fiancé about everything. But... I don't know, I just wanted him here, you know?" Melina nodded again, glancing around the room at the distant faces of their family, all enjoying the party, all caught up in their own lives. Monica's gaze followed hers, and for a moment, there was a brief flicker of something Melina couldn't quite read.

"Don't worry about it," Melina said gently, trying to mask the uncertainty she felt inside. "It'll be fine. He'll be here when it matters."

Monica's lips curled into a small smile. "Thanks, Mel. You always know how to make me feel better."Melina's smile faltered for a split second. *Does she know how to make me feel better, though?*

As the night wore on, the party didn't feel like the joyous occasion it was supposed to be. But still, there was no sign of Sylvester. There was no clinking of champagne glasses in celebration. No stories were being exchanged about the future, or about how lucky Monica was to have found her perfect match. Melina couldn't shake the feeling that something was off. The whole thing, the absence of Sylvester, the way Monica kept looking at the door as if expecting him to walk in at any moment, felt like a façade. The sitting room was getting increasingly crowded, filled with bursts of laughter and a warm hum of overlapping conversations. It seemed like everyone wanted a moment with my sister, either to congratulate her or just to bask in the excitement of her engagement. The air buzzed with joy, and even the usually stiff armchairs looked more welcoming under the soft glow of the overhead lights. Mom entered the kitchen and started gathering the plastic cups, knives, and forks she had brought.

"Please hurry, the guests need refreshments," she said. "Is the tea ready, Mel? Please bring it along with the sandwiches." The atmosphere in the living room was lively and warm, filled with the soft hum of conversation and bursts of laughter. I carried in the tea tray first, careful not to spill, then returned to fetch the sandwiches and a few bowls of crisps and snacks. Gran appeared a moment later, balancing a tray of beautifully arranged cakes, her usual calm presence adding to the sense of celebration. Together, we set everything out, the table slowly filling with homemade treats and the comforting scent of afternoon tea. It was a simple gathering, but it felt special, like the kind of moment we'd remember long after the cups were cleared away. There was something off about the way Monica was barely touching her food, but then again, that wasn't entirely new. She had always been a picky eater, the kind who could spend twenty minutes methodically rearranging a salad without actually consuming much of it. Still, tonight felt different. Her fork moved absently, never quite reaching her mouth, as if she were only pretending to participate in the meal.

Maybe that's how she kept that enviable figure everyone liked to whisper about. Some would call her skinny; others claimed she simply "ate clean," mostly vegetables, a few berries on a plate, and occasionally, a dainty bite of something sweet if it was homemade or beautifully plated. Gran often said she ate like a bird, though Melina sometimes wondered if birds at least ate with more enthusiasm. But Melina had known her sister long enough to recognize the signs. This wasn't just about health or discipline. It felt more like a distraction. Or anxiety. Monica's smile was intact, her voice as composed as ever, but there was a tightness around her eyes that hadn't been there before. Was it the pressure of the engagement? The upcoming party? Or something else entirely?

Melina watched her sister quietly, the questions building silently in her mind, unspoken, but not unnoticed. Monica stood at around five feet, graceful, poised, effortlessly elegant. It was a height that seemed made for her, just enough to be striking without ever drawing attention on purpose. She probably wore a size 6, maybe an 8 on days she'd dismiss with a breezy comment, her figure naturally balanced in a way that drew admiration from relatives and strangers alike. The remarks came often, unsolicited, sometimes even intrusive, yet Monica always received them with a polite smile, as if they were about someone else entirely. But it wasn't just her shape that turned heads; it was the *way* she carried herself. Monica moved like she had been born under the glow of soft lighting, with the quiet self-assurance of someone who didn't need to try. Her gestures were smooth, her posture flawless, and even the simplest things, brushing hair behind her ear, folding a napkin, looked refined. She didn't chase attention. It just... followed her. Melina noticed it all, of course. She always had. And while she loved her sister deeply, she couldn't help but feel the quiet weight of comparison, often unspoken, but always there.

Monica made it look so easy: the style, the charm, the ability to float through rooms like she belonged in every one of them. Melina, by contrast, felt like she was always figuring things out, what to say, how to stand, and whether anyone noticed when she left. She would never admit it aloud, but sometimes she wondered what it would feel like to be Monica, even for a day. To be admired so casually, to be effortlessly composed. To not feel like you had to work at simply existing in your own skin. Still, Monica was her sister. Her best friend, once upon a time. And despite the distance that sometimes grew between them, quiet and slow, like ivy creeping along a wall, Melina wanted to believe there was still a closeness worth salvaging.

Even if she didn't quite know how anymore. She was still watching Monica when her sister looked up from her untouched plate, their eyes meeting across the dining room for the briefest moment. It wasn't awkward, not exactly, but there was a flicker of something. Recognition, maybe. Or an unspoken question neither of them had found the courage to ask. Monica offered a small smile, the kind that looked more practiced than genuine. "You've been quiet all morning," she said softly, her voice low enough that only Melina could hear it over the soft clatter of cutlery and murmurs of conversation from the rest of the table. Melina shrugged, reaching for her glass of water. "Just tired," she said. A simple answer. A safe one. Monica tilted her head slightly.

"You sure? You seem... distracted."

Melina hesitated, her fingers tightening around the glass. *Say something real,* a voice whispered in her mind. *Ask her. Tell*

her. Anything. But instead, she offered the same smile Monica had given her, thin, polite, and hollow.

"I'm fine," she said. "Really."

Monica nodded, but she didn't look convinced. She studied her sister a second longer, then reached across the table and nudged a small plate toward her.

"Gran made the apple tart again," she said. "I know it's your favourite." Melina looked down at the plate, flaky pastry, still warm, the scent of cinnamon drifting up like a memory. She wasn't hungry. Not even a little. But something about the quiet gesture settled in her chest like warmth.

"Thanks," she murmured.

The conversation around them moved on. Plates were passed, stories retold, laughter rising in little waves. But between them, a thin, invisible thread had been tied, fragile, maybe, but still there. Melina glanced at Monica again. She looked perfect, as always. But now, Melina noticed the slight crease between her brows, the way she kept checking her phone when she thought no one was looking. Maybe she wasn't pretending. But it wasn't just Monica's figure that turned heads; it was the way she *moved*. There was a quiet, unstudied grace about her, as though every step she took had already been choreographed by instinct. Whether she was gliding across a room, pausing to adjust a chair, or simply standing still, Monica carried herself with the calm poise of someone who never questioned her place in the world. Her posture was impeccable, her gestures fluid, and her presence magnetic, without a hint of effort or self-awareness. She didn't flaunt her beauty or her elegance.

She often seemed entirely unaware of the effect she had on people. That was part of her mystique; she wasn't trying to be admired; she simply *was*. Her kind of grace didn't belong to the Instagram age; it belonged to another time, like something pulled from an old film reel, all soft edges and quiet glamour. Classic. Understated. Impossible to imitate. To Melina, Monica often felt like a walking contradiction: soft-spoken, yet impossible to ignore; delicate in appearance, yet somehow emotionally unshakable.

There was a stillness to her that people mistook for calm, but Melina had seen the steel beneath it, the quiet resilience Monica wore like perfume: subtle, invisible, but always there. And though Monica never sought the spotlight, it had a habit of finding her anyway. She didn't chase admiration; it followed her, lingered around her like a scent on silk. Even in silence, even in stillness, she was someone people *noticed*. Melina sometimes wondered what that felt like to walk into a room and feel as though the air shifted slightly just because you were in it. To not have to *earn* attention, but to be given it without question. And yet, there was something lonely in it, too. Something Melina couldn't quite name. As if Monica lived in a glasshouse where everyone admired the view, but no one truly stepped inside. Next to Monica, most people seemed to fade just a little, not because she was loud or attention-seeking, but because she carried a quiet confidence that naturally drew the eye. It wasn't the kind of confidence you could fake or rehearse; it was woven into her very being, like it had been stitched into her bones before birth. She didn't dominate a room; she *settled* into it, and somehow, the room adjusted to her.

Not like our brother Eton, who stood well over six feet tall and always looked one sneeze away from cracking his head on a ceiling beam. Eton didn't enter a room so much as *collide* with it. Doorways were narrow escapes. Chairs groaned under him like they'd been warned but hadn't prepared. Where Monica glided, Eton ducked and folded and tried not to knock things over. People noticed him, too, but for entirely different reasons. And yet, in their own ways, both of them had a kind of presence. Monica's was smooth and seamless, like water finding its level. Eton's was more like a boulder in a stream, unmissable, sometimes inconvenient, but undeniably *there*. And me? Well, I always felt like the footnote in that paragraph. Not invisible exactly, just... comfortably unremarkable. Anyway, back to the party

CHAPTER TWELVE

The living room had exploded into the kind of joyful chaos only our family could create. The air was thick with overlapping conversations, shouts of recognition, peals of laughter, and the occasional squeal from a toddler darting between legs. Plates clinked, glasses chimed, and someone had already commandeered the stereo to play a throwback playlist that blended '90s reggae with Aunt May's favourite old-school ballads.

The furniture had been rearranged to make space, armchairs pushed against walls, the coffee table turned buffet stand, and every available surface held either food, drinks, or someone's handbag. Warm light from the fairy lights draped across the ceiling gave the room a cozy, golden glow, as if the walls themselves were leaning in to listen. It wasn't the lavish engagement party Monica once imagined, but in this moment, with the hum of laughter and the smell of Gran's famous coconut rice wafting from the kitchen, it didn't matter. The house was full. And for a brief moment, so was everyone's stomach.

"Mel!" Monica called out from across the room, waving me over with that familiar brightness in her voice. "Come sit with me, we still haven't finished discussing your university studies. "I groaned playfully but made my way toward her, weaving through the crowd.

"I think I've answered all your questions already," I said, raising my hands in mock surrender. "Please, slow down, Monica. That's enough interrogation for one afternoon. I already spent half of last night questioning myself."

She laughed, tossing her hair over her shoulder as she patted the seat next to her. "Oh, come on. I'm just trying to keep up. You never tell us anything unless we drag it out of you." I sank into the chair beside her with a sigh, but I couldn't help smiling. Monica's questions could feel like spotlights, bright, persistent, and a little too direct, but they came from a place of genuine care. It was just her way: curious, intense, and impossible to ignore. Even when she was annoying, she meant well. Around us, the party buzzed with warmth and motion. Laughter rose and fell like music, chairs scraped back and forth, and the scent of freshly sliced cake drifted in on the steam of just-poured tea. Someone in the corner had started a quiet sing-along, the melody drifting lightly above the chatter. For the first time in a long while, it felt good to just *be* there, surrounded by voices I knew, people who didn't need explanations, and a kind of comfort that only came from home. I glanced sideways at Monica. She was still watching me, one eyebrow raised, clearly waiting for more.

"All right," I said with a sigh of defeat, reaching for a slice of cake. "One more question. But only if I get to ask you something next."

Her eyes sparkled with amusement.

"Deal".

I took a slow bite of cake, buying myself a moment. Then, as casually as I could, I turned to her.

"So," I began, brushing a crumb off my lap, "since it's my turn now, can I ask you something about Sylvester?" Monica's smile faltered just slightly, but she recovered quickly.

"Sure," she said, her tone easy, though her fingers fussed a little too long with her teacup.

"Why did he leave so quickly?". "He just arrived this morning," I asked, keeping my voice light. "Didn't even stay long enough to blink, let alone mingle."

Monica gave a small, practiced shrug. "Oh, you know how it is with him, always on call. He got an urgent message from the hospital and had to dash off." I nodded slowly, not entirely convinced. "Right. That makes sense, I guess." Then I added, "But still he came all this way and didn't even stay for the second round of tea. That's unusual, isn't it?" She didn't answer right away.

Instead, she glanced down at her plate, nudging a strawberry around with her fork. "Well, you know Sylvester. He's committed to his work. That's one of the things I admire about him." "Sure," I said, watching her closely. "It's just that... this was supposed to be a bit of a celebration, right? You and him. The engagement."

Monica looked up then, her expression carefully neutral. "The proper engagement party's still being planned. This wasn't... that. Not really. Gran got a little excited, that's all." I leaned back slightly, chewing over her words. There it was again, that quiet deflection. Monica always polished. Always composed. But under the surface, something about Sylvester made her tense. Still, I let it go. For now.

"Well, just don't let him miss the real party," I said with a half-smile. "You'll both have some explaining to do if he vanishes again."

She chuckled softly, but the sound didn't quite reach her eyes. "Don't worry," Monica said, lifting her chin just slightly. "He'll definitely be at the big engagement party, *the one his family is hosting.*" There was a flicker of something in her tone, a hint of satisfaction, pride, maybe, or something just a touch sharper. Her smile turned a shade smug, the kind that said more than her words ever could. Melina caught it instantly. It wasn't just about Sylvester being dependable. It was about who he was connected to. *The Longhorns.* Everyone knew the name. Old money. Serious money. The kind of family whose names ended up on brass plaques and hospital wings. They didn't just have wealth, they had *influence*.

Monica didn't say any of that outright, but she didn't have to. The way she said "his family" carried enough weight to do the talking. Melina smiled politely, but a quiet knot tightened in her chest. She couldn't tell if Monica was trying to reassure her or remind her that she'd landed someone whose world spun on a much bigger, glossier axis. Out of the corner of my eye, I spotted Gran heading toward the kitchen, her stride purposeful and her apron already tied with military precision. Instinctively, I stepped back and pressed myself against the wall, hoping the shadow of the doorway might shield me. If I were lucky, maybe she hadn't seen me. But deep down, I knew better. She didn't miss a thing.

"Mel, I *saw* you," came her voice, light but laced with that unmistakable *do-not-even-think-about-it* firmness. "Stop skulking and get in here. These sausage rolls won't heat themselves." I sighed and peeked around the corner, already caught. Gran stood with one hand on her hip and a wooden spoon in the other, her unofficial sceptre of domestic command. Her eyes twinkled, but she wasn't playing around.

"Come on, love," she added, her smile turning more persuasive. "It's your sister's big moment, and everyone wants to celebrate. Let's make sure they're properly fed while they do it."

I couldn't argue with that logic, especially not when it came wrapped in the scent of warm pastry and Gran's stubborn affection. I stepped into the kitchen with a sheepish grin.

"Okay, okay," I said, rolling up my sleeves. "But only if I get first dibs on one of those sausage rolls." Gran winked. "You know the rule, helpers eat first." It was impossible not to smile back. Despite the chaos and the strange ache that sometimes sat quietly behind my chest when I thought about Monica's engagement, something was grounding about being in that warm kitchen, next to Gran, doing what we'd always done.

"I know," I muttered under my breath as I slowly stepped forward. *She's always having a big moment,* I added silently, though not unkindly. That was just how it felt sometimes, like I was always orbiting around someone else's star. Still, I followed Gran into the kitchen. The clinking of teacups and the smell of freshly baked pastries met me like a familiar embrace. As I tried on an apron, I told myself it didn't matter. Tonight wasn't about me. It was about family, about being present, even when it was easier not to be. I didn't want to admit how much the little things mattered: a hand with the dishes, a warm smile, just showing up. Helping Gran in the kitchen turned out to be a blessing. It gave me purpose, something to focus on, and more importantly, a perfect excuse to avoid yet another round of exhausting small talk with Mr and Mrs Jonas, my well-meaning but relentlessly inquisitive godparents. I could only deflect so many questions about my plans, my future, or whether I was "seeing anyone these days" before my patience wore thin. The clatter of pots and the scent of simmering herbs felt like a shield from all of that. In the quiet rhythm of chopping and stirring, I found a strange kind of peace. Gran didn't ask questions, not the kind that cornered me. She just passed me a bowl, asked for the thyme, or nudged me gently out of the way when I lingered too long by the sink. Her silence was comforting, not awkward. It said, *You're here, and that's enough.*

Mr and Mrs Jonas, on the other hand, operated like a two-person interrogation team disguised as a cheerful couple. They meant well, I knew that. They always had. Growing up, they never missed a birthday, never forgot to send postcards from their travels, and were the first to drop off casseroles when Mom got sick. But now, every question felt like a spotlight I wasn't ready to stand under.

"What are you working on these days?" "Still in that tiny apartment ". Any special someone in the picture?" It was all too much. I knew they asked because they cared, but lately, I didn't know how to give them the answers they wanted. So, I stayed in the kitchen, making more sandwiches beside Gran, and letting the noise of the gathering fade into the background. I liked it better this way. There was something sacred in the small acts of folding napkins, stirring gravy, and passing a spoonful of sauce for Gran to taste. These were the kinds of things that didn't demand explanation. They just were. And maybe, for tonight, that was enough

CHAPTER THIRTEEN

Gran looked over at me, her brow gently furrowed, concern softening her eyes. "Are you all right, Mel?" she asked, her voice low and kind. "You look a little... worn down." I forced a small smile and wiped my hands on a dish towel. "Just tired, Gran," I said, trying to sound casual. "All the shopping and talking, it's been a long day." She didn't say anything right away. Just kept stirring the pot on the stove, the wooden spoon making slow, thoughtful circles. I knew that look. She wasn't convinced, but she wasn't going to push. That was her way, gentle patience that made it harder to pretend I was fine. Gran didn't press me, but her silence left space for my thoughts to creep back in, the ones I'd been pushing aside all day. I busied myself wiping down the counter, but my hands moved on autopilot. What I really wanted to say was, *I'm not just tired, Gran. I'm scared. I heard something I shouldn't have, and now I don't know what to do with it.*

It had been a few days since I overheard that conversation-just, just a sliver of it, really, but enough to rattle me.

Enough to make me look at Monica's fiancé differently. There was something about his family, something hidden beneath the polished smiles and charming toasts. I still wasn't sure what it all meant, not completely. But it didn't feel right. And yet... Monica was so happy. Genuinely glowing. She hadn't smiled like that in years, not since, I stopped myself. No use going there. I glanced over at Gran, who was now humming softly to herself, her rhythm steady and sure. I envied her peace. She made everything seem simple. But this wasn't simple. If I told Monica, it could shatter everything. If I stayed silent, and something happened...My stomach twisted. I stirred the gravy a little too hard.

"Careful," Gran said gently, giving me a sideways glance. "You're going to beat the flavour out of it."

I gave a weak laugh. "Sorry. Guess I'm more tired than I thought."

She didn't answer, just reached over and squeezed my hand.

"Hand me those napkins, will you?" she said with a gentle little smile that stated You will be okay, nodding toward the sideboard. "The ones with the little blue flowers. "I passed them over, and for a moment we worked in companionable silence, just the two of us, away from the noise and excitement. The kettle began to whistle, sharp and shrill, cutting through the muffled laughter from the other room. Gran poured the hot water into the teapot, the steam curling upward like a soft ribbon. "You know," she said as she stirred in the loose leaves, "when your mum got engaged, the house was just as loud. Maybe louder. Your granddad nearly broke the radio dancing."

I chuckled despite myself.

"That sounds like him. "She glanced at me, her expression warm but sharp enough to catch the quiet undercurrent I thought I was hiding.

"You're proud of her, aren't you?"

I nodded. "Of course, I am."

"But…" she prompted gently.

I shrugged, suddenly fascinated by the way the sugar bowl gleamed under the kitchen light. "It's just… she always seems to be the centre of everything. And I'm happy for her, I am. It's just hard sometimes, being the one in the background." Gran didn't rush to respond. Instead, she placed a hand on my arm, grounding me with that simple, steady touch only she could manage. "Being in the background doesn't mean you're invisible, love. It means you see things others don't. You notice the quiet moments. You carry more than people realize." I swallowed, the lump in my throat catching me off guard. She smiled. "And besides, you're not in the background to me. Never have been." The doorbell rang again, followed by another round of cheers from the sitting room. Gran gave my arm a gentle squeeze. "Now, let's go feed the happy crowd before they start eating the furniture."

I smiled, and together we carried the tea and snacks out to the celebration, my heart a little lighter than before. Later, as the party started to wind down and the guests began to leave, Melina found herself standing at the kitchen window once more, staring out at the darkening sky. She could hear the laughter of the family continuing in the background, but it felt distant. Her thoughts were consumed with a single question: *Why wasn't Sylvester here? And what emergency call could have kept him away* from his fiancée? It's strange, although he stated that it is work. It wasn't just about the wedding anymore. Melina couldn't ignore the nagging sensation that Sylvester's absence, his *evasive* absence, wasn't as innocent as Monica believed. Just then, her phone buzzed again. Another message, from an unknown number.

Melina frowned, her brow furrowing as she stared at the screen. At first, she'd thought nothing of probably a wrong number or some spam. But now, with a second message coming through so soon, unease began to creep in. She hesitated, thumb hovering over the screen. Lately, she and her friends had been doing a bit of quiet digging into Monica's fiancé. Nothing serious, just harmless curiosity, or so they told themselves. But suddenly, the timing of the message felt... off. Melina shook her head and forced a small laugh, brushing the thought away.

"I'm overthinking," she muttered, slipping the phone back into her pocket. For now, she chose to ignore it and focus on the preparations around her, but a quiet knot of worry had already begun to form in her chest.

****

After finishing the last of her kitchen chores, Melina sank into one of the worn wooden chairs at the table, letting out a soft sigh. The scent of dish soap and cinnamon lingered in the air, mingling with the quiet rustle of paper as she helped her younger cousin, Leo, with his homework. His brow was furrowed in concentration; pencil poised over a half-finished math problem. After a moment of silence, he glanced up at her with wide, earnest eyes. "Mel," he said, voice low and hesitant, "when are you coming back for good? You never stay long when you visit… I miss you." The question caught her off guard, a quiet ache slipping beneath her ribs. She opened her mouth to respond, but before she could find the right words, Vanda, her fifteen-year-old cousin, who was studying at the counter, looked up from her flashcards and said to her brother.

"I think you just want her to do your homework for you," Vanda said with a teasing grin, nudging Chris with her elbow. "You're not fooling anyone." Chris rolled his eyes but smiled, and Melina laughed, grateful for the momentary lightness.

"Hey, I happen to be excellent at fractions," she said, ruffling his hair. "But I'll only help if you promise not to replace me with a calculator when I'm gone."

He grinned, but the question still hung between them, unanswered. Vanda turned serious for a moment, watching her younger brother.

"But seriously… are you ever going to move back? Or is the city home now?" Melina hesitated, fingers tracing the rim of her teacup. She wasn't sure what "home" even meant anymore. The city had ambition, opportunity, and noise. This house had warmth, tangled roots, and the kind of love that didn't need to be spoken aloud to be understood.

"I don't know," she said honestly, her voice soft. "Maybe one day."

Chris nodded, accepting the answer without pushing, while Vanda went back to her notes. Outside the window, the garden lights flickered on as evening settled in, casting long shadows across the tiles. And for a few quiet minutes, the three of them simply existed together, past, present, and possibility, all gathered around the same kitchen table. Melina laughed softly and continued explaining a math problem. Vanda leaned over the table and added, more thoughtfully this time,

"When I turn eighteen, I'm moving in with Auntie Iris and Uncle Chester. I've already decided. They're like my second parents." Melina smiled, touched by the affection in her cousin's voice. In moments like this, surrounded by family, the distance between her city life and the village felt even more noticeable, and somehow, harder to keep. As the laughter settled and the conversation drifted back to schoolbooks and exam stress, Melina leaned back slightly in her chair, watching her cousins with a quiet smile. Vanda's words lingered in her mind, *"They're like my second parents."* It was said so simply, so matter-of-fact, yet it carried a warmth that wrapped around Melina like a soft scarf.

She glanced over at the small, framed photos lining the sideboard, snapshots of birthdays, holidays, muddy boots, and messy cakes. This house had been a constant through every stage of her life. No matter how long she stayed away, the door was always open, the kettle always on, and someone, Gran, Grandad, or one of the cousins, was always waiting to ask when she'd be back again. A flicker of guilt touched her. She *did* tend to leave quickly. Visits were often squeezed between deadlines, and even when she was home, her mind was half elsewhere, already thinking of what came next. She hadn't meant to be distant; she'd just been… caught up in life. In chasing the future. But sitting here now, with a cousin leaning on her shoulder and Vanda casually planning her adult life around their shared family, Melina felt something shift. These weren't just familiar faces; they were part of who she was. A living, breathing reminder of her roots. She reached for Vanda's notebook and gave her cousin a playful nudge. "Well, if you're planning to live with

Auntie Iris and Uncle Chester (Melina's mom and dad), you'd better get those grades up. They'll expect top marks." Vanda smirked, completely unfazed. "That's exactly why I'm sticking with you tonight. You're my buffer." She rolled her eyes. "I've been dodging Aunt Iris like it's a professional sport. The way she gives me that *principal stare* every time she asks about school. No, thank you."

Mel chuckled softly. "That's what it feels like when you've got an actual school principal in the family. She doesn't even have to say anything, just *looks*, and suddenly I feel like I forgot to do my homework." Vanda nudged her playfully.

"And yet you're the smart one."

Mel grinned, shaking her head. "Smart enough to keep my answers vague and my distance strategic." Vanda laughed. "Strategic distance, love that. You should teach a workshop. I barely made it past the buffet before she pounced."

"She caught me by the punch bowl earlier," Mel said with a grimace. Asked if I'd thought about going back to school. I said I was thinking about it."

"Are you?" Vanda asked, raising an eyebrow.

Mel hesitated, then shrugged. "Not really. But it sounded better than saying, *I'm too mentally fried to even open a laptop right now.*" Vanda gave her a sympathetic look. "Yeah...

I get that. People always want you to have a plan, like life's a checklist. School, job, relationship, check, check, check. But real life's messier."

Mel smiled, but it didn't quite reach her eyes.

"Tell that to Monica. She's got it all lined up perfectly."

Vanda tilted her head.

"Are you okay?"

"Yeah," Mel said quickly, brushing a stray crumb from the counter. "Just… thinking."

There was a beat of silence between them, not heavy, but not light either. Vanda didn't press. She just leaned against the counter and grabbed a cookie from the cooling rack. "Well, for what it's worth, I'm glad you're here. Makes this circus a little easier." Mel looked at her cousin, grateful for the moment of sincerity. "Same. You make a good escape partner."

"And you make excellent excuses for me to avoid responsibility," Vanda said, holding up the cookie like a toast.

"To strategic avoidance and not getting caught".

Mel tapped her water glass against it. "Cheers" to that. Melina laughed, but inwardly, something in her softened. Maybe this visit was more than just a short stay. Maybe it was the beginning of her finding her way back, not just to the village, but to herself.

CHAPTER FOURTEEN

The Telfer family lived in an affluent, tree-lined neighbourhood that rested not in the bustling heart of the city, but on its quiet, well-kept outskirts. It was a distinguished enclave, a place where driveways gleamed, hedges stood trimmed to perfection, and every lawn looked as though it belonged in a gardening magazine. Neighbours still greeted one another politely over wrought-iron fences, and it wasn't uncommon to see a maid in uniform or a gardener tending to flowerbeds on weekday mornings.

Influence lived here; judges, doctors, executives, and the Telfers were no exception. Excellence wasn't just encouraged; it was expected. The family had built their reputation on hard work, public standing, and a refusal to settle for anything less than the best. At the centre of it all stood Mrs. Telfer, elegant, composed, and exacting. As principal of Raytown Secondary School, her name was synonymous with discipline and academic distinction. Parents spoke of her with a mix of admiration and fear, students with respect tinged by apprehension. Her authority extended beyond the school gates. At home, she ruled with the same precision. The Telfer household ran like a well-oiled machine, no clutter, no chaos, and certainly no room for emotional unravelling. Achievements were praised, appearances were maintained, and expectations were crystal clear. Warmth existed, but only in measured doses. Love, while present, was often overshadowed by structure. To outsiders, the family seemed flawless. But to those looking more closely, there was an unmistakable sense of pressure humming beneath the surface, like the ticking of a clock, always counting down to the next goal, the next milestone, the next perfect moment.

Mr. Telfer ran a successful haulage company with over thirty employees and a fleet of trucks that crisscrossed Europe. Though he could have stepped back long ago, he still occasionally took the wheel himself, disappearing for days on long-distance routes. He claimed it was to stay connected to the business, but Melina sometimes wondered if it was just his way of escaping the quiet pressure that filled their home. To outsiders, the Telfers seemed perfectly composed, a family of accomplishment and ambition. But for Melina, being their daughter often meant living in the shadow of expectations she never quite fit. Where Monica met every mark with ease and polish, Melina had always coloured slightly outside the lines. Her choices, her questions, her quieter dreams, they didn't always align with the family blueprint. Though her parents loved her and her siblings, Mel never doubted that their affection often came wrapped in layers of critique and quiet expectations. Their love was present, but it had conditions, unspoken yet deeply felt. Her brother Eton, the second-born and now an accountant in their father's business, had always seemed to fit neatly into the Mold they respected most: practical, predictable, successful by their standards. Mel, by contrast, had walked a very different path, one shaped more by creativity and intuition than certainty or convention. While Monica excelled in academics and climbed a steady ladder of predictable success, Melina had always moved to her own rhythm. She pursued her arts, leaned into compassion, and eventually found her place in a nursing career rooted in care, not prestige. It was fulfilling, but not flashy. Meaningful, but not headline-worthy.

Her parents never openly disapproved, but their approval often came wrapped in subtle suggestions and thinly veiled comparisons. It was Monica who garnered their admiration, Monica, who always did what they expected, who ticked every box, and now stood poised to marry a well-known, well-connected man with a gleaming future. It was everything they'd dreamed of, even if they never said so aloud. And Mel? Mel was once again cast into the quiet shadow of her sister's success.

"Why can't you be more like Monica?" her mother would often say, the words softened by a smile but still sharp enough to sting.

"You should take up business; Monica could even help you find a good job at the bank." It was a familiar refrain. Monica, after all, was the golden standard. She was the assistant manager at one of the most prestigious banks in the city, respected not just for her sharp mind but for her poise and professionalism. Even her colleagues admired her; some openly called her a rising star. Now, with a promotion to branch manager on the horizon, Monica seemed unstoppable.

"She has her master's in business studies," her mother would continue proudly, as if reciting lines from a polished résumé. "I must say, she's very brilliant." Melina had learned to smile and nod, to let the praise for her sister wash over her like background music, pleasant, familiar, and not meant for her. The comparisons came so frequently, so effortlessly, that they no longer shocked her. But they still hurt. Not because she begrudged Monica her success, Mel was proud of her sister, but because she sometimes felt invisible by comparison. It wasn't that Mel lacked ambition. She had simply chosen a different path, one less shiny, less celebrated, but no less important. Nursing required its own kind of brilliance, its quiet strength. But in her mother's eyes, it had always seemed like a backup plan. A nice gesture, but not the kind of thing you bring up at family dinners with pride. Still, Mel carried the weight of those expectations with quiet grace, even as a small part of her longed just once for her mother to look at her with the same awe she reserved for Monica. Her mother would say not always directly, but in the sideways glances, the carefully worded questions, the silence that followed when Mel spoke of her small victories. It wasn't cruelty, just a kind of disappointment they tried to dress as concern. A constant reminder that love, though present, came with terms and conditions Mel could never quite seem to meet. Still, Mel carried on, gently, quietly, building a life on her terms, even as she sometimes wondered if it would ever be enough for them to see her. The comparisons were never cruel, just constant, and that quiet pressure had a way of settling in her chest like a weight she couldn't shake.

Achievements were acknowledged, but always measured against someone else's success, rarely celebrated on their own. Melina had long since learned to keep certain parts of herself tucked away, hidden behind a polite smile and an agreeable tone. It was safer that way, easier than risking disapproval or being misunderstood. And yet, here she was, still trying to find her place in a house that had never fully felt like hers. The walls held memories, yes, but they were tinged with expectation, not warmth. The furniture, the photographs, even the scent of familiar meals carried a kind of quiet judgment that made her chest tighten. Outwardly, they projected the image of a well-balanced, accomplished family, respectable, close-knit, enviable even. But like most families, theirs was woven with contradictions and silences, the kind that don't show up in framed pictures or polite dinner conversations. Beneath the surface lay old grievances, unspoken disappointments, and fragile attempts at a connection that never quite reached where they were meant to go. Melina had become an expert at navigating the family's emotional terrain, stepping carefully between her mother's quiet disapproval and her father's well-meaning but distant encouragement. Eton, with his calm demeanour and impeccable track record, had always seemed to glide effortlessly through their parents' expectations. He was the golden child, the one who did things "right," the invisible standard against which Melina was often measured. Not that he ever gloated or even seemed to notice. That made it worse in a way; his unintentional perfection only magnified her sense of not quite being enough.

She sometimes wondered what it might have felt like to grow up in a home where love wasn't tangled up in performance. A place where she could speak freely, be messy, be unsure, be herself. But vulnerability had never been encouraged here; it was considered a liability, a softness mistaken for weakness. Still, there were moments, fleeting, fragile moments, when the edges softened. Her mother's hand brushing a stray hair from her face, her father's laugh echoing across the dinner table, Eton sneaking her the last piece of pie with a wink. Little things. They didn't erase the distance, but they kept her from giving up entirely. And maybe that was why she'd come back. Not just out of obligation, or for appearances, but for the slim chance that something might change. That one day, this house could feel less like a proving ground and more like home. Vanda crossed her arms and said quietly, "I prefer you over Cousin Monica. At least you talk to me like I matter. Whenever she visits, she barely looks up from her phone, and when she does, it's usually to ask me to do something for her." Her voice dropped, tinged with frustration. "She treats me like I'm some kind of helper, not family. I've had to clean her shoes, do her laundry, even fetch her coffee, like I'm the maid and she's royalty or something. It makes me resent her, even if I try not to."

She glanced at me, her expression guarded, like she was afraid I might defend Monica or dismiss her feelings.

"I don't think she even realizes how she makes me feel. Maybe she just doesn't care."

I reached out and touched her arm.

"You deserve to be treated with respect, Vanda. That's not okay, and you're not wrong for feeling upset about it. Her eyes softened slightly, and she nodded.

"Thanks. Sometimes I just need someone to say that out loud." Vanda's words for a moment, the weight of them settling like dust. It wasn't just petty complaining; there was hurt behind her voice, the kind that builds up in layers when someone you look up to constantly overlooks you.

"She shouldn't treat you like that," I said, my voice low.

"You're not her assistant. You're family."

Vanda gave a small shrug, but her eyes were fixed on the floor.

"I know. But it's Monica. People let her get away with things because she's... well, Monica. Beautiful. Confident. Loud enough to fill a room."

I smiled sadly. "And stubborn as hell." She snorted.

"That too."

A quiet beat passed before I spoke again. "I think I need to talk to her. Not just about how she treats you, but how she talks to everyone, me included. She crosses lines without even noticing. Vanda looked up, a flicker of hope in her eyes. "Do you think she'll listen?"

"I don't know," I admitted. "But someone should tell her. And maybe it's easier coming from me than from you." She hesitated, then gave a small nod. "Just... don't make it a fight. I don't want her to hate me."

"She won't hate you," I said gently. "But maybe she'll start to see you." Although my mother advised against using the word 'hate' and encouraged me to show love and tolerate her behaviour, understanding that her visits are brief." Mel then concluded, "Alright, let's set aside discussions about Monica for now and focus on completing this homework. Afterwards, we can assist Gran in the kitchen, have the usual cocoa, and go to bed early. That night, lying in bed with the glow of my phone screen dimming beside me, I thought about all the small slights I'd brushed off over the years. Monica's teasing. Her assumptions. The way she always seemed to take up all the space in the room, and in the family. Maybe it was time to push back, just a little. Not to hurt her, but to remind her that we were here too. That our voices mattered. That love, real love, means noticing the people who aren't shouting for attention.

CHAPTER FIFTEEN

Melina sat on the old wooden swing beneath the sycamore tree, its weathered ropes creaking gently as she swayed back and forth. The morning sun filtered through the leaves above, casting dappled patterns of gold across the garden. In front of her, Rex and Albi, the family's aging but ever-spirited Australian shepherds, chased each other in wide, looping circles, their tails wagging like they were still puppies. Snappy and Happy, the two shaggy Bobtail cats, lounged nearby in the long grass, batting lazily at falling petals and occasionally flicking their tails with idle amusement.

They were all getting older, just like everything else around her, but something was comforting in their familiar presence. Melina smiled as she watched the four of them play, a quiet warmth settling in her chest. They had been there through every chapter of her life, through scraped knees, broken hearts, and quiet victories no one else had noticed. She leaned back slightly, letting her mind wander. Her thoughts drifted to her college days, the chaotic blur of adjusting to a faster, louder world after the slower rhythm of secondary school. Her grades had been solid, good enough to make her proud, though never quite as flawless as Monica's.

Monica had always soared effortlessly, while Melina had worked quietly, steadily, sometimes invisibly. Their mother had expected brilliance from both of them, sharp, polished brilliance that turned heads and drew praise. Melina had delivered something different: quiet strength, a stubborn persistence, and a growing sense of her path, even when it didn't shine quite as brightly in the eyes of others. She looked down at her hands resting in her lap, her fingers absently tracing the edge of the swing's seat. *I didn't have to be her,* she thought. *I just had to be me.* And for the first time in a while, that felt like enough.

Melina's swing creaked softly in the breeze as she pushed herself gently back and forth, eyes still following the dogs darting through the grass. The cats had long since settled into a sun-drenched nap, stretched out like old royalty on their mossy thrones. The back door creaked open behind her. She didn't turn right away, but she knew the footsteps. Light, measured, confident. Monica. A moment later, her sister lowered herself onto the swing beside her, carefully, elegantly, like she always did. She wore one of her perfectly pressed cardigans and jeans that never seemed to wrinkle. Her engagement ring caught the sun, scattering tiny sparks of light across the garden.

"They still haven't tired themselves out?" Monica asked, nodding toward the dogs.

"They're stubborn," Melina said. "Like us."

Monica gave a soft laugh. "More like you."

They sat in silence for a few moments, the gentle rhythm of the swings rocking them in time. The air between them was familiar, but a little too still, like they were both waiting for the other to speak first. Monica finally broke the quiet. "You've been quiet since Sylvester got here." Melina hesitated.

"Just... tired." By the way, where is your fiancé? He did not get back to the party last night".

"You sure?" Monica asked, her voice gentler now, ignoring Melina's last comment. "I know things haven't always been easy for you. I don't want this weekend to feel like it's about me and him. I want you to be part of it." Melina nodded; her gaze fixed on a patch of wildflowers near the fence.

"I know."

Monica turned to look at her fully now.

"You don't like him, do you?"

Melina paused. She could feel Monica's eyes on her, searching. Hoping. Bracing.

"I don't know him," she said finally. "And I don't think you do either. Not really. " That hung between them, delicate as glass. Monica's jaw tightened just slightly.

"He makes me happy, Mel."

Melina turned toward her.

"I want you to be happy. Truly."

Another long silence stretched out, this one more brittle than the last. Then Monica stood, brushing invisible specks from her jeans.   "I should check on Gran. She wanted help with the apple tart."

"And I'm leaving early, to avoid the rush hour traffic on the motorway," Monica said, brushing her coat sleeve as she adjusted her bag.

"Aren't you going to Mass?" I asked, a little surprised. "You know, whenever the family visits all together, we *always* go to Mass on Sunday."

Monica hesitated for a second before flashing a polite smile.   "Not this time, Mel. I've got a lot on my plate. But... please light a candle for me, will you?"

"I certainly will," I replied, my voice quieter now, laced with something unspoken. There was a pause, brief but thick with meaning. Melina watched her sister turn and walk back toward the house. Her back was straight, her movements composed, every gesture as polished as always. But there was a new slowness in her steps, a heaviness she was trying to hide. Something in the way her shoulders dipped slightly, as if the weight she carried was no longer just from her overnight bag.

Melina stood still, the noise of the party muffled behind her as she watched Monica disappear through the doorway. She didn't know exactly what was bothering her sister, but she could sense it. Something had shifted. And for the first time in a long while, Melina wasn't sure Monica had everything as under control as she wanted everyone to believe. Left alone again, Melina let her swing drift to a stop, the gentle creak of the chain the only sound left in the air. The dogs, finally worn out from their earlier frenzy, flopped down in the shade nearby, panting softly, their tails giving the occasional lazy thump against the grass. The garden, moments ago buzzing with distant laughter and clinking glasses, settled into a hush once more. But the silence no longer felt peaceful. It felt like a countdown. Each second ticked by with invisible weight, as if the breeze itself had paused to listen. The warmth of the morning sun pressed against her skin, but Melina shivered slightly, though she couldn't say why. Maybe it was the way Monica had hurried off. Or maybe it was the hollow smile she'd given when she said she wouldn't be at Mass. Melina glanced at the house, sensing something unspoken nearby. She pulled her knees up on the swing, wrapped her arms around them, and rested her chin on top.

CHAPTER SIXTEEN

Melina reminisced about a time when she wanted a part-time job, not just for the money but for the independence. She was tired of asking for every little thing and weary of the subtle guilt that accompanied it. But her mother, as always, had other ideas.

"Mom, I can handle both," Melina said, trying to keep her voice even. "I'll go to college during the week and work on weekends. Just enough to earn some pocket money, so I don't have to keep asking you." Her mother's expression tightened. "But what about your studying?" she said, arms crossed. "I'd prefer if you focused entirely on your coursework. That should be your only priority right now." Melina could feel the tension tightening around the room like a slowly coiling spring. She knew exactly where this was headed, the familiar pattern, the push and pull. Her mother rarely let things go once she dug her heels in. Sensing the argument forming, she turned to her father in a last-ditch effort.

"Dad, what do you think?" He looked up from his phone, visibly caught between them. "Well…" he began slowly, "I think it depends on how much time the job would take, and whether or not it would affect your grades."

But Melina wasn't fooled. She knew that, often, he deferred to her mother. His opinions had a way of dissolving under pressure, like sugar in tea. Even her grandmother, who always seemed warm and affectionate during solo visits, somehow managed to take her parents' side whenever the whole family gathered at the country house. It turned into a kind of informal tribunal, what her dad liked to call a "family discussion," but which Melina secretly referred to as *The Round Table of Judgment.*

"Melina, how are you planning on accomplish this", "Nan, would say"   "the hours I am going to work will be flexible, I will be in college three to four days weekly, and the days I am not in college, I will be working five to eight hours, when I can, the hours are flexible, I will still have enough time to study and be on top of my course work".   And of course, there was Monica. Big sister. Golden girl. The one who could do no wrong in anyone's eyes. She didn't even need to say much; just a raised eyebrow or a carefully timed sigh could shift the whole direction of the conversation. Melina often felt like she was auditioning for adulthood in a room full of critics, and no matter how well she performed, she never quite got the part.

****

Melina sank into the armchair after dinner, her fingers absently tracing the hem of her sleeve while the discussion still echoed in her head. No one had brought it up again directly, but the silence around it felt thick with unspoken judgment.

She watched her mother in the kitchen, moving with practiced certainty, and her father sitting nearby, eyes half-glued to the football result. They seemed so sure of their version of how her life should unfold, safe, structured, and obedient. But Melina wasn't a child anymore, even if they still treated her like one. She took a breath, then spoke, her voice steady, though her heart thudded against her ribs. "I've thought about it a lot. A weekend job won't stop me from doing well in school. It might help me stay more focused. I'll manage my time. I already do." Her mother glanced over, frowning faintly. "We just want what's best for you."

"I know," Melina replied gently. "But sometimes what's best for me isn't what makes *you* comfortable."

There was a pause. Her father looked up, surprised by the quiet conviction in her voice. Monica, who had been scrolling on her phone across the room, raised an eyebrow but said nothing. Typical. Melina stood, grabbing her empty mug and heading to the kitchen. As she rinsed it in the sink, she could feel the air shift behind her, not quite confrontation, but not dismissal either. Maybe they were listening, if only a little.

CHAPTER SEVENTEEN

Monica resided in an elegant condominium shared with her close friend, Sandra, a location I had visited only on select occasions, typically to fulfil tasks on behalf of others. Whether it was my mother requesting that I deliver or retrieve items Monica had misplaced, my visits were always transactional in nature. I was never invited simply to spend time there or to experience the space as a guest, as someone genuinely welcome. I remember overhearing Monica once, laughing as she told someone over the phone, "Sylvester pays the least, but he acts like he owns the place." Her tone was amused, a little smug. I hadn't even known she lived with Sylvester until then. The condo itself was stunning. Monica had boasted that Sylvester had hired a professional interior decorator, and for once, she wasn't exaggerating.

"The décor is fantastic," she'd said, practically glowing. "Plush carpets, custom furniture, sleek lighting, the place even *smells* expensive." Her tone was light. I had not known she lived with Sylvester until then.

. "The décor is very well done," she stated. "Plush carpets, custom furniture, sleek lighting, the place even has a distinctive scent." She'd said it so effortlessly, with that offhand pride she always carried when things worked out in her favour. And even though she hadn't meant to, it stung. Standing in that perfectly arranged living room, feeling like an outsider in my sister's curated world, I realized something: I didn't belong there. It wasn't just the condo. It was Monica's *whole* life, immaculate, curated, enviably put together. Everything about it gleamed with purpose: the clean lines of her furniture, the subtle scent of eucalyptus and lavender, the tasteful art hanging in perfect symmetry on the walls. Even her fridge was organized. It all spoke of someone who had figured things out.

Although my flat is not as elegant as Monica's, it is quite comfortable, and I love living on campus. I have my en-suite bathroom, for which my parents assist with the rent. Anna and Barbara, my two flatmates and friends, shared a bathroom. We all shared the kitchen and living room, which was quite comfortable. We took turns doing the dishes and cleaning, and when we are swamped with assignments, we hire a cleaner and split the payment. I remember thinking, *I'd love to have a place like this one day.* Not just for the space or the furniture or the view, but because it represented something more. It meant stability. Independence. Pride. I wanted to walk through my own front door and feel like I had built something that was *mine*, not assigned, not handed down, not part of someone else's plan. A space that said, *I chose this. I earned this. I belong here.*

Because deep down, that's what I envied most, not the apartment itself, but the quiet certainty that came with the feeling still lingered. A quiet ache. Not for the condo itself, but for the closeness I didn't have with her, the kind where you're invited over just because someone wants you there. But those brief visits left a lasting impression. The moment I stepped inside, it felt like I'd walked into a magazine spread. Monica beamed with pride as she gave me the tour, boasting that Sylvester had hired an interior decorator. "The place is fantastic," she'd said, gesturing grandly. "Plush carpet, brand-new furniture, everything perfectly in place, and the smell? Like fresh linen and expensive candles." I could only nod in agreement, a little awestruck. I remember thinking: *Someday, I'd love to have a place like this. Not just nice, mine.*

"Mel, are you listening?" Gran's voice snapped me out of my reverie. "Stop daydreaming and hurry up with that sandwich!"

"Oh, sorry, Gran! I'm back now," I said, laughing, shaking the thought from my head as I returned to slicing the tomatoes. It was a week later when the opportunity came, not planned, not dramatic. Just one of those ordinary days that unexpectedly turn into something bigger. Monica had asked me to drop off a box of decorations she wanted for some event Sandra was hosting. I almost said no. I nearly texted, *Can't you come get it yourself?* But something stopped me. Maybe it was curiosity. Maybe it was something deeper, some part of me that still hoped things between us could shift. When I arrived, she barely looked up from her laptop. "Just put it over there," she said, nodding toward a marble-topped counter in the kitchen. The space was still beautiful, still magazine-perfect. And still not mine. I set the box down more firmly than necessary. "You know," I said, trying to keep my voice steady, "I've only ever been here to run errands for you. "Monica blinked, caught off guard.

"What?"

"I've never been invited to see you for a sisterly visit. Just to run errands." She leaned back in her chair, closing her laptop slowly. "I didn't realize it bothered you."

"Well, it does," I said. "You have this whole life, and I'm always watching it from the outside. Even when I'm right in the room." A pause stretched between us. She looked at me with something that wasn't quite

Guilt, but maybe recognition.

"You're not on the outside," she said finally, quieter than before. "I just... I guess I didn't think it mattered."

"It does," I replied. "Not the condo. Not Sylvester. Just feel like I matter to you outside of being your little sister or Mom's messenger. She looked down for a moment, then back at me.

"I'm sorry. I didn't mean to make you feel that way." For the first time in a long while, her voice didn't sound polished or dismissive. It sounded real.

"I've been thinking about that a lot lately," she added. "About how I show up or don't, for people who care about me." I nodded slowly. It wasn't a full resolution. It wasn't a dramatic reconciliation. But it was something. And as I turned to leave, she called out after me.

"Hey. Next week, Sandra's out of town. You should come over. Just us. I'll even let you pick the movie." I smiled, not turning around right away.

"Even if I pick something with subtitles?"

Monica groaned. "Ugh. Fine. But only if you bring popcorn." It was a small thing. But for the first time, I didn't feel like a guest in her world. I felt like maybe–just maybe, I belonged in it too. For me, when Monica said those words, I felt like I should just tell her everything that I had overheard about the Sylvester family. It had been a long, exhausting day, the kind that leaves your limbs heavy and your thoughts slightly frayed around the edges. The house was still alive with the hum of conversation and bursts of laughter, echoing off the walls like leftover energy no one quite wanted to let go of. But I needed a pause, a breath away from it all. So I quietly slipped out of the sitting room, unnoticed, and stepped into the sanctuary of the back garden. The evening air greeted me like an old friend, cool and comforting, wrapping around my shoulders like a shawl woven from silence and dusk. I made my way across the lawn to one of the weathered garden chairs beneath the sprawling chestnut tree, our childhood landmark, steady and familiar. Its broad leaves stirred in the breeze, casting dappled shadows that danced lazily over the grass. The sky overhead was a pale, dreamy blue, fading into delicate streaks of gold and lavender as the sun began its slow descent beyond the rooftops.

I sank into the chair, exhaling slowly, the tension in my shoulders easing as the quiet settled around me like a soft blanket. Somewhere in the distance, a bird chirped its final notes of the day, and a faint scent of lavender floated by from Mum's flowerbeds. I tilted my head back and closed my eyes, letting my thoughts wander freely for the first time in hours. Memories flickered gently behind my eyelids, snippets of laughter, flashes of old conversations, echoes of faces both near and far. I didn't even notice I was smiling. And then, without meaning to, I drifted into a quiet daydream, caught between past and present, wrapped in the kind of peace that only comes in rare, fleeting moments, when the world slows down just enough to let you breathe. Monica was… well, Monica. Beautiful, with a petite frame and long, black, curly hair that cascaded down her back like silk. Her complexion was smooth and glowing, the shade of warm cinnamon, and when she spoke, people stopped to listen, captivated, almost spellbound. She had a quiet confidence that turned heads and a grace that made it all seem effortless.

And then there was I.

CHAPTER EIGHTEEN

Melinda remembered Monica the way one remembers sunlight, bright, undeniable, and always just a little out of reach. Monica had been head-girl during her time at secondary school, a natural leader, effortlessly brilliant, the kind of person teachers held up as an example long after she'd left. A shining star who left a lasting impression. Even now, years later, her name still echoed in the hallways like an old song everyone knew by heart. Most of the teachers were still there, their eyes lingering on Melinda with that familiar, quiet expectation. It wasn't overt, just a subtle look, a slight uptick of interest, as if they were waiting to see if she might be Monica, version two.

It was strange. Ironic, even. Melinda had always been proud of her sister; how could she not be? Monica had this way of lighting up every room, commanding attention without ever demanding it. But pride could sit side by side with something else, something quieter, heavier. Living in her sister's shadow often felt like trying to outshine the sun. No matter how hard Melinda tried, no matter what she achieved, there was always that sense of being slightly dimmer, slightly smaller. The sequel to a story that everyone already thought had ended perfectly. And yet, she never resented Monica, not truly. It wasn't Monica's fault that she shone the way she did. But sometimes Melinda wished someone would look at her without comparing her to a memory. Just once, she wanted to be seen for who she was, not who she reminded them of. We all went to the same secondary school. Mum made sure of that.

"I'm not buying new uniforms every few years," she used to say with a half-laugh, though the edge in her voice made it clear she wasn't joking. It wasn't that we were struggling financially. Mum just had her priorities lined up like soldiers on parade. She believed in spending sensibly, saving for what she called "more important things", house repairs, bulk supermarket trips that could feed an army, and those inevitable, always-at-the-worst-possible-moment emergency dental visits. She ran the household like a tight ship: steady, no-frills, and reliable. But at the centre of it all was love, quiet and unwavering. Firm but fair, with just enough softness to come home to. Hugs were rare, but when they came, they were warm and grounding. Hot chocolate with extra marshmallows was her version of a pep talk. Just then, a sudden bark cut through the quiet and snapped me back to the present. I flinched, heart leaping as though my body hadn't been ready to rejoin the world just yet. A rustle in the bushes was followed by the unmistakable shuffle of Snowy, our overweight, self-important cat, who waddled into view with the air of someone late to an important meeting. The bark hadn't come from her, of course, Snowy could barely summon the energy for a meow these days without sounding like she needed a lie-down afterward. Most likely the neighbour's terrier again, full of noise and nerves.

Snowy paused mid-waddle to glare at me, as if I'd personally arranged the disturbance, then resumed her march with the grace of a potato in motion. I watched her disappear into the tall grass, feeling oddly grounded by her ridiculous presence. For all the noise in my head, the familiar rhythms of home had a way of stitching things back together. I leaned back against the chair and exhaled slowly, listening to the rustle of leaves overhead and the distant clatter of dishes from the kitchen. For a moment, I just let myself exist there, in that strange in-between space where the past tugs at you, and the present feels like it's holding its breath. Lately, I've been thinking a lot about how things used to be. How Mum used to pack our lunches with little handwritten notes when we were younger, just silly drawings or reminders like *Don't forget your PE kit!* or *You've got this, starfish!* She'd call us all kinds of odd little nicknames, depending on her mood:

"starfish," "rocket shoes," "my wiggly worm." It was her way of loving out loud, in the moments between the busy ones. I don't know exactly when it all started to change. Maybe it was when Monica left for university. Maybe it was when Dad's job involved travelling a lot. Or maybe it was just me, growing up, noticing more. The silences got longer, and the house seemed to echo more. Monica became a voice on the phone, always saying how busy she was but how she *really did want to come home soon*. And I, I just became the one who stayed behind. The one who kept the rhythm going while everything else shifted. It's not like anyone ever said it out loud, but I could feel it in the way people looked at me sometimes. Like they were expecting more. Like they were silently asking, *why aren't you more like her?* And the truth is, I didn't want to be Monica. I didn't want to take her place. I just wanted to be me.

Whoever that was. A breeze stirred through the branches above, scattering a few chestnut leaves at my feet. I watched them drift and tumble, and I wondered if maybe that's what I was doing too, just tumbling along, hoping I'd land somewhere that felt like mine. I needed a nap afterward. Probably the neighbour's scruffy terrier again, always finding some excuse to cause a commotion. Snowy paused, gave me a withering look as if my existence had inconvenienced her, and kept moving, tail flicking with offended grace. Snowy couldn't walk fast, ate like a small bear, and panted like a dog while glaring at the back gate. Despite his quirks and flaws, we loved him and considered him perfect.

CHAPTER NINETEEN

The attention surrounding my sister's engagement is affecting me. While I am not envious of her, she enjoys being the focal point. You may perceive me as jealous, but that is not the case. I must prioritize my own needs and upcoming exams. As a university second-year student, I must concentrate on my studies. Currently, I do not have time for relationships, as they can distract me from my academic goals. Failure in my examinations would disappoint my parents and lead to comparisons with my sister, Monica.

Our study group consists of Anna, Barbara, David Summerset, and Lester Duxbury. From the outset, we've managed to collaborate effectively and support one another through the demands of our nursing program. Initially, Anna, Barbara, and I were uncertain about including the two boys. We weren't sure how the dynamic would play out, but to our surprise, they've both proven to be intelligent and respectful contributors to the group. David is the quieter of the two, reserved, almost to the point of being enigmatic. He listens carefully, speaks thoughtfully, and often surprises us with insightful questions or observations. I get the feeling there's a lot more going on beneath the surface, and I'm curious to learn more about him as time goes on.

Lester, on the other hand, is David's complete opposite. Outspoken, charismatic, and a bit of a rebel, he tends to dominate conversations. He's a heavy smoker and has a habit of using profanity, which we asked him to tone down early on. During our first group meeting, Lester opened up about his background. He's the youngest of three children in a very wealthy family. His older brother is a lawyer at their father's prestigious law firm, and his sister is on track to become a cardiothoracic surgeon, just like their mother. Lester, however, has chosen a different path, studying nursing not out of passion, but as a form of rebellion against his parents' expectations.

He talks frequently about his mother, clearly holding her in high regard, but rarely mentions his father except to describe him as authoritarian and unyielding. According to Lester, his father believes in strict rules and unquestioned obedience, something Lester openly resists. His defiance is evident not only in his career choice but also in his demeanour and language. When he repeatedly broke the guidelines we established as a group, Anna confronted him and suggested he consider joining another study group. Lester, to his credit, took the feedback seriously. He admitted that he liked being part of our group because he appreciated how polite and respectful everyone was. He promised to make a genuine effort to follow the rules moving forward. Despite our differences, I think we're beginning to find our rhythm. Each of us brings something unique to the table, and there's potential for real growth, both academic and personal, as we continue this journey together.

Lester's parents had always envisioned a very specific future for him: a career in law, following in the footsteps of his father. He had the grades to make it happen and even received offers from some of the most prestigious universities in the country. But then, seemingly out of nowhere, he chose an entirely different path, nursing. I still remember him saying to me one afternoon, "I want to live my own life, not be told all the time what to do or who I should hang out with." There was a quiet defiance in his voice, like someone who had finally decided to step off a carefully paved road and forge his own way through the woods.

His father, a well-known barrister, and his mother, a consultant in cardiology, come from a lineage steeped in tradition and expectations. Their family owns several ancestral estates, old money, the kind that brings not just privilege but also heavy expectations. Everything about Lester's upbringing seems rooted in legacy, in duty, in doing what's expected. But Lester wants none of it. "They can keep their legacy," he once said flatly. "I just want to be free." Freedom, for Lester, seems to mean more than just career choice—it's about identity, autonomy, and rejecting the image his family tried to shape for him. There's a recklessness to it, a raw edge. Honestly, I suspect he smokes weed. My friends and I have caught the scent on him more than once, and it wouldn't surprise me. He walks through life with the air of someone trying to escape a cage invisible to everyone else—pushing boundaries, testing rules, always rebelling, especially if it gets under his father's skin. Still, underneath the bravado and rebellion, I can't help but wonder what Lester's searching for. Is it freedom? A sense of self? Or maybe just someone who sees him for who he is, not for who he's supposed to be. I remember Lester once mentioning, almost in passing, that his family knows Monica's fiancé's family, the Longhorns. According to him, they're not just wealthy; they're powerful, with deep ties in business, politics, and private circles most people never gain access to. "Old money knows old money," he said with a smirk, as if that explained everything.

The way he spoke about them made me pause. There was something in his tone. not quite admiration but not disdain either. More like wariness. He didn't go into much detail, but it was clear the Longhorns were a family people noticed and remembered. Lester seemed to know more than he was willing to share, which made me wonder what exactly he knew and why he held back. It struck me then how small the world can be when you're dealing with circles of influence. I couldn't help but feel a strange tension behind his words, as though there was more to the story, something unspoken, maybe even uncomfortable.

****

Waking up in the country is an experience all its own. The early morning sounds drifted in through the slightly open window: the roosters calling out to the rising sun, dogs barking in the distance, and the faint hum of a tractor starting up somewhere across the fields. The comforting aroma of freshly baked bread rolls and sizzling breakfast filled the air, pulling me gently out of sleep even before my eyes opened.

Visits to the country always promised warm bread, hearty breakfasts, and the kind of quiet you can't find in the city. Snowy, the family's pampered Ragdoll cat, made it her personal mission to wake me up whenever I stayed over. Sure enough, she was already in my room, perched beside the bed and meowing persistently. Her fluffy tail swished as she tried to climb up, not stopping until I sat up. I couldn't tell if she was hungry or simply playing alarm clock, but her mission was clearly accomplished. Groggy but smiling, I slowly rolled out of bed and made my way to the bathroom. I brushed my teeth, splashed warm water on my face, and glanced at the clock above the sink, 7:30 a.m. It was early, especially after the party last night, and my thoughts still lingered on conversations and moments that kept me tossing and turning.

I hadn't expected to get up so soon, but something about being in the country always brought out a different rhythm in me. Despite the fatigue, I always tried to rise early when visiting. There's a kind of magic in the stillness before the day truly begins. The landscape looks softer, quieter, and more alive. I wanted to make the most of it. My usual ritual included a morning walk around the farm and beyond, accompanied by Rex and Hollie, my grandparents' loyal Labrador retrievers, and sometimes, though rarely, by Snowy, if she was in the mood.

I quickly got dressed and reached for the dogs' collars hanging by the back door. The rich, mouth-watering smell of bacon and fresh bread wafted through the house. Gran was already in the kitchen, just as she always was, no matter the day. Sunday mornings were no exception. For her, baking was a kind of devotion, almost spiritual. Even with Mass to attend later in the morning, she found time to make everything from scratch: warm bread rolls, golden-brown cakes, thick-cut bacon, and sometimes even scones with homemade jam.

"You need a strong appetite in this house," she always said, her hands never idle, moving from oven to stovetop with practiced ease. Snowy had given up on her mission to come along and now lay curled beside the fireplace, half awake. One of the dogs barked, and I noticed her eyelids twitch open. She gave me a slow, judgmental blink but stayed in place, clearly deciding breakfast was more important than the walk. "Come on, you guys, let's go!" I called out, clipping the collars onto Rex and Hollie. They leapt into action, tails wagging and tongues lolling in anticipation. The air outside was crisp and smelled of dew and eucalyptus. The sky was painted in soft streaks of pink and gold, and the distant hills glowed under the early morning sun. With the dogs bounding ahead and the quiet hum of the countryside around me, I felt a calm settling into my chest. The kind of peace you don't notice when you're caught up in the noise of everyday life.

Today felt like the start of something, not just another country morning, but something meaningful, even if I couldn't quite name it yet. Walking around the farm early in the morning provides fresh air and the scent of freshly baked bread. Melina was breathing in these aromas. She felt she could walk for miles without stopping. As Melina walked, her mind wandered to what her friend had mentioned about her sister's fiancé, Sylvester. he seems polite and respectful. He comes from a wealthy family background, and her parents are fond of him. Her entire family appears to admire him, including her grandparents. Something doesn't sit right. He says he's studying to become a surgeon, long hours, endless debt, years of training ahead, yet his house looks like something out of a luxury lifestyle magazine. We've only visited once, and even then, it was brief. Strangely, none of us has met his parents. They supposedly live abroad, moving between continents for business, but no one knows what that business is. The details are vague, intentionally so, it seems. There's a kind of silence surrounding his family. A curated distance. And then there's the rumours, the one I overheard entirely by accident, during a conversation I wasn't meant to hear. Something about ties to cartels and other... dangerous groups. The kind of secret that makes your stomach turn and your thoughts spiral. It's hard to believe, and yet, that's what eavesdropping does: it feeds suspicion. Now I can't stop thinking about it. I need to know more. I *have* to know more. Snapping out of her thoughts, Melina suddenly realized how quiet everything had become. Too quiet. She hadn't heard the dogs in a while, and a flicker of worry crossed her face. Her heart skipped. What time was it? Could she miss her train?

Panic stirred in her chest. Rex and Hollie were adventurous and sometimes got into trouble, especially if left unsupervised around the livestock. If they chased the hens again or wandered off into the bushland, her grandfather would not be pleased. He'd warned her before. She started calling for them, her voice sharp against the still morning air. No response. Her pace quickened to a run as she made her way across the farmyard, boots crunching on gravel and damp grass. The property was vast fields, sheds, and pockets of trees. The dogs could be anywhere. Then she heard it, barking. Loud, persistent, and coming from the far side of the farm near the hen house

"Rex! Hollie!" she called, breathless as she approached. She rounded the corner to find the two Labradors in full excitement mode, tails wagging, barking furiously at a flock of squawking hens. The birds flapped in all directions, feathers flying, as the dogs darted playfully back and forth in a chaotic dance. Melina groaned.

"Oh no, not again."

She rushed over, grabbing their collars and pulling them back.

"Leave them alone! You're going to get us both in trouble." The dogs calmed a little, panting happily as if proud of their morning mischief. Melina looked around to make sure none of the hens were hurt; thankfully, just ruffled feathers and one very annoyed rooster. Still catching her breath, she glanced back toward the house. Between the dogs, the train, and the questions crowding her mind about Monica's fiancé and his mysterious family, the day was already off to a chaotic start. And something told her it was only going to get more complicated from here.

"Good morning, Grandad," stated Melinda.

"Good morning, Mel," replied her grandad. "Why are you running and chasing the dogs? They always come here in the morning whenever I am in the hen house, don't you remember?"

"They always followed me around the farm doing my chores; they knew the time I would be out. You should go inside and get ready if you want to catch the train," her grandfather said, his voice gentle but firm. "I'll drive you to the station, don't keep me waiting."

"Thank you, Grandpa," Melinda replied, flashing him a grateful smile before hurrying into the house. She took the stairs two at a time, her mind already racing ahead to her return to university. She couldn't wait to see her friends again, to dive back into their animated conversations about the upcoming engagement party. Something was comforting in the buzz of student life, predictable, open, hers. Just as she began tossing clothes into her weekend bag, a familiar voice rang through the house.

"Mel! Breakfast is ready!" her grandmother called sharply from the kitchen. Melinda paused, groaning softly to herself. No matter how rushed the morning, no matter the urgency of a train schedule, one rule never changed at her grandparents' house: everyone must sit down for a proper, healthy breakfast. It wasn't a request, it was a ritual, as firmly rooted in the household as the old grandfather clock in the hallway. As a child, she had resented it. Mornings at the table often turned into showcases, mostly of Monica's achievements. Awards, grades, glowing teacher reports; all served up between mouthfuls of eggs and toast. Melinda had become skilled at stirring her porridge slowly, hoping no one would ask what she'd done that week. Compared to Monica's spotlight, her efforts always seemed to fade into the background.

But now, older and more self-assured, Melinda understood the deeper intention behind the tradition. Breakfast wasn't just about food; it was about connection, about grounding everyone before the day pulled them in different directions. Even if it still carried echoes of comparison, it also held memories of warmth, of family, of the kind of structure that, in its way, had helped shape who she was. With a resigned smile, she zipped up her bag and headed downstairs, ready to take her place at the table. Her grandfather looked up from his newspaper. "What are you up to, Mel? Well, I was just having a word with one of my friends about the engagement party, because Anna is very good at organising, and we could all come up with something elaborate for Monica and Sylvester. We were thinking of the engagement party, the theme, tying historical rituals to modern expressions of commitment." That caught their attention. Her grandmother blinked. "You're helping with the engagement party?"

Melinda nodded. "If Monica allows me."

"Have you asked her yet?" Gran inquired.

"No," Melinda replied. "I'll call her tomorrow when she's more settled."

"Well," her grandmother said, softening, "that sounds useful."

Melinda glanced down at her plate, hiding a small smile behind a sip of water. *Useful* wasn't exactly a glowing endorsement, but in this house, it passed for high praise. It was the closest thing to approval she'd received in weeks, and that, in itself, felt like a quiet triumph.

"I thought you were driving back with us, Mel," her mother said, her tone more assuming than questioning.

"Aren't you going to Mass with us today, Mel?" her grandmother chimed in, already reaching for her purse as if Mel's answer wouldn't change her plans.

"Can you stay another night? I thought you said you had Monday off for a study day," her aunt added, folding a napkin neatly in her lap, as if the matter had already been settled. The questions came in a gentle chorus, overlapping and clashing like waves against rocks, each one well-meaning but filled with the unspoken expectation that Mel's time was theirs to take. She hesitated for a moment, catching her father's quiet glance from across the table, unreadable as always. After a brief pause, she smiled softly. "Sure, I'll go to Sunday Mass," she said, her voice calm but resigned. "And I'll head back early Monday morning." The answer seemed to satisfy them. Conversations resumed, chairs scraped, plates passed. But Mel's mind drifted, already counting the hours until she could reclaim the quiet of her own space again.

CHAPTER TWENTY

The morning after the engagement party unfolded in a gentle hush. Soft Sunday light filtered through the lace curtains, casting delicate patterns across the worn wooden floor. The excitement of the night before had faded into the quiet hum of breakfast dishes and murmured conversations, the comforting rhythm of a house preparing for Mass.

Melinda lingered in the kitchen doorway, holding a cup of tea that had long since gone cold. She'd planned to leave early, to escape the familiar tangle of family expectations and unspoken tension, but something in the stillness, or perhaps the warmth in her grandparents' voices as they asked her to stay, softened her resolve. Her young cousins, still in pyjamas, were begging for just one more day. Despite the complications that always seemed to rise to the surface during these visits, Melinda found herself agreeing. One more night wouldn't hurt. Meanwhile, Monica and her parents were quietly gathering their things. They'd decided to skip Mass and make the long drive back to the city mid-morning. There were murmurs of schedules, traffic, and early starts on Sunday. Still, they paused long enough to join the rest of the family for a quick breakfast, coffee, toast, and a few last photos by the front porch, before slipping away with hugs and promises to "see everyone soon." Melinda watched as other family members and their cars pulled away from the gravel drive, a quiet ache settling in her chest. The house, already returning to its Sunday rituals, felt a little emptier. But there was still time, one more evening to sit with her grandfather on the porch, to help her grandmother peel vegetables for dinner, to remember why, even when it was hard, she always came back. The kitchen smelled like toasted bread, brewed coffee, and a hint of cinnamon, comforting scents that enveloped Melinda as she entered. The table was already set: a jug of orange juice, neatly stacked slices of buttered toast on a plate, scrambled eggs steaming in a ceramic bowl, and small glass jars of homemade jam lined up like soldiers on parade.

Her grandmother stood at the stove in her apron, flipping the last pancake with practiced ease. Her grandfather was already seated, reading the morning paper, glasses slipping down his nose.

"Sit, sit," her grandmother said, waving a hand without looking up from the sizzling pan on the stove. "No one leaves this house on an empty stomach."

Melinda slid into her usual seat at the long wooden kitchen table and poured herself a glass of orange juice. Her eyes drifted to the spot across from her. Monica was already there, sitting in her old place as if she'd never left.

The kitchen buzzed with cheerful chatter. Everyone was still talking about the surprise engagement party from the night before, how beautifully it all came together, how shocked Monica looked when the lights came on, and everyone shouted, "Congratulations!" Now, the conversation had shifted to what Monica's plans were for the wedding.

"Have you thought about a venue yet?" Aunt May asked between bites of toast.

"Not really," Monica replied with a smile. Sylvester and his parents are providing the venue, and I know it will be grand. "It still feels unreal. I mean, last night!" engagement party, sorry Sylvester was not here to meet the rest of the family and friends, but I will make sure they meet him before the wedding, if possible, because his schedule is very hectic. The air was filled with the comforting clatter of plates and the rich smell of buttered toast, fried eggs, and brewed coffee. It was one of those rare mornings when the whole family was gathered in one place, laughing over breakfast and slipping into the rhythm of familiar routines, each person offering advice, teasing Monica, or reminiscing about their own wedding stories. Melinda smiled quietly to herself, but a small knot tugged at her stomach. Something about the night before still clung to her, specifically, the way Sylvester had left. It hadn't been abrupt, exactly, but there was a tension in his eyes, a stiffness in his goodbye that unsettled her more the longer she thought about it. No one explained why, and when she tried to ask her mother about it later, she was told to leave it alone. She tried to push the feeling aside, just as she had tried to forget the conversation she'd accidentally overheard a few weeks ago, muffled voices, the name *Longhorn*, and something else, something darker. At the time, she couldn't quite make out the details, but there was a word that stuck in her mind like a splinter: *cartels*. It had been whispered like a secret too dangerous to name.

Since then, Melinda and Anna had taken to digging around when they could, online searches, quiet questions, careful observations. It could've been nothing. Gossip. Rumours wrapped in paranoia. But still, the unease lingered like smoke after a fire, and Melinda couldn't shake the feeling that something wasn't right. She glanced across the room where Monica was laughing with their younger cousins, her engagement ring catching the light. Melinda's chest tightened. No matter how vague or uncertain the threat was, she knew one thing for sure: she would protect her sister, no matter the cost.

And if there *was* something beneath the surface of the Longhorns' charm and wealth, something dangerous, then, then Melinda intended to find it before Monica got pulled in too deep. The family had made an unspoken agreement to avoid the subject. Every time his name hovered at the edge of conversation, someone changed the topic or clinked a glass just a little too loudly. Even Monica had plastered on a cheerful smile all morning, pretending like nothing had happened. But Melinda saw it, the flicker of tension in her sister's jaw, the way she kept glancing at her phone as if waiting for a message that hadn't come. Then, right as Grandma brought over a plate stacked with freshly buttered scones, Aunt May, never one to hold her tongue, blurted out, "Monica, what happened to your fiancé last night?" The room fell silent. A spoon clinked against a saucer, and someone coughed. Monica's smile faltered for a split second.   "He had to deal with something urgent," she said quickly, eyes fixed on her plate. "Work stuff."

"On the night of his engagement party?" Aunt May raised an eyebrow.

"Come on, darling. That's not normal. He didn't even say goodbye."

Melinda held her breath. She wasn't the only one who had noticed something was off.

"I'm sure it was important," Monica said, more firmly this time. "He didn't want to leave either. He just... didn't have a choice."

No one said anything. The silence stretched uncomfortably before Grandma cheerfully announced, "Tea, anyone?" as though that would stitch the conversation back together. But Melinda couldn't ignore it. Something wasn't right, and deep down, she suspected Monica knew it too. Melinda stirred her juice absentmindedly, barely listening as the conversation around the table resumed in a carefully upbeat tone. Her thoughts drifted to a few days earlier, when she had gone to the Sylvester family estate on an errand for her mother. Monica wasn't home yet, so she'd been asked to drop off a box of invitations and wait. She hadn't meant to eavesdrop. The door to the study was slightly ajar, and she had paused in the hallway when she heard voices, two men speaking in hushed but urgent tones.

"It's too soon. He wasn't supposed to propose until the matter was resolved," one of them said.

"He panicked. He's trying to keep her in place before everything unravels."

Melinda's heart had thudded in her chest. She had crept away quickly, not wanting to be caught listening, but the words stayed with her. At the time, she wasn't even sure she'd heard right. Maybe she had misunderstood. But after last night, after Sylvester disappeared just before the party, she wasn't so sure anymore. Maybe it *was* true, what people whispered about the family. She needed to dig deeper. Just as Aunt May opened her mouth again, clearly not done with the subject, Melinda's father quickly jumped in, smiling a little too brightly.

"Monica, darling, if you want to beat the traffic back to the city, you really should be leaving soon."

"Yes, yes," her mother chimed in. "We don't want you stuck on that motorway all evening. You know how dreadful it gets this time of day."

Monica glanced between them, clearly recognizing the distraction for what it was, but she nodded.

"You're right. I should get going."

Melinda watched her sister rise from the table, still trying to play the part of the glowing bride-to-be, even though the shadows under her eyes betrayed her. Melinda wanted to say something to her if she was okay, if she believed whatever excuse Sylvester had given her. But the words wouldn't come. Not yet. Instead, she stood too, helping Monica gather her things, her mind already racing. If there was something hidden, something wrong, she would find it. She had to. The clatter of breakfast dishes had quieted, replaced by the gentle hum of movement around the house. The sun was already climbing high, its light filtering through the lace curtains and warming the kitchen tiles.

"It's getting late," Grandma said, glancing at the old clock on the wall. "If we don't leave soon, we'll be walking in after the first hymn."

That was all it took to set everyone in motion. Chairs scraped back, napkins were folded, and half-full cups of tea were abandoned as the family began preparing for Sunday Mass, a ritual as old and ingrained as any family tradition they kept.

"Has anyone seen my church shoes?" Uncle David called from the hallway.

"In the laundry room, where you left them last week," came the dry reply from Aunt May.

Melinda rose from the table and carried her glass to the sink; her mind was still clouded with thoughts of Sylvester. But the familiar rhythm of Sunday morning helped push the unease to the side, at least for now. Her mother was already at the coat rack, straightening scarves and handing out folded umbrellas, just in case the weather turned. Her father buttoned his jacket and gave Melinda a small nod, the kind that said *Hurry along, no dawdling today*. Monica was nowhere in sight, most likely upstairs, quietly gathering her things before the drive back to the city. It wasn't surprising. After everything that had happened at the engagement party the night before, especially Sylvester's unexplained disappearance, she probably wanted to avoid yet another round of family interrogation. The looks, the whispers, the questions no one dared ask outright, it was all too much. Melinda stood in the hallway, her eyes drifting toward the staircase. A part of her wanted to go up, to check on Monica, maybe even try to talk to her. But another part hesitated. Would Monica even want to talk? Would she open up or shut down the moment Sylvester's name came up?

The weight of everything unsaid lingered in the silence of the house. Melinda shifted uneasily. The family was still buzzing with speculation, some of it whispered too loudly to be considered polite. Melinda had heard enough to know that people were starting to wonder if Monica knew more than she was letting on. And truthfully, so was she. She took a step toward the staircase, then paused. Maybe this wasn't the time. Or maybe this was exactly the time, before Monica left, before the distance made it harder to ask the questions that had been keeping Melinda up all night. She exhaled slowly and whispered to herself, *"Just talk to her."* Then, without waiting for more doubt to creep in, Melinda started up the stairs and then stopped.

CHAPTER TWENTY-ONE

It wasn't that Melinda begrudged her sister's success. Monica had worked hard. She was smart, polished, and ambitious. But the way the room shifted around her, the subtle change in posture, the extra attention, the way compliments were served as easily as the fruit salad, it left Melinda quietly wondering whether anything she did would ever feel quite as impressive. The dining room felt unusually calm. Someone passed around a plate of toast. Someone else poured coffee. Gran hummed a hymn under her breath as she laid out preserves. It was the kind of quiet that invited reflection, the kind that made Mel feel both comforted and exposed. She watched the way her uncle folded his napkin with practiced ease, how her cousin reached for the honey without asking, how Gran's eyes shifted across to Monica's sitting on the chair where she had sat last night.

"Are you okay, dear?" her grandmother asked gently, placing a warm hand on Monica's arm.

"Yes, Gran," Monica replied with a soft smile, but it didn't quite reach her eyes. She tried to appear composed, but the question had touched a nerve. Ever since the night before, she'd been replaying everything in her head, Sylvester rushing off without a proper goodbye, the vague excuse from one of his cousins about an "urgent matter," and the way no one seemed to want to talk about it. She had tried to brush it off, to tell herself it was just bad timing or some emergency. But the truth was, she didn't like it. Not one bit. Something felt off, and it wasn't the first time. As she smoothed down the sleeve of her coat, her jaw tightened ever so slightly. She would call him later, no more polite texts or waiting for him to explain. This time, she'd demand answers. He owed her that much, especially after vanishing on the night of their engagement party. Still, she kept the smile in place, knowing everyone was watching her more closely than they let on.

And all the while, the thought simmered beneath the surface: *Should I tell her? Should I have told her already?* The secret sat with Mel at the table, uninvited but ever-present, tightening its grip with every sip of lukewarm coffee.

"Betsy announced, "It's time to prepare for church." Whenever the family visits, she ensures they attend church services. As devout Catholics, the entire family was raised in the Christian (Catholic) faith. Although

186

some members no longer practice Catholicism, they maintain respect for the church and their family's traditions. Additionally, attending church provides an opportunity to reconnect with relatives and friends who have not been seen for a long time. Jeremy and Betsy (Melinda's grandparents) were chatting while the rest of the family got ready for church upstairs.

"I love when they visit," said Jeremy. "It's just like when they were kids and we'd all go to church together." "That's true," replied Betsy. "It's a shame Monica and the others cannot make it this Sunday to Mass. Hopefully, next time, when they visit, they will not have to leave so soon. Let's get ready; we don't want to be late for the service. Father James will be watching me come through the door and quizzing me after church." For being late again. But you are always late said Betsy with a laugh.

"Melinda, are you ready?" her grandmother called from the front door, her gloved hands folded neatly over the worn leather cover of her Bible. Melinda came down the last step of the staircase, fastening a small earring. "We barely use the Bible at church anymore, Gran," she said with a smile. "Everyone just reads off their phones." Her grandmother gave a small chuckle, adjusting her scarf. "I know, dear, but your grandpa and I are old-fashioned. There's something about holding the real book. The pages, the smell... It's how we've always done it." Melinda glanced at the well-thumbed Bible in her grandmother's hands, edges soft from years of use, a ribbon bookmark peeking out from somewhere in Psalms. There was a quiet dignity in how she held onto tradition, even when the world moved on around her.

"I get it," Melinda said softly, reaching for her coat. "It's kind of nice, actually." Her grandmother's eyes crinkled with a smile.

"One day, you might feel the same."

Just then, the sound of car doors opening outside signalled that the others were already heading out. The morning sun shone through the frosted glass panels of the door, casting a warm glow across the hallway.

"Come on then," Gran said. "Before your grandfather starts the engine without us."

Melinda followed her out; the Bible was now tucked under her grandmother's arm like a treasured companion. For a brief moment, as they stepped into the fresh morning air, the world felt calm, even if only on the surface.

"Yes, coming," Melinda replied, slipping on her cardigan. She took one last look around the now-empty kitchen, the hum of the morning giving way to the solemn hush of Sunday tradition. Whatever secrets were hiding behind those polite smiles and careful distractions, today was not the day they would surface. But soon. As they walked toward the car, Melinda slowed her pace just slightly, watching Monica waving them off to Mass

Now's the moment, Melinda thought. She could tell her Gran, she changed her mind about Mass, saying she is tired and wants to spend the time with Monica and tell her about her theory or what she overheard. Ask her gently if everything was okay, if she wanted to talk about Sylvester. She could even mention what she'd overheard at the estate. It had been bothering her for days, gnawing at the edge of her thoughts like a loose thread she couldn't ignore. But something stopped her. Maybe it was the way Monica's smile had flickered earlier, forced and fragile. Or maybe it was the familiar weight of a Sunday morning, the whole family dressed in their best, wrapped in the quiet reverence that came before Mass. It didn't feel like the right moment. Not yet. Melinda sighed and climbed into the back seat beside her younger cousin, tucking her gloved hands into her lap.

I'll talk to her another time, she told herself. *Later, when we're alone, when it won't feel like an ambush.*

The car pulled away from the driveway, tires crunching softly over gravel. Outside, the village passed by in a blur of budding hedgerows and stone walls warmed by sunlight. Inside the car, the mood settled into a familiar quiet, everyone mentally preparing for church, for hymns and prayers, and maybe, if the sermon ran long, a few stifled yawns. But Melinda's mind wasn't on the service. It was still on Monica. And on Sylvester. And on the uneasy feeling that something important was being hidden, just beneath the surface.

She looked out the window, telling herself she'd wait, but deep down, she knew that time was running out to keep pretending everything was fine.

CHAPTER TWENTY-TWO

The small village church stood at the end of a winding lane, its ancient stone walls partly covered in ivy, the bell tower casting long shadows across the churchyard. It was the same church the family had attended for generations, a place of christenings, weddings, and quiet farewells. Melinda stepped inside and was immediately wrapped in the familiar scent of polished wood, incense, and old hymnals. The hush of the sanctuary settled over her like a heavy quilt, soothing and stifling all at once. She followed the family into their usual pew near the front, where sunlight spilled through the stained-glass windows in soft patterns of colour, or the first time in a long while, Melinda found herself sitting through Sunday Mass without Monica or her parents beside her. The absence felt strange, like a missing piece in a well-rehearsed routine. They had left earlier that morning, traveling mid-morning to avoid the usual weekend traffic back to the city. It made sense, of course, but it didn't make it feel any less hollow. The pew beside her, usually filled with Monica's quiet presence and the occasional whispered joke during a long sermon, sat empty. Melinda tried to focus on the service, but her eyes kept drifting to that space, her thoughts lingering on her cousin's strained smile and forced calm the day before.

She realized, in a way she hadn't before, just how much she'd come to rely on Monica's presence. Despite everything, despite the tension surrounding Sylvester, Monica had always been a steady part of family life, a link between childhood memories and their slowly diverging adult lives. Melinda shifted in her seat as the choir began the Gloria. The notes soared through the chapel, but they couldn't quite fill the ache of that empty space beside her. She wondered if Monica had called Sylvester yet, and what he'd said if she had. Part of her wanted to reach out immediately, to ask. But another part of her hesitated, unsure of how deep this rabbit hole really went. After the final hymn, as the congregation began to rise and file out into the sunlight, Melinda lingered a moment longer, staring up at the stained glass above the altar. A quiet resolve settled over her.

Next time I see her: she though, I won't hold back.

Sunday Mass unfolded as it usually did, calm, familiar, steeped in ritual. The sunlight streamed in through the stained-glass windows, casting jewel-toned patterns on the wooden pews. Father James stood at the altar, delivering a homily that was both heartfelt and reflective. After nearly twelve years in the parish, he had grown into a steady, reassuring presence, filling the role left by Father Jeffery, who had retired not long before. His words that morning touched on kindness and quiet strength, and Melinda found herself unexpectedly moved.

After the final hymn, the congregation slowly made its way out, pausing to greet Father James at the doors of the church. His handshake was warm, his smile sincere, as he exchanged pleasantries with parishioners.

"Hello, Betsy," he said, shaking Melinda's grandmother's hand. Then, turning to her, he added, "And Melinda, how are you? I've heard about your sister's engagement party, Monica, isn't it? I couldn't visit yesterday because I was at the hospital, providing last rites to one of our long-time parishioners. "Melinda nodded politely, offering a small smile.

"Hello, Father James. It's lovely to see you again. I understand, you had responsibilities. You were needed."

Father James returned the smile with a gentle, knowing warmth. "

"That's very gracious of you, Melinda. Thank you. I trust university life is treating you well?"

She nodded again, this time more genuinely. "It has its challenges, but I'm managing."

"Good,"

He said with a nod. "It's a time for stretching your wings. And please, do pass on my heartfelt congratulations to Monica. An engagement is a beautiful milestone; may it bring her joy and strength."

"I will," Melinda said softly, though a flicker of something unreadable passed through her eyes. She'll be happy to hear that." Father James paused, as if sensing there was more beneath the surface, but chose not to press. Instead, he gave her a warm pat on the arm before moving on to greet the others. Melinda watched him go, the smile still on her lips, though her thoughts had begun to drift elsewhere.

****

Father James gave her arm a brief, comforting pat.

"You always struck me as a thoughtful one. Don't let the noise of the world dim that." Melinda felt her chest warm, caught off guard by the genuine kindness in his words. As they stepped away from the church steps and into the crisp morning air, she realized how rare it was to be seen, to be really seen, without the shadow of comparison.

"I'm going to the church Hall for a cup of tea, Aunt May said to Melina.

"That's okay," May said warmly, offering a quick smile before turning to greet Father James, who stood near the church doors in his familiar green vestments. He was doing what he always did best, shaking hands, exchanging kind words, and offering quiet blessings to parishioners as they filed out of the pews. The air was filled with the gentle hum of post-service conversation; a mix of reverence and comfort that made Sunday mornings feel like home. Mr. and Mrs. Jonas greeted

Father James with warm smiles and a few friendly words about the sermon and altar flowers. Father James replied humbly, though his eyes scanned the crowd.

"I'm so glad you enjoyed the service," he said, nodding earnestly. "Now, don't forget, there's tea, coffee, and plenty of biscuits waiting in the church hall. Make sure you help yourselves before the good ones are gone." His tone was playful, but with just enough encouragement to get people moving. He gently stepped away, his hand already outstretched to the next person in line, continuing the delicate balance of priest and host. There were so many faces to greet, so many quiet moments of connection to make. May lingered for a moment, watching him work his way through the crowd, a soft smile playing at her lips. Something was comforting in the routine of it, the familiar cadence of community life, the shared rituals, the little kindnesses that stitched everyone together week after week.

In the church hall, the air was filled with the warm, familiar murmur of post-service conversation. Parishioners clustered in small groups, some lingering near the tea table, others seated at folding chairs pulled into cozy circles, chatting over steaming mugs and plates of homemade biscuits. The scent of freshly brewed coffee mingled with the sugary sweetness of cakes and the occasional burst of citrus from squash drinks poured for the children. Laughter and chatter rose in waves, punctuated by the high-pitched squeals of children darting between tables, chocolate smudges on their fingers, plastic cups in hand. Some played an impromptu game of tag near the coat racks while others clutched half-eaten biscuits, their Sunday shoes scuffing lightly against the linoleum floor. It was lively, a little chaotic, but warmly so, the kind of atmosphere that felt stitched together by habit, history, and heart.

Earlier, as the congregation had filed out of the pews, Jane, a respected elder of the parish with an uncanny ability to command attention without raising her voice, had made her usual announcement. "Tea, coffee, and biscuits in the hall," she'd said with a cheery nod, "and squash for the little ones. You know the way." Her tone was light but practiced, as though she'd been delivering the same line for decades, which, truthfully, she had. Now, the ritual played out as it always did, adults catching up on news, children weaving through their legs, and the comforting hum of community wrapping the room like a soft quilt. It was a cherished tradition: after Mass, the congregation would gather in the modest but cozy hall, where trestle tables were laid out with warm drinks, homemade cakes, and the comforting crunch of digestives and shortbread. During the colder winter months, however, the parish sometimes set up the refreshments just inside the church doors, offering tea, coffee, and biscuits before anyone had a chance to step out into the chill. It was a thoughtful adjustment, practical, yes, but also quietly inclusive. No one had to brave the cold walk to the hall, and no one was left out, especially the elderly or those with little ones in tow. It turned the exit into a pause, a shared moment of warmth before heading back into the world.

The refreshments, lovingly brought in by the parishioners themselves, weren't just about snacks; they were about community. Over steaming mugs and plates of sweets, people caught up on each other's lives, swapped stories, shared news, and discussed everything from upcoming church fundraisers to local events and family milestones. Children played underfoot while older members lingered, their conversations laced with memory and quiet laughter. But today, the warmth lingered not just in the tea and conversation, but in the sense of familiarity, a ritual that wrapped around the community like a well-worn shawl. For most, it was just another Sunday.

For Mel, it was one of those quiet, sacred rituals that wrapped the world in a sense of calm, if only for a moment, even while her thoughts remained tangled and restless beneath the surface. She stood near the back of the church hall, cupping a mug of tea that had already begun to cool, watching the gentle chaos unfold, children darting between chairs, older parishioners catching up in clusters, laughter rising and falling like a familiar hymn.

On the surface, it was comfortingly predictable. But inside, Mel felt anything but steady. Her thoughts kept drifting to Monica, bright, beaming Monica, who had looked so radiant the night before, her hand never far from her fiancé's. Mel had smiled, clapped, and even offered a toast. But behind every word, behind every smile, sat the quiet thrum of worry.

What if I'm wrong? What if I misunderstood what I heard?
She replayed it constantly, clipped, urgent tones, the strange comment about "keeping it buried," the sudden silence when she'd turned the corner. Something about it had felt off. Not just gossipy or careless, *wrong*. Like a secret that had teeth. And yet, the idea of telling Monica now, in the middle of all this joy, felt almost cruel. She had waited so long to be happy. Mel couldn't bear the thought of planting doubt in her mind without proof, of becoming the reason her cousin looked at her future with suspicion instead of hope. Still, the unease sat with her like a second shadow, quiet but insistent. Because if something truly *was* wrong, and she said nothing... She took a sip of her tea, barely tasting it. Across the room, someone laughed. A child spilled juice. Life moved on, warm and ordinary. But Mel couldn't shake the feeling that something beneath it all was beginning to shift. The post-service social gathering stretched on for a comfortable forty-five minutes, filled with the soft clinking of teacups, polite laughter, and the rustle of

biscuit wrappers. Conversations ebbed and flowed, about the sermon, the weather, and, unsurprisingly, Monica's recent engagement.

As usual, the Jonas family took charge of tidying up. As caretakers of the church hall, they moved with quiet efficiency, stacking chairs and wiping down tables. Other parishioners, including Melinda's parents and younger brother, stayed behind to lend a hand. The familiar rhythm of teamwork made the clean-up feel less like a chore and more like an extension of the gathering. Melinda, however, quietly slipped out through the side door before Mr. and Mrs Jonas could catch her for another chat about Monica. She wasn't in the mood to be cornered with congratulations meant for someone else.

The cool air outside felt like a small relief, wrapping around her as she made her escape. Inside, a group of relatives huddled near the tea urn, chatting animatedly about wedding plans, venues, colours, and the dress, of course. May, ever the practical one, raised a hand and gently interjected, "Let's not get ahead of ourselves. It's Monica's wedding, remember? Let her decide." One by one, families waved their goodbyes and filtered out into the late afternoon sun, promising to catch up again tomorrow. The sense of community lingered, even as they all went their separate ways.

That earned a few chuckles and sheepish nods, and the conversation shifted to lighter topics. The cheerful atmosphere carried everyone through the last of the tidying, and soon the hall was spotless again. Chairs stacked, lights off, and doors locked.

CHAPTER TWENTY-THREE

The church bells chimed softly behind them as Melinda and her grandmother walked down the quiet street, their shoes crunching gently against the gravel-lined path. "I saw you, Mel, trying to hide from your Godmother, her Gran said with a gentle smile. Melinda laughed and linked arms with her. The Sunday air was crisp and carried the faint scent of pine from the neighbouring yards. For a while, they walked in silence, the kind that was more habitual than uncomfortable. Her grandmother finally broke it.

"That was a lovely homily. Father James always knows just what to say." Melinda nodded.

"He does. He has a gentle way about him... It's nice."

Her grandmother adjusted her purse on her shoulder. "You know, he used to ask after Monica all the time when she was still at home. She used to help with the youth group. "

"I remember?"

Melinda smiled politely.

"I remember." She repeated slowly, more to herself.

A beat of silence passed.

"She's very excited about the engagement party," her grandmother continued. "It's going to be a big event. So many people are asking about it, friends, neighbours, even old colleagues of your grandfather's." Melinda glanced down at the sidewalk as they walked, watching her shadow stretch long and thin beside her in the afternoon light. "That's good," she said softly. "I think it'll be a lovely celebration." Her tone was measured, but her thoughts were elsewhere.

Much bigger and better than the one we did yesterday, she added silently. Out loud, she continued, "I think Monica just went along with it because she knows Sylvester's family will be planning something, probably *the* engagement party of the year." Gran gave a low chuckle beside her. "Hmm, just imagine what the wedding's going to be like," she said, adjusting her scarf as the breeze picked up. "His people seem like they do everything on a grand scale. Champagne and chandeliers, I expect." Mel smiled faintly, but the curve of her lips didn't quite reach her eyes. "Yeah... probably swans and fireworks too." There was a pause between them, brief but not empty. Gran glanced sideways at her, a flicker of concern softening her features.

"You sure you're all right, love? You've been a bit quiet today." Mel hesitated, then nodded quickly. "Just tired, that's all." But the words felt thin in her mouth. Because what she wanted to say was still locked somewhere behind her ribs: what if **something's not right with Sylvester's family? What if** *Monica's walking into something none of us fully understand?* But she didn't say it. Not yet. Instead, she tucked her hands into her coat pockets and kept walking, her shadow stretching ahead of her like a question she didn't yet have the answer to.

Her grandmother turned to her, her tone gentler now. "And I'm glad you're involved, even if it's just helping out a bit." Melinda paused, unsure whether to feel grateful or dismissed. *Just helping out a bit.* She kept her voice even. "I'm actually coordinating part of the program with Nia. We've been planning for weeks." Her grandmother seemed to consider this. "Well, that's more than I realized," she said, her tone softening slightly. "You always were the quiet one. Sometimes people overlook the quiet ones until they're doing something important." Melinda wasn't sure if that was a compliment or a caution, but she let it hang in the air between them. As they rounded the final corner toward the house, her grandmother added, "You're not Monica, Melinda. But you have your way. Don't lose that. "Melinda looked at her, a flicker of surprise crossing her face. It wasn't

exactly approval, but it felt close, maybe even closer than her grandmother had ever come before.

She smiled faintly.

"Thanks, Gran."

And for the first time in a while, she meant it.

****

It was late evening, just after Sunday Mass. Mum, Dad, and Monica had already left for the city, their goodbyes still lingering faintly in the air. I was glad I'd decided to stay another night. I had Monday off for study anyway, and the quiet felt like a gift. Dad had promised to transfer some money into my account. He mentioned it briefly, leaning in with a half-smile and muttering,

"Okay, punkin." *"Don't worry, I'll sort you out."* He'd said it in front of everyone, so I let it slide, even though it made me feel slightly like a child again.

"It's always lovely to have you here, Mel," Gran said warmly as I stepped into the kitchen. "Supper will be ready shortly."

"I could've helped," I offered, already knowing she wouldn't let me.

"Oh, it's just some leftovers from yesterday, no trouble at all," she said, waving a hand like the thought of me lifting a finger was unthinkable. From the front room, I could hear Aunt Jen's unmistakable voice rising above the soft murmur of conversation. Subtlety had never been her strong suit; she hadn't quite grasped the idea of an "indoor voice," and she thrived on lively chatter, especially when it skirted the edge of gossip. Tonight, however, there was no scandal to be had. She, Uncle Sylvan, and Grandad were deep in discussion about the evening Mass, their voices layered with reverence and the occasional chuckle.

They were still unpacking Father James's homily: how moving it had been, how he'd managed to strike just the right balance of grace and conviction. They replayed key moments, debated whether the choir had chosen the right hymns, and lingered over the details the way only a tight-knit family could, where even the smallest moments felt worth remembering. A few minutes later, Gran's voice rang out from the kitchen, clear and commanding, slicing through the comfortable noise like a dinner bell from another era. "Supper's ready!" she called, in that way only she could, with the kind of authority that made even the most stubborn cousin straighten up and head to the table. We were having vegetable soup, still warm and fragrant, served with freshly baked bread rolls that Gran had made earlier that morning. There were also bits and pieces from the party, cold meats, pickles, and potato salad that had somehow gotten better overnight, and more.

"It's like having another party," Aunt Jen said brightly, reaching for a bread roll. "Only quieter, and with better seating."

The sound of chairs scraping against the floor and footsteps moving toward the kitchen followed. Our kitchen had always felt like the heart of the house, wide and open, with a big rectangular table taking up half the space. We all found our seats: Grandad, Gran, Aunt Jen, Uncle Selvin, Aunt May, Uncle Buster, and I. It felt intimate, even with the leftover laughter from earlier still echoing faintly in the corners.

"Don't touch that yet, Sylvan," Gran scolded with a teasing glare as Uncle Sylvan reached for a roll before grace had been said.

"Just testing if it's still warm," he said with a wink, drawing a few laughs.

We bowed our heads for a quick blessing, Grandad's voice low and gravelly, but steady as he gave thanks for family, food, and safe travels. When we lifted our heads, the sound of cutlery and clinking glasses quickly replaced any silence. Plates were passed hand to hand, overflowing with food by the time they reached the end of the line.

"So, Jen," Gran said mid-bite, "you were saying something earlier about Father James's message?"

Aunt Jen, never one to shy away from a spotlight, jumped back in.

"I just thought it was beautiful how he said, 'Faith isn't about having all the answers, it's about showing up with your heart open.' That hit me, you know? It's been a long week." Uncle Sylvan nodded, unusually quiet for a moment. "Yeah... it made me think about Dad. He always just showed up. Even when things were rough." A gentle hush fell across the table, one of those rare, sacred pauses where the air itself seemed to hold its breath. Gran broke it gently. "Well, he'd be proud of you all. Even if you can't sit through a service without whispering like schoolchildren."

Laughter returned, and just like that, the heaviness lifted. We moved on to lighter things: who had baked the better pie this year, whose kids were growing the fastest, whether the rain would hold off long enough for a walk after supper. I sat back for a moment, watching the ebb and flow of voices, hands, and laughter, and felt that quiet, grounding presence of family. The kind of warmth that sticks with you long after the plates are cleared and the stories have all been told. Everyone chuckled, and for a moment, the clatter of spoons and soft chatter filled the room like music. I dipped my bread into the soup and looked around the table, at familiar faces lit softly by the yellow glow of the kitchen light, at hands that had built this life, at a space that had always made room for me. And just like that, I felt it again, that strange, grounding comfort that came from being exactly where you belonged, even if just for one more night.

"So," Aunt Jen said, stirring her soup with unnecessary enthusiasm, "what *did* you think of the engagement party, Mel? Be honest now, I saw you sitting near that cousin of his with the unfortunate moustache."

Uncle Sylvan choked slightly on his bread roll and muttered, "That thing looked like it was glued on in a hurry."

Laughter rippled around the table. I smiled, trying not to seem too guarded.

"It was lovely," I said, carefully. "Well put together. Monica looked… happy." I paused for a moment, then added,

"She always did know how to make an entrance." I let the conversation swirl around me, a warm blend of teasing, questions, and familiar rhythms. But under it all, I felt a small, persistent tug in my chest, like something I couldn't quite name. I'd watched Monica smiling all day yesterday, watched her glide from one guest to the next like she was born to be at the centre of things. But there'd been a moment—just one one-one-one-where I caught her expression falter, just for a second, when she thought no one was looking. Uncle Sylvan said, between spoonful's of soup,

"How's university treating you, Mel?" All eyes turned to me. I swallowed quickly, buying a second to find the right answer.

"It's good," I said, nodding. "Busy, but good. Lots of reading. A mountain of it."

Aunt Jen gave a dramatic sigh. "Ugh, I don't miss that. I remember trying to read *Great Expectations* in two days; it took me a week. Didn't understand a word of it. Still passed, though."

"By copying my notes," Nan pointed out with a smirk.

Aunt Jen grinned. "Well, I had to get creative. You were the clever one, always scribbling away in your notebooks."

"I can see where Monica gets it," Uncle Sylvan added.

The mention of Monica made my stomach tighten slightly, though I smiled politely. "Yeah, she's always been a planner," I said. "Got her whole future mapped out since she was twelve."

"That sounds about right," Grandad chuckled. "She was the only child I've ever seen take minutes during a family meeting."

"Mel was the one always rearranging the spice rack," Gran added. "Alphabetically."

Everyone laughed, and I laughed too, even though I could feel a little knot in my chest. They meant it kindly, but I couldn't help feeling like the footnote in Monica's story, again. The *also-smart-but-in-a-different-way* sister.

****

I worked part-time as a Health Care Assistant on the gynaecology ward, and to my surprise, I genuinely loved it. At the time, I still held onto the dream of becoming a journalist, traveling the world, writing powerful stories, and maybe even appearing on television. I had always imagined myself chasing headlines in faraway places, the way bold, fearless women do in the movies. Perhaps, deep down, I also wanted to shine in a way that would outdo my older sister Monica. There's still a trace of that old sibling rivalry between us, the kind that never quite fades, no matter how grown-up we pretend to be. But something shifted.

Working on the ward changed me. I started seeing things differently: life, people, pain, and strength. Each shift brought stories that weren't written on paper but lived through real women and families. Slowly, journalism faded from my mind. The excitement of deadlines and newsrooms didn't compare to the quiet fulfilment I found helping someone through recovery or simply listening when they needed a kind voice. I stopped imagining myself in front of a camera and started picturing myself in scrubs. I wanted to be a nurse. Melina gave it her all, with 100% effort and a full heart. It wasn't just about following in her grandmother's footsteps or even keeping up with Monica anymore. It was about finding something meaningful, something that finally felt like *hers*. She wanted her parents to be proud of her, yes, but more than that, she wanted to be proud of herself.

"Okay, Aunt May," she said one Sunday afternoon while helping her fold laundry, "I'm in my second year now, and the studying is intense. So many modules, articles to read and write, it's honestly harder than I expected." Aunt May looked over her glasses and gave her a knowing smile. "I know you can do it. You're bright, focused, and more talented than you give yourself credit for. Melinda laughed, shaking her head. "I don't even think about journalism anymore. And if I did go into media, I'd probably work behind the scenes, writing, editing, maybe production. Quiet stuff. I never really liked being the centre of attention."

"Good,"

Aunt May teased, a mischievous twinkle in her eye. "You don't want to outshine your sister Monica. She's the one who likes the spotlight, always has, taking centre stage, all that attention. Let her have it." They both chuckled, the tension between pride and rivalry melting into something gentler, more affectionate. And in that moment, Melinda felt it clearly; she wasn't in competition anymore. She was on her path, and for the first time, it felt just right. That smile means she was just making fun of Monica. She said, "What are you studying again, love?" Aunt Jen asked, her voice a little softer now, maybe sensing the shift.

"Nursing", I said, "just like Gran". "I'm hoping to rise to the top when I graduate.

"Ooh, nursing, she said brightly. "That suits you. You were always the quiet one, always reading under a blanket somewhere." You were always helping animals and people.

"I wasn't that quiet," I said, smiling. "Just... observant."

"That's the best kind," Grandad said, pointing his spoon for emphasis. "The ones who notice everything. Makes you good company and dangerous in a debate." That made me smile for real. Grandad always had a way of making his words feel like gentle medals. As the soup bowls emptied and plates were passed around for leftovers, the conversation drifted to memories of past parties, who had said what, who had danced with whom. I mostly listened, letting their voices wash over me like waves. It felt safe, like I didn't have to be anyone. Just Mel, in Nan's kitchen, on a quiet Sunday night.

"Okay, Aunt May," I said, setting my spoon down. "It's my second year now, so there's a lot of studying, and a lot of patients to care for." Aunt May's eyes widened. "You already get to look after patients?"

"Don't be silly, May," Gran said, giving her a look over her glasses.

"She does," Gran added proudly. "And I know she'll do a good job, just like I did when I was nursing. Only now, everything's degrees and registrations. Not like in our days when we learned as we went."

"I think it's wonderful," Aunt May said, nodding. "Takes a strong stomach and a soft heart." Then Aunt Jen piped up, her voice laced with that teasing tone she used when she wanted to stir the pot. "At least she won't outshine Monica. I don't think Monica would like that."

She smiled as she said it, *that* smile. The one that meant she was only half-serious and fully poking fun. We all knew how Monica loved the spotlight. She was born for it. The kind of person who entered a room and assumed everyone had been waiting. I laughed because I knew Aunt Jen wasn't being cruel, just cheeky. "Don't worry, I've got no plans to upstage Monica."

"She wouldn't let you anyway," Aunt Jen quipped with a wink, and we both started laughing.

"What's so funny?" Uncle Sylvan asked from the other end of the table, raising a curious brow.

"Oh, just girl talk," Aunt Jen replied breezily, waving a hand. I caught her eye and smiled. I knew what she was doing, lightening the mood, reminding me I had a space here that was mine, even if Monica's shadow sometimes stretched longer than it should. Gran pushed her chair back. "Alright now, it's getting late. Off to bed, all of you. Mel, remember you've got an early start tomorrow."

Everyone stood slowly, chairs scraping against the floor, dishes clinking as they were gathered. I helped stack a few plates before following the others out of the kitchen, the warmth of supper and laughter still clinging to the air. But as I climbed the stairs to the guest room, a quiet thought tugged at me from somewhere deep inside: the world outside this house would start up again tomorrow. The train rides, the textbooks, the expectations. And when it did, I wasn't quite sure which version of me I'd be expected to bring, Monica's little sister, the student nurse, or someone I was still in the middle of becoming. I paused at the landing and looked back toward the kitchen, where the lights still glowed and where faint voices echoed. For tonight, I didn't need to choose. I was just Mel. And that was enough. That night, sleep found me slowly. The bed in the guest room was familiar but just different enough to make rest a negotiation. The ticking of the hallway clock drifted in through the crack under the door, a rhythm I hadn't heard since childhood. I let my eyes close, letting the sounds of the old house wrap around me, floorboards settling, the faint hum of the fridge downstairs, the whisper of the wind through the cracked-open window. And then, like stepping through a veil, I was back...

We were in the schoolyard, Monica and I. The old red-brick building rose behind us, tall and stern, with ivy curling up its sides like it was trying to climb away. It must have been lunchtime; kids were scattered across the grass, eating sandwiches and kicking footballs, their voices layered like overlapping waves. Monica was standing just a few steps ahead of me, laughing, as always, surrounded by people. Her uniform was crisp, her hair in its perfect high ponytail. She was telling a story, something funny, and everyone was hanging on her every word. Even I was. But then she turned to me, smiling, and beckoned.

"Come on, Mel," she said, her voice brighter than the sky.

"Tell them the bit about the dog! "I hesitated, suddenly aware of all the eyes on me. My voice caught in my throat. I could feel the heat climbing my neck, the way it always did when attention turned my way. But Monica kept smiling, patient, waiting. And then I started to speak, but the words didn't come out right. They tumbled over each other, awkward and too fast. A few kids giggled. Someone muttered, "What?"

I looked at Monica, but her smile had faltered, just slightly. Just enough for me to see it: that flicker of disappointment. Suddenly, the crowd blurred, the colours of their uniforms bleeding into each other like watercolours left in the rain. The sky dimmed. Monica turned away, her back to me now, her laughter blending with the wind until I couldn't tell if she was laughing at me or just forgetting I was there. The dream shifted again, the way dreams do, becoming something more abstract, a hallway with endless doors, voices whispering behind each one, all just out of reach. I walked slowly, unsure which one to open. Then I heard Nan's voice, soft and distant: **"You don't need to follow to be seen, love. You've got your own story."**

I turned, but no one was there.

And then I woke up.

The early light had just begun to filter through the lace curtains, brushing the walls with gold. For a moment, I lay still, blinking against the quiet.

The dream clung to me like mist, that strange echo of Monica's voice, of my own silence, of Gran's impossible words. I wasn't sure what it meant. Maybe nothing. Maybe everything. But as I sat up, rubbing the sleep from my eyes, I felt something I hadn't before, not clarity exactly, but a small space opening in my chest. A space where I could start to breathe as myself.

CHAPTER TWENTY-FOUR

The house was still hushed when I woke properly. That early kind of silence, the kind that settles over everything like a blanket, broken only by the creak of an old pipe or the soft rustle of trees outside the window. I sat up slowly, letting the dream dissolve somewhere behind me. The light through the curtains had grown stronger, laced with the golden blush of early morning. For a moment, I stayed there at the edge of the bed, grounding myself. A new day, and with it, the world is waiting to start up again. I dressed quietly, folding the spare nightclothes Gran had left out for me the night before. My bag was already packed, books, charger, planner, and the Tupperware container Gran had pressed into my hands last night with leftover bread rolls and a slice of fruit cake "just in case."

Downstairs, the kitchen smelled faintly of fresh coffee and last night's soup. Gan was already at the table, dressed in her usual housecoat and slippers, reading from a small prayer book. She looked up and smiled when she saw me.

"Morning, love. I thought I'd be up before you."

"You usually are," I said, and we both smiled.

She closed the book gently. "Want a bit of breakfast before you go? I've got toast and eggs, nothing fancy."

"Just toast is fine," I said, easing into the chair across from her. "I don't want to miss the train."

She moved efficiently, her hands practiced, spreading butter, setting down a mug of tea without needing to ask how I liked it. Everything she did held a kind of unspoken care, the kind that wraps itself around you without fuss or ceremony. As I ate, we didn't say much. We didn't need to. There was something comforting about the clink of the butter knife, the distant sound of birds in the garden, the steady rhythm of the world beginning again.

When it was time to go, I stood and wrapped my arms around her.

"Thanks for everything, Gran."

She hugged me back, warm and sturdy. "You be good, Mel. Take care of yourself, and don't run yourself into the ground with that course. You've got nothing to prove."

"I know," I whispered, even if I didn't fully believe it yet.

"Give your mum a kiss from me. And your sister."

I hesitated, just for a second.

"I will."

Grandad appeared then, in his cardigan and slippers, rubbing sleep from his eyes. He gave me a gentle pat on the back, then slipped something into my hand, an envelope, probably with a bit of cash folded neatly inside.

"Just a little top-up," he said gruffly, pretending to look at the clock instead of me.

"Thanks, Grandad," I said, slipping it into my bag without opening it. "I'll put it towards my travel card."

He grunted in approval and offered me a wink. A few minutes later, I was standing at the front door, the cool morning air brushing my face. My small suitcase bumped softly against the floor as I reached for the handle.

"Go on then," Gran said, giving me a gentle nudge. "The world's waiting."

As I stepped out onto the porch, the sun was just beginning to climb above the trees, casting long, golden shadows across the gravel. The house stood behind me like a quiet sentinel, steadfast, familiar, full of stories. I pulled the door shut behind me and started down the path. Not Monica's sister. Not just the girl who stayed an extra night.

Just Mel. Heading forward.

WALKING IN MY SISTER'S SHADOW

PART TWO

CHAPTER TWENTY-FIVE

On Monday morning, Melina returned to Bridge Heath by train. She had politely declined her aunt and uncle's offer to drive her back the night before, citing study, though the truth was simpler. Their constant bickering, even when well-meaning, left her feeling like a sponge wrung dry. The train, in contrast, offered her something precious: silence. No running commentary about motorway exits, no half-argued detours, no political debates turned into backhanded family grievances. Just quiet, and time.

It was a mid-morning train, off-peak, mostly empty. The kind of quiet only a Monday could offer, when the weekend rush had subsided and the weekday commuters had already vanished into office buildings and lecture halls. She stepped onto the near-deserted platform with a small sigh of relief, found her carriage, and slipped into a window seat facing forward. The fabric of the seat was worn, the heater just a little too warm, and the carriage smelled faintly of coffee and old newspapers. She took off her coat, folded it behind her head like a cushion, and leaned back. Outside, the world rolled by in a blur of hedgerows, sleepy fields, and skeletal trees stretching skyward against a pale, washed-out sky. She didn't really sleep. She never did on trains. But it didn't matter. That light, liminal state, where the body rested and the mind drifted just beneath the surface, was exactly where she did her best thinking. Her eyes hovered half-closed as the rhythmic clatter of the tracks formed a soft, hypnotic percussion beneath her thoughts. In that stillness, everything seemed to float into place. The weekend's images, Monica's party, Gran's kitchen, the hushed dream that still clung to her, gently reassembled themselves like puzzle pieces finding the corners. She thought of Monica's face during the toasts: poised, proud, but with something unreadable behind the eyes. She thought of Gran's words, *"You've got your own story."* It echoed now, not just as comfort, but as a challenge.

She reached into her bag and pulled out her notebook: not the one she used for lectures, but the one she kept for moments like this. She flipped past old scribbles and fragments of thoughts, then found a clean page. She didn't know what she was going to write yet. But she clicked her pen, stared out at the rolling countryside, and waited. Not long after, she began. She loved watching the world blur past the train window, fields unravelling like green ribbons, distant farmhouses tucked beneath the rise and fall of gentle hills, and the occasional flicker of a village station flashing by like a forgotten postcard. Each stop ushered in a fresh wave of passengers: some rushed and flustered, clutching takeaway coffees and tangled headphones; others calm, unbothered, as though the train were simply a moving extension of their home. Melina studied them with quiet interest. She never stared, just observed, carefully and from a distance. What shoes they wore, what bags they carried, the way they settled into their seats or hovered near the doors as if always half-ready to escape. It was a habit she had nurtured for years, something between a game and a meditation. She would tuck each stranger into a little imagined story: a woman in a navy coat became a tired surgeon heading home after a night shift; a teenager with an oversized backpack was running away to start a new life somewhere anonymous and exciting.

Her university friends teased her about it, especially Anna, who once dubbed her *"the train psychologist"* after catching her mid-stare on a London-bound journey. But Melina didn't mind. It was her quiet ritual, her way of grounding herself. While some people journaled or meditated, she collected silent narratives. There was something deeply soothing in it: a reminder that the world was full of lives larger than her own. That her worries were small and moving, just like the train, always in motion, never stuck. More than anything, watching people like that helped her reset. It pulled her out of herself, especially when the weight of expectation or comparison pressed too heavily on her shoulders. It gave her perspective. Everyone was going somewhere. Everyone had something to carry. And yet, for a few brief moments, they all shared the same space. A carriage full of strangers, heading in the same direction, for now. She smiled softly at the thought and leaned back in her seat, eyes following a flock of birds that lifted off from a field, their wings cutting clean lines across the sunny sky. There was something about solo travel that reset her. No one to talk to, no obligations, just the gentle forward motion of the train and the slow, unfolding countryside. It gave her room to breathe, to step outside the swirl of daily life and just *be*.

As the train rolled past fields dotted with sheep and rows of terraced houses, Melina pulled her coat tighter around her shoulders. There was a faint chill in the air, despite the weak sunshine slanting through the window. A part of her dreaded returning to Birmingham, not because she didn't like the city, but because returning meant stepping back into the fast pace of university life: lectures, deadlines, group projects, and the endless buzz of conversation. Still, she felt a certain readiness this time. The weekend had done her good, despite her aunt's sharp comments and her uncle's exaggerated sighs. Seeing her cousins, the smell of familiar cooking, even the chaos: it grounded her in a way Birmingham never quite could.

She glanced across the carriage. An older woman sat a few seats down, knitting with quiet focus, her needles clicking gently in rhythm with the train's movement. A teenage boy further along tapped away on his phone, earbuds in, lost in his world. It struck Melina how many lives were always unfolding side by side, each carrying its weight, its own rhythm. She pulled out her journal from her bag, a soft leather-bound one with the corners slightly worn, and uncapped her pen. It had become a habit lately, jotting down whatever came to mind during these journeys. Sometimes it was a thought, a quote, a fragment of dialogue she'd overheard. Today, she started writing about clarity, how silence and motion together could bring her back to herself. A few stops before her final destination, she decided to give Monica a call.

Monica's phone buzzed loudly on the nightstand, slicing through the quiet of the morning. She groaned, barely lifting her head from the pillow. *Who on earth is calling at this hour?* It was Monday, her day off, and she'd been looking forward to sleeping in, especially after the long journey back last night. She'd purposely travelled early Sunday to avoid the usual family pressure to attend Mass. She just wasn't in the mood for incense and small talk. She reached blindly for the phone, blinking at the screen. A part of her considered ignoring it. *Let it ring,* she thought, rolling onto her side. *I deserve a lie-in.* But then a possibility crept into her mind, *maybe it's Sylvester.* A small smile played at the corners of her mouth despite herself. After the little stunt he pulled on Saturday, disappearing halfway through the engagement party, she wouldn't put it past him to call and explain himself with some charming excuse. Typical Sylvester. But the moment she saw the caller ID, her expression changed. The smile vanished. *Melina.* Monica stared at the name for a beat, her brows knitting together with a mix of confusion and irritation. She tapped the screen and brought the phone to her ear.

"What is it, Mel?" she snapped, her voice sharp and groggy. "You just woke me up! Couldn't this wait? What's so urgent that you *have* to call me this early in the morning?" and a pleasant good morning to you too, sister dearest", stated Melinda cynically. "

"Don't be cynical, Mel. It's beyond you. What do you want?" Monica grumbled, rubbing the sleep from her eyes as she shifted against the headboard. Melina's voice came through the speaker, light but firm.

"It's just after 11:30. I figured you'd be awake by now. I was calling to see how the engagement party planning is going, and if you need help with anything." There was a brief pause. Monica sat up slightly, something about Melina's tone making her more alert than she wanted to be.

"You call 11:30 *early*?" Monica said with a dry laugh, the sarcasm curling around her words. "Honestly, Mel."

"I'm sorry, Monica," Melina said, a little more softly now. "I just thought… I'd like to help with the planning. I know Mum and Dad are going full throttle with this grand version they're imagining, and, well, I thought you might want a hand."

Monica let out a sharp, amused scoff.

"You? Help with my engagement party?" she repeated with a touch of theatrical disbelief. "Have you completely lost your mind? You and your little friends running around, turning it into some artsy disaster? No, thank you." She paused just long enough to make her point sting. "That party at Gran's was fine, for the country crowd. I appreciated your input. But this one, this is *the* party. The real one. Sylvester and I are planning it together with his parents. It's going to be elegant, tasteful, *controlled*." As a matter of fact, Sylvester's cousin is hiring a party planner. Melina stayed quiet for a moment. Monica could almost hear her chewing over a response, deciding whether to push or let it go. Melina stayed quiet for a moment. The silence on her end was heavy, and Monica could almost hear her thinking. When Melina finally spoke, her voice was calm but edged with something sharper, concern, maybe, or quiet defiance.

"You know, Monica… sometimes I wonder if you actually want help or if you just want control."

Monica's eyes narrowed.

"Excuse me?"

"I'm not trying to take over," Melina continued, more measured now. "I just thought you might need someone in your corner. You sounded exhausted the last time we talked. And the way Mum's going on, it sounds like she's steamrolling you. Don't tell me this is all fun for you." Monica opened her mouth to snap back but hesitated. Her jaw tensed.

"It's not about fun," she said finally, quieter now. "It's about getting it *right*. Sylvester's family expects a certain standard. His mum keeps dropping hints about the venue, the guest list, even the flower arrangements, and I can't give them any reason to think I'm not good enough." Melina softened, hearing the edge in her sister's voice start to crack.   "Monica… no one gets to decide if you're good enough. Least of all, some posh people worried about centrepiece symmetry."

"You don't get it," Monica said, the veneer of confidence slipping.   "They see me as the loud girl from a working-class family with too much lipstick and too many opinions. I have to prove I can belong in *their* world."

There was a beat of quiet between them.

"I *do* get it," Melina said gently. "Maybe not exactly the way you feel it, but I know what it's like to pretend you're fine when you're crumbling under pressure. Just... let me be there. Not to fix things. Just to stand beside you. You don't have to do this alone." Monica let out a breath she hadn't realized she was holding. Her fingers tightened around the phone.

"Mel tapped her screen and brought the phone to her ear. Monica, are you still there?

"Yes, Monica's voice, smooth and sharp like polished marble. "I was beginning to think you were screening my calls." Mel forced a small smile that no one could see. Monica, I'm on the train, and the Wi-Fi It's sometimes not so great. Mel bit back a sigh. *Here we go.*

"What's up?" she asked, trying to keep her tone neutral.

"Everything okay?"

"Well," Monica huffed, "if you must know, I had to smooth things over with Sylvester's mother *again* because someone decided to throw an impromptu country-style engagement party without *consulting* me."

Mel blinked, stunned by the casual dismissal. "Monica… you were there. You smiled through the whole thing."

"I smiled because I'm good at being gracious," Monica snapped.

"And because I didn't want to embarrass Mum and Dad. But really, Mel? Paper bunting? Jam jars with wildflowers. I mean, what were we, auditioning for a wedding in a farmer's field?" Mel's jaw tightened. "It wasn't about style. It was about family. About Gran being able to celebrate you."

"Well, next time, leave the celebrating to people who understand taste," Monica said flippantly. "Sylvester's parents are hosting the engagement party of the year, something *proper* in the next few weeks. Champagne, live quartet, city views, the whole thing. Maybe then we can pretend this little village tea party never happened." Mel paused, gripping the phone tightly. Her heart pounded, not with anger exactly, but with something heavier. Disappointment. Maybe a bit of sadness, too.

"Right," she said quietly. "I'll be sure to wear something appropriate for pretending."

There was a pause on the other end, just long enough for Mel to wonder if the bite in her words had landed.

"Anyway," Monica said briskly, "you *are* coming, aren't you? Sylvester's parents want everything to look... well, balanced. Like we're all from the same world."

Mel let the silence stretch a beat too long, just enough to make it uncomfortable. Finally, she said,

"Sure. I'll be there." Monica hesitated, testing the waters.

"What about my friends? Can I bring them too?"

A pause. Then Monica's voice came through, cold and blunt. "I met your friends briefly. Not really my scene. I know the Lester family will be there; he's decent. You can bring Anna. I'll think about the others." The line went quiet for a second before Melina mumbled, "Okay, that's fair," and ended the call. Monica set the phone down and let herself sink into the bed, staring up at the ceiling fan as it spun in lazy, uneven circles. The tension in her shoulders began to loosen, just slightly, like a knot that had started to give way but still held tight in places. Maybe letting someone in wouldn't be the worst thing after all. But almost immediately, the quieter voice in her mind, the one she usually tried to drown out with noise and busyness, spoke up, dry and unforgiving.

You only said that to end the conversation.

She closed her eyes and exhaled, slow and tired. The kind of tired that came from months, years, of emotional balancing acts. Pretending was second nature now, like muscle memory. Smiling when she didn't want to, nodding along when she didn't agree, making space for people she wasn't sure she could trust. The truth was, she didn't want Mel to ruin this, not again. And not because Mel wasn't trying. But because Mel didn't fit, not here. Not with these people. Not in this version of Monica's life that she'd worked so hard to build. And her friends, loud, unpredictable, full of questions, they didn't fit either. She could already imagine the looks, the forced small talk, the subtle judgment lingering under the surface like smoke. She wanted this gathering to go smoothly. Quietly. Without tension or side-eyes or anyone pulling focus. Just once, she wanted something to feel simple. But simplicity came with a cost. And that cost, often, was honesty.

CHAPTER TWENTY-SIX

As the train neared Bridge Heath station, the landscape began to change. Fewer trees, more concrete. Warehouses, apartment blocks, graffiti-scrawled bridges. The stillness she'd found on the journey began to retreat, replaced by the familiar thrum of city life approaching. But this time, she held on to the calm a little longer. She looked out at the city coming into view and thought I'm ready for this week. Whatever it brings, I'm walking into it steadily and clearly.

Mel wasn't surprised by Monica's outburst. She'd seen it coming, really. Monica had always been dramatic when things didn't go exactly her way. Spoiled, self-centred, and relentlessly determined to stay at the centre of everyone's attention, Monica had perfected the art of making every situation about her. Their parents had indulged her for as long as Mel could remember, smoothing over her tantrums, bending to her whims, calling it "sensitivity" or "passion" when it was really just entitlement. Now, it was clear even they couldn't rein her in. And Sylvester, Monica's charming, deep-pocketed fiancé, wasn't helping. If anything, he seemed to encourage it. He doted on her like she was made of glass and gold, giving her everything she asked for with a smile and a credit card. Designer shoes, spontaneous weekend trips, and champagne brunches, it was all part of the package. And Monica soaked it up like sunlight. Mel just shook her head, feeling more worn out than angry. She had long since given up trying to keep up with Monica's endless demands or call out her flaws; what was the point? Some people were too wrapped up in their own reflections to ever see the cracks, let alone admit they were there.

With a quiet, almost resigned sigh, Mel began gathering her things slowly, her fingers tracing the edges of her bag as the train station came into view ahead. The familiar hum of commuters, the sharp scent of diesel and cold metal, grounded her for a moment, a small reminder that life moved forward, with or without her involvement in Monica's drama. She glanced once more at the fading outline of the family home behind her, feeling the weight of unspoken worries settle like a stone in her chest. Somewhere deep inside, she wished things could be different. But for now, all she could do was keep moving.

****

Monica was fuming. Her silly little sister had woken her up for nothing. She knew perfectly well that Monica had driven down late the night before, and on a Sunday, no less, when the motorway was practically a parking lot, clogged with people returning from their weekend getaways. Monica had taken a precious day of annual leave specifically so she could sleep in and recover. And then this, an early morning call from Mel, of all people, disrupting what was meant to be a rare, peaceful morning.

She tossed back the covers and sat up, still simmering. The engagement party was still bothering her, too. She hadn't been consulted, not even given a hint. Everyone kept insisting it was a *surprise*, but Monica wasn't fooled. It was disorganized, homespun, and, most irritating of all, clearly driven by Gran and Mel, as if their quaint little village ideas could somehow pass for a proper celebration. She ran a brush through her hair with jerky movements. Now she had to smooth things over *again* with Sylvester's parents, who had asked, politely but firmly, why they hadn't been informed or invited. Monica would have to spin the story delicately: downplay the bunting and fairy lights, emphasize the good intentions, and lay the blame gently at the feet of her well-meaning little sister and traditional grandmother.

"It was just a small, local gesture," she rehearsed under her breath.

"Something simple that my Gran wanted to do… your younger sister helped organize it… You know how sentimental village families can be." She sighed. This wasn't the narrative she wanted for her engagement. Not jam jars and Victoria sponge cakes. She wanted chandeliers, silk napkins, and Instagram-worthy elegance. And now she had to spend the afternoon damage-controlling *that* party just to keep things on track. She picked up her phone again, hesitating before sending a message to Sylvester. Need to talk later.

My family got a bit carried away this weekend. I'll explain. I'm sure she'll try to bring her university friends to *my* party, Monica thought with a scoff, pulling the covers over her legs again. I'll have to find a way to stop her. Maybe she can bring one or two, *if* they're presentable. If their credentials are good. Otherwise, no. She still didn't understand why Melinda had chosen to go to university in *Bridge Heath* of all places. She had the grades to apply to a decent London University, *better* Universities, even. But no, she had to run off to the Midlands like some rebellious heroine in a budget drama. They'd never been close as sisters, not really. Monica had tried, especially in their teens, to guide her, to bring her up to her level. She'd always believed Mel could be shaped into something elegant, refined. But it didn't take.

"I told Mum and Dad," Monica muttered aloud. "She's a wayward girl. They kept saying she'd grow out of it, but she didn't. She grew *into* it." Now, Monica thought, it's too late to train her. She's set in her odd, soft-hearted ways. Her thoughts wandered back to the few times she'd met Mel's university friends, unpolished, awkward, overly familiar. Monica had done her best to be polite, but the whole group gave off an energy she couldn't stand: too casual, too underwhelmed, too comfortable in their mismatched clothes and inside jokes. They didn't care how they looked, didn't try to impress anyone. It baffled her. She remembered one particular visit, Mum had insisted they stop by the campus unannounced, eager to "see how Mel was settling in." Monica had reluctantly agreed, hoping at least to find something redeemable. Instead, they were met with a dorm room that smelled faintly of instant noodles and half-damp towels, and a crowd of students who greeted them with lopsided grins and cluttered mugs of tea. One young man stood out slightly; something about his watch and the way he spoke suggested money, but Monica couldn't recall his name. It didn't matter. None of them did. And then there was Mel's obsession with working part-time at a nearby hospital, clocking long hours between lectures. Monica had asked her once, genuinely puzzled, why she felt the need to work.

"You have your student grant," she'd said. "Mum and Dad already give you money every month. What's the point of running around on hospital wards like some overworked porter?" Mel had just smiled, unbothered as always. "It's not about the money. I want the experience, something real, before placements start.

I want to know what I'm doing when I get there." Monica had blinked at her, baffled by the earnestness. *Real experience?* Monica couldn't imagine choosing that kind of stress when you didn't have to. But then again, that was Mel all over, choosing effort, mess, and meaning over ease, polish, and appearance. Mel's answer still gnawed at her. "I want the experience," she'd said with that maddening calm. "It'll help during placements. I'll understand the wards better, the patients, the rhythm of it all." Monica had rolled her eyes at the time, and even now the memory made her bristle. So noble. So unnecessarily *earnest*. Like something out of a charity brochure.

"And nursing," she muttered aloud, her voice sharp in the quiet room. "Of all the professions she could have chosen." She let out a sigh, exasperated. "I even suggested she consider becoming a Physician Associate. It's more advanced. More professional. More respectable." Mel had smiled vaguely and said she'd think about it, but Monica doubted she ever had. She was too busy trying to be the saint of the ward. Still, there was time, just enough, perhaps, for Mel to change course. She *should*.

Fuming, Monica flopped back onto the pillows, the duvet twisting uncomfortably around her legs. She stared up at the ceiling, willing her racing mind to slow down. But her jaw was still clenched tight, her thoughts refusing to settle. It wasn't just the party or the phone call or even Mel's ridiculous job. It was the way everything always seemed to bend to her sister's quiet orbit, how she could be soft-spoken and scatterbrained and still be taken seriously. Monica had spent years mastering the art of control, of elegance, of being listened to. And yet somehow, Mel always managed to draw attention without even trying.

CHAPTER TWENTY-SEVEN

Her phone buzzed on the nightstand, pulling her from her spiralling thoughts. She glanced at the screen. *Mum.*

Monica let it ring once more before answering, composing her voice into something close to pleasant.

"Hi, Mum."

"Oh, good, you're awake," her mother said in that brisk, chirpy tone that always felt slightly rehearsed. "We didn't wake you, did we?" Monica hesitated. "I was resting. I took today off for a reason."

"Yes, well, I just wanted to check in. Your father and I were talking about the engagement party. It turned out quite sweet in the end, didn't it?"

Sweet. That was the word they were using now?

"If by 'sweet' you mean hastily thrown together and painfully underdressed," Monica replied, sitting up straighter.

"I told you both, I should've been consulted. It's my engagement, not a bake sale." Her mother sighed on the other end. "Monica, it was meant to be a surprise, something thoughtful from Gran and Melinda. You know how she fusses over family traditions." Monica scoffed. "Well, next time, maybe they could try 'thoughtful' with a little less bunting and fewer fairy lights."

There was a pause.

"Anyway," her mother said, voice tight, "we're going to see Sylvester's parents this afternoon. Your father wants you to come along. Just to clear the air, make sure everyone's on the same page." Monica closed her eyes. "Let me guess, you want me to do the apologizing?"

"Not *apologizing*," her mother said, a touch too quickly. "Just smoothing things over. Explaining that it was a small family gesture, not meant to exclude anyone." Monica gritted her teeth. *Damage control. Again.* All thanks to her sister and Gran's quaint little fantasy.

"Fine," she said at last. "I'll get dressed and meet you there. But next time, can we try planning something that actually reflects *my* taste?"

"We'll talk about it later," her mother replied. "Just be polite, please. And no drama." The line went dead. Monica threw the phone back onto the bed and exhaled slowly, her eyes narrowing.

"No drama", she echoed under her breath.

"Right".

Monica adored her immaculate, spacious three-bedroom condo, a sleek, modern flat nestled in one of London's trendier boroughs. Each bedroom had its en-suite bathroom, high ceilings, and soft ambient lighting that looked like something out of a luxury magazine. The master bedroom, hers, of course, was the crown jewel: a walk-in closet, a rainfall shower, a velvet-upholstered king-size bed, and a private balcony with a view of the city skyline. It was, in her words, *"to die for."*

She shared the apartment with her longtime friend Sandra, although this morning, their usual camaraderie was noticeably tense. Sandra had left early for work, still fuming about not being invited to the engagement party. Monica had tried to explain, *repeatedly*, that it wasn't *her* event, that the whole thing had been a surprise organised by Melinda and Gran. But Sandra wasn't having it.

"I thought I was your best friend," she'd snapped, keys jangling in her hand. "I shouldn't be hearing about your *surprise* engagement party through Instagram stories!" Monica had rolled her eyes.

"Sandra, we're planning the *real* party later, the big one. You'll be on the guest list. The other thing was just… family, village stuff. Honestly, it wasn't even my idea." Sandra had stormed out with little more than a mumbled "Sure," the front door clicking shut a little harder than usual. Monica sighed, sipping her green smoothie in silence. It was too early for drama, but then again, that seemed to follow her lately. Still, she couldn't complain too much. The apartment lease, twelve months of luxury, was paid for in full by her fiancé, Sylvester. That had been his engagement gift, one of many. He'd said once they were married, they'd buy a proper house together. Something modern, but grand. Monica had already started saving ideas on Pinterest. Sylvester doted on her in ways that still made her friends envious. He bought her designer handbags "just because," flew her out for weekend getaways, and never hesitated to say yes, whatever she wanted, whenever she asked. At first, she'd been a little skeptical. A young registrar doctor with this much wealth? But Sylvester had explained it all one evening over champagne. "

"After I completed my training as a surgeon, I'm going to be a professor soon," Sylvester said, almost offhand, as they waited for their takeaway in a quiet street in one of his family's luxurious cars. "But most of my income doesn't come from the hospitals or the private sectors; My family owns businesses across the UK, Europe, and even the States. I get a family allowance. Think of it like... early inheritance."

He'd said it without arrogance, but with the kind of calm assurance that made it clear: this wasn't a boast. It was just the truth. For Monica, that changed everything. Not because she was after wealth and power, she'd always worked hard, had ambition of her own, but because it meant stability. Sophistication. A future she didn't have to build alone. She hadn't needed much convincing after that. When her parents came to visit the condo for the first time, a high-rise with concierge service and a doorman who greeted them by name, they had stood in the foyer for a moment, looking quietly stunned. Her mother had smiled too broadly and asked if the marble was real. Her father tried to play it cool but kept glancing at the artwork like it might fall off the wall if he got too close.

That's when Monica explained. She told them about Sylvester's family, how they owned commercial properties, tech ventures, and something to do with green energy. She didn't pretend to understand it all. What mattered was that they were established and respected. And generous. She even added, with a calm smile, that his parents would be helping with the engagement party. The real one, the one with an actual guest list, a hired planner, and monogrammed menus. The one that would appear in society columns, if not literally, then at least in spirit, the one that matters. The one Melinda wouldn't be planning. And even though she would never admit it out loud, that last part brought Monica a quiet, guilty kind of satisfaction, not because she disliked Mel, but because, for once, everything felt like it was unfolding the way it was supposed to. Monica remembered the conversation clearly. Her mother had been standing in the kitchen, arms folded, eyes bright with determination.

"I'm buying my daughter her wedding dress," she had declared, the way some mothers announce a sacred vow.

"And whatever else she needs. That's our tradition."

At the time, Monica had tried to explain that most of the costs were already covered. Sylvester had transferred a substantial amount into their joint account for exactly that purpose. "The wedding planner is handling everything," Monica had said gently, hoping to deflect her mother's intensity.

"It's all taken care of."

But her mother had waved a dismissive hand. "That doesn't matter. The planner can do whatever they like, but I'm buying my daughter her dress. It's not just about money, it's about love, family, and doing what mothers do." In the end, Monica gave in. It wasn't worth the pushback, and in truth, a small part of her appreciated her mother's insistence. It felt grounding, something familiar amid the whirlwind of luxury venues, cake tastings, and floral arrangements discussed over champagne. They began the hunt for *the* dress in earnest, touring several exquisite bridal boutiques across London, places with quiet lighting, mirrored walls, and assistants who addressed Monica as "Miss Telfer" and brought her chilled water in crystal glasses. They even scoured exclusive online collections, designer showrooms, and private ateliers. Her mother, sharp-eyed and unrelenting, was in her element. She'd taken to the role with enthusiasm, inspecting fabrics and asking pointed questions about stitching and cuts.

At one point, her mother suggested bringing Melinda along. "It would be nice to have both my daughters there," she said with a hopeful smile. But Monica had hesitated. "Mel has assignments. She's got a lot going on with university and with her placements, at the hospital, she has too much going on right now," she'd replied, choosing her words carefully. The truth was more complicated. While she loved Mel in a sisterly way, they were never close. Mel was thoughtful and dependable, but she didn't exactly *fit* into Monica's world. She didn't care about designer labels, didn't know the difference between Vera Wang and Vivienne Westwood, and wasn't impressed by private drivers or champagne lounges. Monica's two best friends, Sandra and Gracie, on the other hand, understood the assignment. They knew fashion, had taste, and weren't afraid to voice it. Still, her mother had insisted, at least once.

"She's in the bridal party, Monica. One fitting won't ruin her studies."

Melinda reluctantly attended an appointment. It had been a blur of soft fabrics, excited chatter, and flashes of camera phones. The girls laughed and posed in front of three-way mirrors, gushing over silk veils and feather-trimmed trains. A chauffeur had driven them all, Sylvester's idea, of course, and Monica had only brought two members of the wedding planning team, despite having five at her disposal. She trusted her mother's opinion and her friends' instincts. The planners were there more as insurance than anything else.

CHAPTER TWENTY-EIGHT

The train pulled into Bridge Heath station with a soft screech of brakes. Melinda stepped off, her bag slung over one shoulder, and exhaled slowly. The weekend had left her emotionally wrung out, and as she scrolled through her phone to book an Uber, she felt the tension in her shoulders begin to ease.

The ride to her flat near the university took longer than usual. What was typically a ten-minute drive stretched into twenty, slowed by the usual Monday afternoon congestion. Cars inched along the busy street, their drivers impatient and tired, already transitioning into commuter mode. She leaned her head against the cool windowpane, her breath fogging the glass slightly as she watched the familiar rows of buildings flicker past like a reel of half-remembered memories. Despite the warmth of her family's company over the weekend, there was a quiet relief in returning to her own space, a small but comforting corner of the world that was entirely hers. The thought of slipping off her shoes, reheating leftover curry, and curling up on the sofa with her favourite book brought a soft smile to her lips. It wasn't just the quiet she missed; it was the solitude, the sense of autonomy that her flat represented. The flat she shared with her university friends was modern and airy, filled with natural light that poured through wide windows and softened the minimalist décor. Though modest in size, it carried just enough warmth and personality to feel like a proper home rather than a temporary student rental. Each of the girls had added their own touches over time, framed photos, throw pillows in mismatched patterns, string lights twinkling above bookshelves stacked with textbooks and takeout menus. It was lived-in, chaotic at times, but full of laughter and life. Mel's room was her sanctuary. Tucked at the far end of the flat, it came with a small en-suite bathroom, an absolute luxury she never took for granted, especially after long hospital shifts or emotionally draining weekends with family. Her space was calm and uncluttered, a contrast to the more vibrant shared areas. She kept it simple: soft grey bedding, a tiny potted plant on the windowsill, a stack of journals by the bed. It was the one place she could retreat to and breathe, uninterrupted.

The kitchen was communal, a space of both cooperation and chaos. They cooked there, sometimes together, when schedules allowed, and sometimes in shifts, with pasta pots and mugs of tea constantly rotating on the hob. Cleaning duties were shared as best they could manage. They had an unspoken agreement: whoever had the time would tackle the mess. And when exams loomed or they all hit burnout, they'd pitch in for a professional cleaner, grateful for the small luxury of a sparkling oven and scrubbed-down counters.

Despite its flaws, the occasional plumbing hiccup, the noisy neighbour downstairs, the too-thin walls, the flat was theirs. And that meant something. It was where friendships deepened over late-night chats and cheap wine, where they learned to live semi-independently, and where they quietly began to shape the outlines of the adults they were becoming. It wasn't cheap, nothing in this part of town was, but the place was worth it. Clean, well-located, and peaceful when she needed it most. As the Uber pulled up in front of her building, Mel smiled faintly. *It's good to be home.*

She paid the fare, murmured a thank-you to the driver, and let herself in with her key. The hallway was quiet. Her roommates were almost certainly still asleep; they'd gone out the night before to a birthday party for someone's sister, and judging by the group chat, it had been a late one. Mel was glad she'd skipped it. They all knew that big parties weren't really her thing, especially not after the kind of weekend she'd just had. She needed rest, not music, dancing, or more small talk. She stepped into her room, dropped her bag onto the floor, and sat on the edge of her bed, letting the silence settle around her like a warm blanket.

Finally, she thought, *some space to breathe.*

Melinda had planned to call her grandmother as soon as she got settled, but exhaustion took over. She lay down for a moment and inadvertently drifted into a deep sleep, waking only when loud, persistent knocking rattled her door. Groggy and disoriented, she rubbed her eyes and glanced at her phone. *Over five hours?* She blinked in disbelief. She shuffled to the door and opened it to find her flatmates, Anna and Barbara, standing there with snacks in hand and curiosity practically written across their faces. Despite each having their rooms, the three shared a spacious kitchen and had long since become more like sisters than just roommates.

"There she is, Sleeping Beauty," Anna teased as she stepped inside, her ponytail bouncing. "We were beginning to think you'd gone into hibernation." Barbara grinned and dropped onto Mel's bed. "So? Spill. How was the big village engagement shindig? Did the *Princess* make a grand entrance?" Mel sighed, a wry smile tugging at her lips. Anna always referred to Monica as *'the princess'*, and frankly, it wasn't far off.

"No changes there," Mel replied. "She was exactly as dramatic and self-involved as usual." Anna raised an eyebrow. "Did you finally say something to her? I swear, if it were me, one sharp sentence and she'd shut right up."

Mel shook her head and sat down beside Barbara. "No. She's still my sister. As snobby and rude as she can be, I'm not about to start a fight with her, especially not without being sure."

Barbara tilted her head.

"Still about the thing you overheard. The family secret?" Mel nodded slowly. "Yeah. I've been thinking about it nonstop. I just… I feel like I need to know more before I make any moves." Anna frowned. "Why not just ask Sylvester the next time you see him? Get it straight from the source."

"Don't be ridiculous," Barbara cut in before Mel could respond. "What if the information's wrong? What if there's more to it than what she overheard? I'm with Mel; she should get the full picture before doing anything. You don't just throw accusations at people like that, especially not in a family setting."

"Exactly," Mel said, grateful for Barbara's level-headedness. "This isn't just about Monica; it could affect my relationship with my whole family. If I handle it wrong, it could blow everything up. I need to be careful. Thoughtful." Anna sat down beside her with a huff.

"You're a better person than I am, Mel."

Mel chuckled softly.

"No, just tired of drama."

There was a brief silence as the three girls exchanged looks, mutual understanding hanging in the air.

"So… do you want the tea first or food?" Barbara asked with a grin.

"Both," Mel said. "But make the tea strong. I have a lot to figure out. A knock at the door interrupted their conversation, followed by familiar voices.

"Hello, ladies!" David called out cheerfully. "Can we come in?" Mel opened the door to find David and Lester, two friends from their study group, grinning on the other side.

"We're heading out to grab some supper," David continued. "Thought we'd see if you wanted to come along. Figured it's a good excuse to catch up, and get all the gossip from Mel, of course."

Anna perked up immediately. "Are you guys treating us?"

Lester chuckled and nodded. "Yep. My treat tonight."

"Well, in that case," Barbara said, already grabbing her jacket, "lead the way!"

They started to walk to one of their favourite eating place, just around the corner from their flat. They were all chattering and laughing about one of their tutors at Uni, but for Mel, it wasn't saying much; she had a lot on her mind. She had to try to concentrate on her studies. "Mel, what's your answer?" Lester, please repeat the question. I didn't hear the first time". Are you okay, Mel? Said David You seem a bit off; you should be excited about your sister's upcoming wedding." Yes, I am okay, just thinking about the assignment. She looked across to the girls, signalling for them not to say anything. Because Anna was just about to tell them about Mel's sister's fiancé, Anthony, and the secret. "Mel, is your sister marrying this guy named Anthony Sutherland?

"Do you know him asked Mel. "Well, yes and no, saw him a few times when I was younger, at a family function. He seems a decent guy. I heard he is a big-shot doctor or surgeon. Yes, he is a cardiologist surgeon, said Mel. "Enough of doctor and surgeon talk, I am hungry said David, as the restaurant came into view, and they all entered the restaurant. The evening air was cool and pleasant as the group strolled down the quiet street toward their favourite local restaurant, just a ten-minute walk from their building. The sun had dipped below the skyline, casting a soft orange glow over the pavement. Streetlamps flickered to life, and the occasional breeze rustled the trees lining the road.

David walked ahead with Anna, the two of them animatedly debating which takeaway spot made the best samosas on campus. Barbara and Lester lagged just a few steps behind, chuckling at their banter. Mel walked in the middle, her hands tucked into her hoodie pockets, soaking in the easy rhythm of the evening. For the first time since she returned from the village, she felt herself relax.

"So," Lester said, falling into step beside her, "you're going to tell us what really happened over the weekend? Or are we waiting until the food arrives?" Mel smirked. "Depends. How much are you buying me?"

"Starter, main, and dessert," he said. "With extra naan if you spill everything." "Be careful of this one, said Barbara, who preferred to be called Barbie. David turned around mid-stride.

"Please don't listen to her. "And don't hold back. We want the good stuff. Family drama, passive-aggressive cake-cutting, whatever you've got."

Mel chuckled. "There was cake. There was drama. And there was Monica, of course."

"Say no more," Barbara added with a grin. "That already sounds like a trilogy."

Mel hesitated for a beat, then said more softly, "Actually... something strange did happen. I overheard something about Sylvester's family, something serious. I haven't told Monica yet." The group slowed down slightly. Anna turned to Mel and suggested caution since Lester's family knew them. "Lester is fine, though I haven't told him much. How serious is it?" Anna asked.

"I'm not sure yet," Mel replied, carefully choosing her words. "But it didn't feel right to me. And I don't want to inform Monica unless I'm certain." They walked in thoughtful silence for a few moments.

"That's fair," Lester said finally. "But also... don't sit on it too long. If it's something that affects her: her future, she deserves to know."

"I know," Mel said quietly. "I just need to figure out the right way. And the right time."

David nudged her gently. "You're one of the most thoughtful people I know. You'll figure it out."

Mel offered a grateful smile.

"Thanks. I just hope I don't regret waiting."

As they rounded the corner and the warm lights of the restaurant came into view, the group began chatting again, lighter this time, letting the comfort of friendship carry them forward.

CHAPTER TWENTY-NINE

The restaurant buzzed with its usual weekend warmth, faint music playing overhead, the low hum of conversations, and the occasional clatter of cutlery. They were seated at a booth near the back, under a hanging pendant lamp that cast a soft golden hue over the table. Menus in hand, David leaned over to Anna.

"You're getting the butter chicken again, aren't you?" Anna raised a brow. "And you're getting the lamb biryani. We all play our roles." Lester laughed as he slid into the booth beside Mel.

"Some things never change."

The waiter came, took their orders, and David did, in fact, order the lamb biryani. After handing back the menus, the group fell into relaxed conversation. Barbara sipped her water and turned to Mel.

"So, back to this Sylvester thing. Do you think it's... dangerous? Or just messy?" Mel paused, swirling her glass absentmindedly. "I don't know. It was something I overheard part of a conversation. I didn't catch everything, just enough to make me uneasy."

"What did you hear?" Lester asked gently.

Mel glanced around, then lowered her voice. "It was about money. Debt. Something his parents are covering up. Someone, one of the Jonas family friends, mentioned that the family might not be as financially stable as they pretend to be, or be involved with the Cartels/or some other very dangerous organisations. David whistled softly. "That's big. Especially with how flashy Sylvester is.

"Exactly," Mel said. "And Monica... she's all in. Planning her life around this perfect image. If it's not real, I don't know how she'll take it."

"Do you think he knows?" asked Barbara.

"I'm not sure," Mel replied.

"And that's part of the problem. What if he does? What if he's hiding it from her, too?" The food arrived just in time to give them a pause: plates of steaming curries, soft naan, and fragrant rice. For a few minutes, they ate in silence, the table filled with appreciative hums and the occasional spice-induced cough from David. Mel, though, picked at her food.

"Hey," Anna said softly. "You don't have to carry this alone, you know. We've got your back. Whatever you decide to do." Mel smiled faintly, her eyes warming. "Thanks. I think I just need to get my facts straight. Then maybe I'll talk to Gran... she knows more than she lets on." Lester nodded. "Good call. Start where it's safe."

"And whatever you find out," Barbara added, "just remember, Monica might be your sister, but that doesn't mean she'll thank you for telling the truth." Mel let out a quiet breath. "I know. But I'd rather her be angry at me now than devastated later." Their conversation faded into lighter topics as they finished their meal, jokes about classmates, upcoming exams, and whose turn it was to do the next round of kitchen cleaning. But beneath it all, Mel's mind stayed half-rooted in the village, in the overheard words and uneasy truths waiting just below the surface. "Just try to enjoy your meal, said Lester and Barbara at practically the same time. Across from her sat Anna, sharp-eyed and sharper-witted, and David, quiet but always watching, always calculating. They were her oldest friends, her only real ones, if she were honest, and the only people she trusted with this.

"So," Anna said, leaning in. "You're sure she doesn't know anything?"

Melina shook her head. "Not a clue. She's been floating on a cloud since Sylvester proposed. If she even *suspected* something, she'd be in denial." David sipped his espresso, eyes narrowed. "And you're sure about what you heard?"

"I know what I heard," Melina snapped, then softened. "Sylvester and his father. They were talking about keeping the truth from Monica. Like she was just... part of a plan." Anna exchanged a glance with David.

"Well," she said, "we looked into it, like you asked. And remember the Longhorns' and Lester's parents go back a long way. I always suspected that there was something shady about Sylvester and his family. Anna tapped a finger against her cup. "Then that's what we do. We dig deeper. We watch. We get the proof. And when the time is right, we show her."

They sat around the table at the dimly lit restaurant, half-finished plates in front of them, the hum of quiet conversation and clinking silverware filling the space between their words. The topic had shifted from light banter to something far more serious, what Melinda had overheard about Monica's fiancé and his family's alleged ties to the cartels. David leaned back in his chair, his expression unreadable as he swirled the last of his drink. "You don't just blow up someone's life over rumours," he said, voice low but firm. "You wait until the foundation is already cracking. Then, and only then, you show them the fault lines. Let them see it for themselves." Melinda nodded slowly, her fingers wrapped tightly around her glass. She wasn't sure if that made her feel better or worse. David glanced across the table. "And let's not forget, Mel, Lester's family knows them. Isn't that right?" he added, turning his attention to the quiet figure beside him. Lester shifted uncomfortably in his seat, avoiding Melinda's eyes. "Yeah... my family's familiar with them," he admitted. "Not close or anything, I've only met them a few times at events. That's all. Nothing deep." His tone was careful, too careful, as if he was trying not to stir something he couldn't control. Melinda studied him, her mind spinning. She trusted Lester, but the word "cartel" wasn't something you could easily brush aside, especially not when Monica's future might be tangled up in it. There was a long pause before she spoke again. "So what now? Do I just sit on this until it becomes undeniable?" David gave a slow, measured nod.

"You wait. And you watch. Truth doesn't stay buried forever. Especially not with people like that." The weight of what they weren't saying pressed heavily in the air between them, as the waiter came by to clear their plates. For the moment, the conversation stopped, but the unease lingered, sharp as a knife just beneath the tablecloth.

CHAPTER THIRTY

After paying the bill, Melina and her friends stepped into the cool evening air, their breath forming clouds as they walked back to the university flat. The mood was lighter now, with earlier heavy conversations set aside for the moment. Sensing her lingering worry, the others instinctively tried to lift her spirits. Laughter started to bubble up between them as someone made a joke about their perpetually late professor and the chaos that always ensued on Monday morning lectures.

"Don't forget we've got that seminar at nine," Ann groaned, wrapping her scarf tighter around her neck. "If Dr. Sanders asks me one more time to define the theoretical framework for my dissertation, I might cry." Melina chuckled, grateful for the distraction. "You'll be fine," she said, nudging Ann playfully. "At least you don't have back-to-back lectures until 4 p.m."

"That's true," chimed in Ava. "Mel, you basically live in the lecture halls. You should be charging rent."

Their banter continued as they walked down the familiar streets, the golden glow of streetlamps casting long shadows on the pavement. The rhythm of their footsteps and laughter filled the silence between cars and the occasional barking dog in the distance. By the time they reached their building, Melina felt the heaviness in her chest ease just a little. It wasn't gone, not completely, but being surrounded by people who cared, who knew how to pull her back into the present, was exactly what she needed. As they climbed the stairs to their flat, she let herself smile. Whatever tomorrow held, class, more questions about Monica's fiancé, or just the next cup of tea and lecture notes, at least she wasn't facing it alone. Melina exhaled, for the first time feeling like she had a plan—and allies. She didn't know how this would end. But one thing was clear:

She couldn't protect Monica by staying in the shadows anymore.

The dress fitting felt like a scene from a film. Champagne flutes were topped off. Delicate macarons were served on silver trays. Monica had done her research on the planners; she always did, but in moments like these, it was her mother and friends she leaned on. Mel had mostly sat in the corner, smiling politely, occasionally nodding when asked, but mostly silent. She didn't interrupt. She didn't criticize. But neither did she contribute. That was just Mel. Simple. Unbothered. Content with her way of living. She wasn't interested in luxury shoes or matching bridal tiaras. Monica had accepted that long ago, but it still felt like a quiet gap between them, a thread of distance, neither had found the courage or reason to close. The planner, of course, had been Sylvester's idea. Hand-picked, or rather, recommended by his cousin Mary-Jane, a tall, impeccably dressed woman who practically glided into every room she entered. Mary-Jane was the CEO of one of Sylvester's family businesses, from his mother's side, and she moved in circles that included celebrities, diplomats, and fashion royalty. She'd taken one look at the original venue and said, "No, darling. You need something with *presence*."

Monica had been unsure at first. Mary-Jane's world was dazzling, almost too perfect. But the wedding planner she recommended came with glowing reviews, a pedigree of society weddings, and an eye for luxury that made Monica feel both intimidated and oddly safe. Still, she kept her mother and friends close. Not because she doubted the professionals, but because she wanted to feel like a bride, not just a client. As she watched her reflection in the mirror that day, draped in ivory silk, she felt a flicker of something warm. Not joy, exactly. But something adjacent. A quiet pride. A sense that maybe, just maybe, everything was coming together. Even if Mel didn't understand this world…Even if Monica sometimes questioned how she'd landed in it herself.

PART THREE

ENGAGEMENT &

WEDDING PREPARATION

CHAPTER THIRTY-ONE

A few weeks ago, Melina surprised Monica with an intimate countryside engagement celebration. It was a warm and genuine moment filled with laughter, hugs, and emotional toasts. Now, everything had changed dramatically. The grand engagement party had finally arrived, this time orchestrated by Sylvester's parents with all the flair and formality that came with their social status. They had spared no expense. A professional party planner hired by their cousin, Mary-Jane, had been brought in early to handle every detail, from the floral arrangements and five-course menu to the imported string quartet and custom lighting. Everything was tailored to Monica's taste, or at least, what Sylvester's family believed her taste to be.

Monica's engagement had quickly become the talk of the town. It was an exclusive affair, hosted at an elegant estate just outside the city, where only a carefully selected guest list had been invited. The invitations had arrived on heavy cream cardstock embossed with gold lettering, no digital RSVPs here. Local socialites, distant relatives, university colleagues, and a smattering of high-profile business connections all buzzed with anticipation. Whispers floated through salons and cafés in the days leading up to it, who would be attending, what Monica would wear, how extravagant it would be. Some were genuinely happy for her. Others were drawn in by curiosity or the subtle pressure to be seen at such a high-profile event. Melina couldn't help but feel the shift in atmosphere: this wasn't just a celebration, it was a performance, polished and precise, designed to impress.

As the day approached, Melina found herself caught between excitement for her sister's engagement and a strange sense of unease she couldn't quite shake. There was something about the perfection of it all that made her skin itch. It didn't feel like Monica, at least, not the Monica she had shared late-night snacks within their university flat or comforted through heartbreak. This Monica was poised and glowing under chandeliers, but somehow... distant. Still, Melina smiled, slipped into her dress, and told herself to trust the moment. For Monica's sake, she would play her part and keep the shadows of doubt for another day.

The event was scheduled to take place at one of Sylvester's family estates, a large property located in the countryside. The decorations included chandeliers under silk-draped marquees, numerous floral arrangements, and live music. Sylvester, Cousin Mary-Jane is the party planner with her team of five, and will also be the wedding planner, and with the rest of the family, will organize the event with considerable effort. It was designed not just as an engagement but also made a significant impression. As the sun dipped below the horizon, casting a warm golden hue across the estate, the engagement party began in full swing. Luxury cars lined the cobblestone driveway, and guests in designer gowns and tailored suits began to arrive, each one greeted with champagne and a smile from uniformed staff. The estate, with its ivy-draped balconies and manicured gardens, shimmered like something out of a dream. Melina and her friends stood near the entrance, momentarily stunned by the grand gesture. They had seen impressive events before, but this was something else entirely. From the glistening ice sculptures to the live quartet playing beneath the illuminated pergola, every detail had been executed with precision and opulence.

"This is insane," whispered one of Melina's friends. "It's like a royal wedding."

Before Melina could respond, Monica approached them, radiant in an off-white gown that sparkled subtly under the fairy lights. She smiled warmly, but her voice held a gentle firmness.

"Mel, just enjoy yourself tonight, okay? Don't worry about anything. The caterer and the planner have everything under control, really," she said, her tone more instructive than reassuring. Melina forced a smile and nodded, though something in Monica's eyes made her pause. It wasn't nerves, Monica was always poised. It was something else. Behind her polished exterior, Melina sensed a flicker of unease. But tonight wasn't the time to question it... or was it? Melina watched Monica disappear into the crowd, her gown trailing behind her like a whisper. The smile had never left her face, but it was that tight, practiced kind of smile, the kind you wear when something isn't quite right.

"Did you see that?" Melina murmured to her friend, Anna.

"See what?"

"Monica. That smile. The way she brushed me off so quickly. It's not like her," Melina said, her brows furrowed.

Anna shrugged. "She's probably just overwhelmed. This place is like a movie set. I'd be stressed too if I had to host something this extravagant." But Melina couldn't shake the feeling. There had been something odd ever since she arrived. The staff were polite, but stiff, as if trained not just in service but in silence. She'd overheard a hushed conversation near the kitchen, something about a last-minute change in the seating chart and a name that had been removed abruptly. And earlier, when Melina wandered a bit too far from the main patio, she passed a room with the door ajar and caught a glimpse of Sylvester's mother on the phone, her tone sharp and urgent.

"No, absolutely not. He can't come here tonight. If he does, everything falls apart. Do you understand me?" Melina had paused, hidden by the corner, heart racing. The voice was clipped, controlled, but the words stuck in her head like thorns. Back in the glow of the celebration, everything looked perfect. Laughter echoed across the lawn, crystal glasses clinked in toasts, and Monica moved through it all like a graceful swan. But Melina had known her long enough to see the cracks in her composure. She reached for a glass of champagne from a passing tray but barely sipped it. Something wasn't right. And now, she had a gnawing feeling that whatever it was, it had to do with Sylvester, and the family secret she'd overheard just a few days ago. Melina hadn't meant to interfere; Monica had made that clear. *Let me have this*, she'd said with a smile that didn't quite reach her eyes. But as the evening unfolded, and the shadows began to stretch longer across the manicured estate grounds, the glamour of the celebration began to feel more like a mask than magic.

Melina's instincts twisted inside her like a storm cloud held too long. What if this wasn't just nerves? What if her silence tonight turned out to be the worst kind of betrayal? What if Monica was walking straight into something dangerous, and Melina said nothing, did nothing? She turned the question over and over in her mind, torn between the fear of ruining her sister's night and the deeper fear of not ruining it *enough*. If she spoke up, Monica might accuse her of jealousy, of trying to sabotage her engagement, and the fragile trust between them could snap. But if she stayed quiet...

Melina swallowed hard, glancing at her sister across the candlelit patio. Laughter echoed in the distance. Champagne flowed. And the shadows only deepened. For now, she said nothing. But the silence weighed heavily than any words she could have spoken. Growing up, Monica had always been the golden one, the firstborn, the favourite. Graceful, composed, effortlessly adored. Melina, the younger by three years, had spent most of her childhood watching her sister from the sidelines, both in awe and in quiet resentment. She admired Monica; *everyone* did. But admiration came with a shadow. Where Monica strove for perfection, Melina questioned it. She was the one who noticed the tension behind a smile, the unspoken things left hanging in a room. She didn't mind messiness, didn't fear mistakes. Monica, on the other hand, treated failure like a personal betrayal. Everything she touched had to shine. And somehow, she always made it look easy.

Melina had spent her life trying not to live in comparison, but in moments like this, with music drifting on the night air and fairy lights blinking in a curated dreamscape, it was hard not to feel like the outsider again. The one who saw too much and said too little.

"Melina!" a voice rang out, pulling her sharply from her thoughts. It was Anna, one of Melina's friends, from the University, already flushed from champagne and the thrill of the evening.

"Come join us! This party isn't just fabulous, it's *extravagant*!"

Melina offered a small smile, forcing herself to nod and turn toward the glowing patio. But her mind lingered in the shadows, where her questions still lived unanswered. Just as the string quartet transitioned into a soft rendition of *Clair de Lune*, the mood of the evening shimmered with enchantment. Guests twirled on the dance floor, laughter spilled like champagne, and Monica stood beside Sylvester near the floral arch, graciously accepting congratulations from the guests. Then it happened.

A sharp *crack* split the air, not gunfire, but the unmistakable sound of a microphone being snatched off a stand. The music screeched to a halt, feedback whining through the speakers. Heads turned. At the far edge of the lawn, near the terrace stairs, a man had taken the mic from the band. He was dressed in a dark suit, slightly dishevelled, with a look of furious determination in his eyes. No one seemed to recognize him, at least, not right away. But Sylvester's face drained of colour.

"You think your family can erase people, Sylvester?" the man shouted, voice echoing over the stunned crowd. Think! again."

Gasps rippled through the guests. Monica turned sharply, her expression a mixture of shock and confusion. Sylvester started forward, but his mother reached out and grabbed his arm, her nails digging into his sleeve. Melina stood frozen, heart pounding. She didn't know who the man was, but instinct told her *this* was what the family had been trying to keep quiet. The name was removed from the guest list. The secrecy. The urgency in Sylvester's mother's voice.

"I kept quiet for years," the man continued. "But not anymore. You lied to them. You lied to *her*," his voice cracked as he pointed directly at Monica, "and they deserve to know the truth."

Melina's hands clenched around her clutch. She had tried to stay out of it, but now, whatever was hidden beneath the surface was coming undone in front of everyone. The crowd was no longer whispering. They were silent, breath held, waiting. As murmurs rippled through the shaken crowd and the staff discreetly worked to steer guests back toward the garden pavilion with polite reassurances of a "minor incident," Monica slipped away with a few close friends, her expression unreadable. Sylvester was swiftly pulled aside by his mother, her voice low and urgent, while the man with the microphone was escorted off the estate grounds under the quiet supervision of security. Not far from the unfolding commotion, beneath the warm glow of antique lanterns beside a trickling stone fountain, the two sets of parents found themselves gathered, whether by quiet design or happenstance, none of them questioned it. Chester Telfer, Monica's father, a reserved man with a deep, calming voice forged through years in pastoral ministry and community leadership, broke the silence first.

"That was more than just a scene. That was a warning."

Iris Telfer stood at his side, arms folded tightly across her chest. Her elegant evening dress did nothing to soften the concern on her face. "And it wasn't just random. That man knew exactly who to confront, and why." Reginold Longhorn, Sylvester's father, adjusted his cufflinks and gave a practiced, composed nod. "We'll look into it. Some extended families have a habit of showing up when they're least wanted." Sandy Small, one of Sylvester's cousins, offered a poised smile, though her eyes flickered with irritation. "He shouldn't have been anywhere near the property. It won't happen again."

"With all due respect," Chester said carefully, Monica is our daughter. And this wedding is just months away. If there's anything, *anything*, we need to know, I'd rather hear it from you than from a stranger with a microphone. Reginald's tone remained cool.

"There's nothing that affects Monica directly. That man is an old complication. A disgruntled cousin. Whatever he intended to say, it would've been exaggerated."

"Or it might've been the truth," Berdie said quietly, her gaze steady. "What concerns me is not the interruption; it's Sylvester's face when it happened. He wasn't surprised. He looked... cornered. "Sandy's tone hardened, though she kept her composure. "Sylvester has been under enormous pressure. This event was a major production. You can't expect him to remain calm when someone tries to ruin it." Chester held her gaze.

"We're not here to argue. But we are here to protect our daughter. If this engagement is going to proceed, we need transparency. Secrets have a way of surfacing, sometimes right in the middle of a celebration."

Reginald offered a faint nod.

"Let's stay focused on what matters. Monica and Sylvester love each other. The wedding is still on schedule, and anything unresolved will be handled quietly."

Berdie exchanged a glance with her husband, her voice measured.

"Handled, *how*, exactly?" Sandy smoothed her silk shawl, her answer just as composed.

"With discretion."

A brief silence fell between them. In the distance, music began again, soft and uncertain, trying to restore the illusion. Chester's voice cut through gently. "Then, for their sake, let's make sure this is built on more than appearances. Before the atmosphere could fully unravel, Sylvester's parents swiftly acted. Reginald and Sandy stepped onto the small stage near the bandstand, each of them projecting the poise and authority expected of one of the town's most influential families. Berdie gently took the microphone, her voice smooth and composed despite the tension still lingering in the air. "Ladies and gentlemen, please allow us a moment," she began, her smile calm but firm. "We deeply regret the unexpected interruption this evening. The individual who spoke out is, unfortunately, a troubled distant relative with a long history of erratic mental behaviour. We assure you, nothing he said holds any truth or merit."

Reginald stepped forward beside her, his expression grave yet controlled. "This evening is about celebrating love and the future of two remarkable young people. We ask that you disregard the outburst and enjoy the rest of the night. Thank you for your understanding." There was a pause, awkward, uncertain, but polite applause followed, hesitant at first, then more confident as the band resumed playing. Guests exchanged looks, some skeptical, others relieved to have a reason to move on. But the unease remained, like a hairline crack in fine China, nearly invisible, but impossible to forget.

CHAPTER THIRTY-TWO

Melina stood in the hallway, the hum of voices from the living room barely reaching her. She'd slipped away from the conversation with her parents- just a small break, a moment of quiet. The air was thick with unspoken expectations, and she needed a second to breathe. As she turned towards the kitchen, she could hear the familiar sound of her fiancé's parents chattering, their voices warm, but something about the tone made her stop mid-step,

"I'm telling you, Reginold, we must do something about it. This can't keep going! It was Sylvester's parents. Berdie, her voice was low but edged with urgency.

"I know! Reginold replied, a sigh escaping his lips. "But what do you want me to do? It's been this way for years". Melina's pulse quickened. She didn't want to eavesdrop – she never had, not like Anna and the rest of her friends. But the conversation felt too important, too loaded to ignore. She leaned slightly against the doorframe, straining to hear without being noticed.

"I'm not saying we should tell them everything, but she can't just keep living this lie. It'll destroy them both. I'm not ready to lose him over something like this". Bertie's voice shook on the last few words, and Melina's stomach dropped.

"And if we don't tell her? If we keep this secret, and it comes out later? "What then?" Reginold's voice was tight, like he was holding something back.

"We don't have a choice, Reginold. The family will crumble if she finds out. It's better if she never knows: better for all of us". Berdie's tone was final. Melina's breath caught. The family secret. She had suspected that something was off for months now- her sister's fiancé had always seemed like a picture-perfect son, but Melina had noticed cracks. Small things. The way his parents seemed just a little too eager to keep him near, the long hours spent on the phone late at night when he wasn't home. But -this was something else. Her fiancé. Their future. Was it all built on a lie? Her mind raced, the pieces falling together in chaotic flashes. What had they been hiding? And why? She wanted to turn around, to run back to the living room, to pretend she hadn't heard any of it. But the words: "it'll destroy them both", echoed in her mind.

"What the hell could it be?" She whispered under her breath, her hands trembling. She could feel the weight of the secret pressing down on her chest, suffocating her. The kitchen door creaked, and Melina froze. Reginold's footsteps were nearing. She didn't know how long she had been standing there, but now, she felt exposed, like she had crossed a line she couldn't uncross. In a panic, she stepped back, but her foot hit the edge of a chair, knocking it slightly askew. The noise was like a shotgun in the quiet house. The door swung open, and Reginold appeared, looking startled. His eyes narrowed in confusion when he saw her.

"Melina, you alright?"

For a moment, her mind went blank. She knew she had to say something-anything-to cover her tracks.

"Uh. Yeah", she managed, forcing a smile. "I just, uh, thought I heard something". His gaze lingered on her for a beat too long, and she could tell that he wasn't convinced. But he didn't push it. Instead, he let out a tight chuckle and turned to walk back into the living room.

"Well, don't stay out here too long.. You will catch a cold".

Melina stood frozen, the knot in her stomach tighter than ever. He hadn't caught on, but she couldn't shake the feeling that something had just changed, irreparably. Her fingers brushed against the edge of the counter as she steadied herself, taking a long, shaky breath. She had heard enough. But what was she supposed to do with it now? There is a secret about this family, and the weight of it had already begun to pull her in a direction she wasn't sure she was ready to go. Melina's mind buzzed like a live wire, each thought twisting and knotting itself tighter with every passing second. She had managed to return to the living room without raising suspicion, but her thoughts were a million miles away. Her hands, still trembling, clutched her glass of wine so hard her knuckles went white. Monica was perched on the armrest of the couch, laughing with their parents, as if everything was just as it always had been. The picture-perfect family. The same one that had always put her sister at the centre of everything. The same one that had always made Melina feel like a shadow. But now, it wasn't just Monica's perfect world she was fighting against; it was her fiancé's family, too.

The more Melina tried to focus on the conversation around her, the more distant it felt, like she was trapped inside a glass bubble. Every word seemed muffled, every laugh too bright, too hollow. Her gaze shifted to Monica, who was basking in the glow of their parents' praise.

"You're so amazing, sweetheart. I don't know how you managed everything so well". Their mother's voice was soft and adoring.

"I'm just lucky", Monica said with a modest smile, the kind that made the room feel warmer, more perfect. Melina's stomach twisted. *Lucky?* Or was it all just part of the show? Her thoughts circled back to the conversation she had overheard. The more she thought about it, the clearer it became that there was something catastrophic beneath the surface. Something that would tear her fiancé's family apart. It wasn't just a small scandal; it was a betrayal, a betrayal so deep it would change everything. And there she was, trapped in the middle of it. Monica caught her staring. Her sister's eyes softened, the kind of look Melina had learned to expect from her – always caring, always concerned.

"You okay, Mel?" Monica's voice was gentle, almost too gentle. Like she was asking if Melina needed help, if she needed anything at all. But it only made Melina feel more isolated.

"Yeah", Melina managed to force out, her voice strained. "Just… tired, I guess".

Monica nodded, then turned back to their parents, who were continuing to shower her with compliments. Melina's gaze drifted back to the door, half-expecting to see Joseph standing there again, but the hallway remained quiet. She wanted to scream, to rip the façade off their perfect lives. But what would that do? She wasn't even sure she could make sense of it herself. The secret wasn't just a revelation; it was a fracture, and she wasn't sure if revealing it would be like opening a floodgate or simply letting the dam collapse completely.

CHAPTER THIRTY-THREE

The house had quieted down by the time Melina retreated to her room.

The evening had passed in a haze of awkward silences, forced smiles, and polite conversations. In times like these, she missed her Aunt May; she knew how to liven up a room or prolong a conversation. She sat at the edge of the bed, the cool sheets brushing against her legs, and let her head fall into her hands. Her thoughts whirled, disjointed, as she replayed the conversation she had overheard. Reginold and Berdie Monica's in-laws sounded so certain, so terrified of what would happen if the truth came out. They were desperate to keep their son's perfect world intact. But what about her world? What about the truth?

The decision weighed heavily on her. She needed to tell someone in the family; her friends knew some details, but not everything. The burden was too much, as it would change everything. But who could she tell? Melina couldn't shake the weight in her chest as the memory resurfaced, when she and Anna had visited the Longhorns' estate a few weeks ago and unintentionally overheard a hushed conversation behind the library doors. The voices had been low, tense, laced with urgency and warning. They hadn't caught every word, but what they did hear had stopped them cold, mentions of "keeping things quiet," "not drawing attention," and most chillingly, a name loosely associated with cartel dealings whispered like a curse. At the time, Melina had tried to dismiss it. She told herself it was just gossip, maybe even a misunderstanding. Rich families always had secrets, didn't they? And surely Monica, bright and thoughtful Monica, wouldn't be involved with someone whose family carried that kind of shadow.

But the doubt lingered. It gnawed at her in quiet moments. There were times she had nearly told Monica everything, late at night when they were alone, or during casual phone calls when the subject of the wedding would come up. But each time, Melina stopped herself. She knew Monica would deny it fiercely. Love had a way of blinding even the sharpest minds, and Monica was deeply, unquestionably in love. Still, what Melina overheard tonight, another cryptic conversation between two unfamiliar men standing just outside the ballroom, had confirmed what she feared all along. This time, there were no half-heard phrases or uncertain names. It was clear. Something wasn't right with Sylvester's family. There was an undercurrent of danger, of calculated secrecy, woven just beneath their polished exterior. And now, standing in the middle of Monica's glittering engagement party, Melina felt utterly alone with what she knew. How do you tell her sister that the life she's stepping into might be built on lies and danger? How do you pull someone back from the edge when they don't even see the drop? Her hands trembled slightly as she reached for her drink. One thing was certain: this couldn't stay buried much longer. She thought about Monica. She thought about the years of watching her sister shine, the way everyone adored her. Monica had always been the golden child, the one who could do no wrong. And Melina?   She had always been the background noise to Monica's symphony. But now, with the secret in her hands, Melina wondered – did she owe Monica the truth? Or would telling her destroy the only real relationship she had left in the family? Her brother Ethan has been nice to her sometimes, but he always looked up to Monica, knowing she is the second child.

Melina's fingers clenched around the edge of the duvet as the question gnawed at her. Do I protect the illusion? Or do I destroy it? She closed her eyes, but the answer didn't come. The silence of the room was deafening, the kind of silence that only made her feel more alone. She thought back to the way Reginold and Berdie had spoken, how they practically begged each other to keep the secret, to shield their son from fallout. The fear in their voices had been palpable. This wasn't just about keeping up appearances; this was about survival. And Melina? What was her survival in all this? She thought of Monica again, her perfect, flawless sister. Could I do that to her? But the more she sat with it, the clearer it became.

The truth couldn't stay buried forever.

****

The morning light filtered through the blinds, casting long shadows across the room. Melina had barely slept. Her mind raced all night, caught between the loyalty she had always shown to her family and the overwhelming knowledge that everything was about to change. She stood in front of the mirror, staring at her reflection, the decision weighing on her shoulders. Her phone buzzed on the nightstand, the name flashing on the screen: Monica. Melina hesitated for a moment, her heart thudding in her chest. She swiped to answer, her voice barely a whisper when she spoke.

"Hey"

"Hey, Mel. Everything alright?" Monica's voice was warm, but there was a hint of concern there, like she could sense the unease in Melina's tone. Melina swallowed, forcing herself to sound normal. "Yeah, I'm fine. Just…tired, I guess".

"You have been saying that a lot lately", Monica said teasingly, but it felt like an accusation.

"You sure you're, okay? You know you can talk to me about anything".

Melina's heart skipped a beat. She could hear the sincerity in her sister's voice, but she couldn't shake the feeling that telling Monica would destroy something that could never be rebuilt. The tension in Melina's chest built, suffocating.

"I'm sure. Just give me some time, okay?"

There was a pause on the other end, and Monica's voice softened. "Alright. Just know I'm here when you're ready". Melina closed her eyes and let out a shaky breath. "I know," she murmured, her voice barely above a whisper. The conversation had drifted from politics to philosophy, and now, dangerously, into whispered truths neither of them was quite ready to face.

"Oh, Mel… last night was perfect. Well, almost perfect," Monica said, tossing her hair back with a sigh. "Until that lunatic of Sylvester's showed up unannounced. Can you believe it? Just strolled in like he owned the place. They should have had him arrested."

She shook her head, indignant. "I told Sylvester, make sure he's banned from the wedding. I won't have anyone ruining the most important day of my life." Melina forced a tight smile, trying to keep her voice even. "Maybe… maybe he knows something you don't. About Sylvester. About his family." Monica's eyes snapped to hers, fiery and defensive.

"Don't be obnoxious, Mel!" she snapped. "You don't know what you're talking about." The words hung in the air between them, sharp and unyielding. Melina opened her mouth, heart pounding. This was it. She was going to tell her. About the conversation she and Anna had overheard. About the rumours, the whispers, the warnings no one dared speak aloud. But something in Monica's expression stopped her cold. Not now, she thought. Not like this. I can't upset her more than I already have. Monica looked away, her anger softening into something more wistful. She smoothed the skirt of her dress, fingers tracing invisible creases. "He's not like other guys, you know?" she said quietly. "There's something about him… like he's seen real darkness, but he chooses light. With me." I almost said it right then. Almost told her that the darkness wasn't behind him, it was still clinging to his name, his blood. But how do you break someone's heart with the truth when they're building a life on a lie? Instead, I said,

"You really love him."

She looked up, startled, like it had never occurred to her that I might doubt it.

"Of course I do. I *need* him."

Melina swallowed hard. She almost said it then. Almost told her that the darkness Monica spoke of wasn't some poetic past; it was present. It was alive. It was stitched into Sylvester's name, etched into his family's legacy, lurking just beneath the polished surface of their perfect parties and curated smiles. But how do you shatter someone's world with the truth when they're so desperately trying to build a life out of it? So instead, Melina said nothing. She sat in silence, nodding gently, carrying the truth alone, until the moment came when she could no longer keep it hidden. Monica tilted her head, studying Melina more closely. Her earlier irritation had faded, replaced by something softer, concern, maybe even guilt. She reached out and gently squeezed Melina's hand.

"You've been quiet lately," she said, her tone lower now. "Is everything okay?"

Melina offered a small, practiced smile. "I'm just tired, that's all. Long shifts, late nights. You know how it is." Monica wasn't convinced, but she didn't press. Instead, she gave her sister a playful nudge and changed the subject, her voice brightening like it always did when she talked about the wedding. "Well, you'd better get some rest because the wedding is going to make this engagement party look like a warm-up brunch." Melina laughed softly, grateful for the shift in tone. "You mean it's going to be even more extravagant?" Monica grinned. "Please. There'll be fireworks, a live band, real champagne, not the watered-down stuff, and don't get me started on the dress reveal. I'm going full princess mode, Mel. Like, couture runway meets royal wedding. "She leaned in with a smirk. "And you, my dear, will be right there beside me in your gorgeous bridesmaid gown, *if* you don't keep eating your feelings." Melina raised an eyebrow. "Seriously?" Monica held up her hands, laughing. "I'm just saying! Those fittings are *not* forgiving, and I already told the seamstress you were a size down from last time." Melina rolled her eyes but couldn't help smiling. "I'll take that as your strange, slightly offensive way of saying you love me."

"Exactly." Monica leaned her head against Melina's shoulder for a moment. "I do love you. And I want everything to be perfect, for both of us. So please… smile a little more, okay? Don't let the stress of everything weigh you down. This should be a happy time." Melina nodded, the weight in her chest pressing tighter. She wanted to believe Monica was right. That this was just stress and not something more dangerous, unravelling behind the scenes. She forced another smile, this one a little steadier.

"I'll try. For you." And she meant it. Even if the truth was clawing at the back of her throat, Melina wasn't ready to ruin her sister's dream, not yet. But dreams built on secrets had a habit of collapsing, no matter how beautiful they looked from the outside.

CHAPTER THIRTY-FOUR

The hospital hallway smelled like antiseptic and coffee. Sylvester preferred it that way. Clean, focused, far from the shadows his last name carried.

"Dr. Longhorn," **a** nurse called as he scrubbed out of surgery. "You've got a call. Says it's urgent, family."

He tensed immediately. Family rarely meant *good* news. He took the call in his office, jaw clenched. His mother's voice filled the room, smooth, composed, dangerous.

"You haven't confirmed the wine list for the reception," she said.

"You called the hospital for *wine?*" he snapped.

"Don't be dramatic, *mi amor*. We're investing in your future. The least you can do is respect the effort. "Sylvester leaned back in the chair, eyes closed. "You mean the money. Blood money. Cartel money." A long pause.

"We gave you the world," she said quietly. "Do you think your scholarships came from nothing? Your internships? That penthouse you proposed to her in?"

"I earned my degree," he said through gritted teeth.

"And who paid for the school? Who paid for the *clean records* when you got caught with that little incident in France? I could have taken care of that myself, or Dad. His breath caught. That had been buried. Long ago. Or so he thought.

"You can pretend to be clean. But without us, you'd still be hiding behind your mother's skirts, not playing God in a white coat."

He stared at the framed photo on his desk, Monica, laughing in the sun, the day they moved into the condo. A life built on lies. But he loved her. That part, at least, was real.

"Just get through the wedding," his mother said softly. "After that... well, your father may want to speak to you." The line went dead. No one asked why her hands shook when she reached for her coffee.

"Can you believe it's finally happening?" Monica said, breezing into the kitchen in a silk robe, her phone pressed to her ear. "Six days! Sylvester is flying in from his conference tomorrow. He said he has a surprise for me." Melina forced a smile.

"You excited?"

Monica's face softened. "More than anything. It finally feels like… like we're becoming our own family, you know? Not just escaping the one we were born into." Melina flinched at the word *escaping*. Monica didn't know she was marrying into something far worse. and playlist songs, and I'm wondering if someone's going to put a bullet in my head before the wedding." Sandra touched her shoulder. "You're not crazy. You're just the only one awake." Melina looked back at the house. Her father laughed at something. Monica twirled in the living room, practicing for her first dance. All of them are smiling. All of them are clueless.

"They don't see it," Melina whispered. "They're all wearing blindfolds. And I'm the only one who knows we're walking into fire." Melina nodded, not because she was brave, but because she didn't have a choice anymore. The line went quiet again. Then her grandmother added, softer:

"Call us if you need anything. No matter what." When the call ended, Melina sat alone in the silence, heart pounding. They didn't know. Not exactly. But maybe they knew enough.

****

The weeks and months went by so quickly, after much preparation and event planning for Monica's wedding, even Melina's didn't have anything to do with the planning. The family hired a wedding planner. Melina is still wondering when she is going to tell Monica about Sylvester's family. She was trying to gather some information and evidence to show Monica, but was met with a dead end on her side.

"What are you going to do, Mel?" asked Anna, her friend, I don't know yet, but I think I have to tell her. I will try to find the right time to tell her. Monica stood on the pedestal in the centre of the boutique, arms raised as the seamstress adjusted the hem of her gown. Sunlight poured through the window, making the beading on her dress shimmer like morning frost. Monica didn't answer. Lately, she had noticed it too, the way Melina's eyes never quite met hers. The distracted pauses. The tension she couldn't explain. For a second, worry crept in. But it vanished just as quickly when the door chimed, and a florist entered with bouquet samples.

"Oh!" Monica turned, grinning. "These are from Sylvester, aren't they?" The florist smiled, holding out the arrangement: gardenias and pale blue delphinium. "He said to tell you it's a surprise for your 'something blue.'" Monica's heart fluttered. It's kind of him, and very thoughtful, she said, smelling the flowers, which smell gorgeous. I swear it's even more beautiful than the last time," their mother gushed, dabbing at the corner of her eyes with a crumpled tissue. Her voice trembled slightly, the moment clearly overwhelming her. "My first daughter… a bride." She gave a soft, teary laugh as she reached out to straighten a fold in Monica's gown.

"Are you crying, Mom?" Monica teased gently, raising an eyebrow. "It's not even the wedding yet." Her mother smiled through the emotion. "Just happy, dear. You look perfect in that dress. Absolutely perfect." Monica offered a small smile in return, but her gaze drifted back to the mirror. Her reflection shimmered in ivory and satin, but her eyes weren't focused on herself. Instead, they lingered in the space beside her. Empty. Quiet.

"Where's Melina?" she asked suddenly, breaking the silence. Her mother waved a dismissive hand as she busied herself folding the tissue. "Oh, she mentioned something about a group project. Honestly, your sister's been distant lately. You know how she gets when she's in one of her moods." Monica's smile faltered. "She still hasn't done her final fitting. I don't want her to miss anything, or worse, show up in something last-minute and out of place." Her mother sighed. "She'll come around."

"No, please, Mom, just arrange for her to come in this week. I don't care how busy she is. She's my maid of honour. I *need* her."

Their mother gave a nod, reaching for her phone.

"Yes, dear. I'll take care of it."

But Monica's eyes didn't move from the mirror, still locked on that space where her sister should have been, her partner in everything since childhood. A faint crease formed between her brows, barely visible beneath the makeup. Something was off. She could feel it.

CHAPTER THIRTY-FIVE

THE WEDDING

The final day had arrived. The wedding day.

After months of planning, consultations, fittings, and endless mood boards, it all came together like clockwork. The wedding planner, personally recommended by Sylvester's cousin Mary-Jane, had exceeded expectations. Monica had been skeptical at first, but in the end, she had to admit it: Mary-Jane knew what she was doing. The team she chose moved like a polished machine. Every detail was executed with precision and grace, just the way Monica liked it. Outside, the air smelled of pine, polished stone, and privilege. The Longhorn Estate looked like something out of a film set: wide stretches of manicured lawns, a centuries-old manor with ivy crawling up the stone façade, and staff so discreet they seemed to appear and disappear at will. The place spelled money. Old money. Power. Legacy and secrets.

Monica's wedding had quickly become the social event of the year, or at least, that's what everyone whispered. The invitations shimmered like pressed gold, sealed with a family crest most people didn't recognize, but instinctively respected. The floral arrangements looked hand-painted. The venue was so exclusive, it didn't even appear on Google Maps. This wasn't just a wedding. It was an exhibition of status. And Monica? She was glowing. She always glowed. Since we were children, she carried that sort of magnetism, the kind that drew people who came in before they even realized it. Teachers loved her. Neighbours adored her. Strangers complimented her hair in grocery stores. I'd learned early on how to exist in that light without expecting any of it to reflect on me. Smile. Be helpful. Be quiet. That was my lane.

"Mel, can you grab the box of centrepieces from the car?" Monica called, not even turning from the full-length mirror where she was practicing her speech with the poise of a seasoned diplomat.

"Sure," I said, already rising before anyone else moved. I always did. That was my role: the sister who didn't complain. The quiet one. The reliable one. She looked stunning. Even I had to admit that. Dressed in a custom-made gown that clung and flowed in all the right places, she looked like she had stepped straight off the cover of *Bridal Vogue*. Her skin glowed, her eyes sparkled, and the delicate tiara perched on her head made her look, not like a princess, but like a queen who'd known from birth that the crown was hers.

"You look beautiful, Monica," I said softly.

That part was genuine. I meant it. I didn't lean in to kiss her cheek. Her makeup was flawless, and I knew better than to risk smudging it and getting a sharp reprimand from her or one of the stylists circling her like attentive bees. Instead, I blew her a kiss from a safe distance. She caught it with a practiced smile, eyes never leaving the mirror.

"Thanks, Mel," she said, as if I were part of the scenery, pleasant, familiar, functional.

The bridal suite buzzed around us, hairdryers, laughter, Champagne corks, and last-minute adjustments. Her friends fluttered about in matching silk robes, snapping selfies and talking in excited, overlapping voices. The wedding planners hovered in the background, clipboard in hand, ticking boxes and coordinating with earpieces. Monica thrived in this atmosphere. She belonged to it. I slipped away quietly to fetch the centrepieces, walking past rows of white orchids and tall glass vases already arranged on banquet tables like a scene from a dream. Guests were starting to arrive, stepping out of chauffeured cars in silk, sequins, and bespoke suits. Photographers clicked away. Somewhere, I could hear the string quartet warming up. It was perfect. Every inch of it. And still, a part of me, some small, uninvited feeling, stood just outside the glow. Watching. Wondering. Knowing I wasn't made of the same dazzling material. I loved her, truly. But I didn't always understand her. Or maybe she never understood me. But for today, that didn't matter. Today was her day. Her fairy tale. And I would be exactly who I always was: the sister in the wings, quiet and dependable. The one who would never let her down.

****

The wedding was perfect.

Or at least, it looked perfect.

White roses spilled like water from the altar. A string quartet played Vivaldi so flawlessly that it didn't sound real. Monica stood beneath the arch in a dress that shimmered like starlight, her veil catching the soft breeze. She looked like every little girl's idea of a princess. No one would ever guess there was something rotten at the centre of it all. I stood to the side, one foot behind the line of bridesmaids, watching it all unfold, like a scene in a movie I didn't audition for. My fingers clenched the program so tightly that it creased in my hand. I had barely slept since I found the photos, the newspaper clipping, the truth about Sylvester Longhorn, and the girl who disappeared. I'd tried to confront him. He brushed it off with a tight smile and a hand on my shoulder that lingered just a second too long. You don't want to ruin your sister's big day," he said. He was right. And he was wrong. Because it wasn't just about the day. It was about what kind of life Monica was walking into. What kind of family was she marrying into? What kind of man she thought she knew. The officiant began to speak. My chest tightened with every word.

The song played as Monica walked down the aisle with her dad. Dad looked dashing and was a proud father, looking radiant.

"Dearly beloved, we are gathered here today..." My eyes met Monica's. She smiled at me. That soft, radiant Monica smile always made people feel safe. Loved. I couldn't breathe. She didn't know. No one did. And maybe she deserved to know. Maybe she deserved to be angry at me for telling her. But wasn't that better than her finding out ten years from now, too late to leave? I took a step forward. Just one. I wasn't even sure what I was doing, whether I'd call out, walk down the aisle, or simply collapse from the weight of it all. Then I felt a hand close around my wrist. It was Sandra, Monica's best friend. Her eyes locked onto mine, calm but firm.

"Don't," she whispered. "Not now."

I froze. Because in that moment, I realized: I wasn't the only one who knew. I followed Sandra out of the chapel. Not by choice, she all but dragged me by the wrist, heels clicking like gunshots on the marble floor. No one noticed. Everyone was too busy watching Monica say her vows under a chandelier of white roses. We stepped into a side hall lined with portraits of the Longhorns' ancestors, smug men with stern faces and cold eyes. Their silence made it worse., I yanked my arm back.

"What the hell was that?"

Sandra turned, her face calm and unreadable. "You were about to ruin everything."

"She deserves to know the truth." Her lips curled, not quite a smile. "You mean *your* truth?"

"I have proof, Sandra. The photos. The clipping. Sylvester Longhorns and his family are not who you think they are.

"Oh, I know *exactly* who he is."

That stopped me. She stepped closer, her heels silent on the marble floor, her tone dropping to a low, almost intimate whisper.

"You think you're the first person to uncover something dark in this family?" Sandra's eyes narrowed slightly, her lips curving into a faint, knowing smile. "Please. Sylvester has skeletons stacked so high they need their own estate. Closets lined with mahogany, locked behind antique brass, polished weekly." Her voice was smooth, almost amused, but there was a steeliness beneath it, a warning dressed up as conversation.

"And Monica?" she went on, letting the silence hang just long enough to twist the knife. "She doesn't care. Never did. She wants the crown, no matter how bloodstained it is. If there's power to be had, she'll wear it like perfume." The words hung between them, heavy and sharp. Then Sandra tilted her head, her eyes flickering with something close to mischief. Or maybe cruelty.

"But really," she continued with a dry laugh, ", which family doesn't have a few skeletons in the closet? Come on. Even yours, I bet." She gave a slow, deliberate smile, the kind that didn't reach her eyes.

"Especially yours."

The room felt colder somehow, though nothing had changed. The same soft lighting. The same scent of gardenias and expensive candles. But everything had shifted. It wasn't just what Sandra was saying; it was how easily she said it. Like she had seen this play out a dozen times before. Like she knew exactly how this story ended. And Monica? Monica knew too.

"That's not true," I said, my voice shaking. "She doesn't know. She wouldn't go through with this if she did."

Sandra gave a soft, bitter laugh.

"You really believe that?"

Something shifted in her expression. Her voice softened, but not with kindness. "You don't get it, Melina. She always wins. She gets the family, the money, the fairytale. And you? You're still the girl holding her train. But here's the thing: if you want to blow it all up, I won't stop you. I'll *applaud* you."

"You told me *not* to do it."

I said 'don't,' not because I care about Monica, but because I want her to fall." Her eyes gleamed. "Let her say her vows. Let her believe it's real. Then *you* be the one to take it away." The silence that followed felt like pressure underwater.

"You're disgusting," I whispered.

"Maybe. But at least I'm honest." She took a step back, arms folded.

"So, what's it going to be, Melina? Are you going to play the quiet little sister like always, or are you going to finally step out of the shadow and burn it all down? The champagne was flowing like water. Everyone was laughing, dancing, and toasting to "forever." From a distance, it looked like a dream. But I knew better. I stood at the edge of the tent, half in the shadows, watching Monica twirl under a canopy of fairy lights. Her dress sparkled with every turn. She looked radiant, too radiant for the truth that hovered, unspoken between us; I hadn't told her. Not yet. I still wasn't sure if I was protecting her... or myself. Across the lawn, Reginold Longhorn stood stiffly in a group of older guests, laughing a little too hard. His eyes met mine once, just once, and the look he gave me wasn't fear. It was a challenge. Sandra was right about one thing: Monica always wins. But this time, I held the match that could burn the whole thing down.

"You, okay?"

Monica's voice broke through my thoughts. She stood beside me now, flushed from dancing, veil clipped back like an afterthought. She looked genuinely happy, the kind of happy I hadn't seen in her since we were kids. Before the world decided she'd be the golden one. I forced a smile.   "You look beautiful." She laughed, brushing hair from her face. "Tell me something I don't know." Then she softened.

"Seriously, though, you've been quiet all day. You're not... mad at me, are you?"

The question caught me off guard. "Why would I be mad?"

"I don't know," she said with a small shrug. "It's just... this day, this life, it feels like too much sometimes. Like maybe I don't deserve it. And you've always been the grounded one. The one who sees things for what they really are." My throat tightened.

"I'm not trying to leave you behind," she added. "I want you there. In my life. This family... they're intense, sure. But Sylvester's good. He loves me." Sylvester, the groom. The person pretending to be Monica, or is he? Does Monica know the type of family she has married into?

"Monica..." I began, but the words caught in my mouth.

"What?"

"I just want you to be happy," I said instead.

She smiled again and pulled me into a hug. "I am. I really am."

She didn't see the look Sandra gave me across the tent. It wasn't encouragement. It was *daring*. And suddenly, the secret didn't feel like something I was holding. It felt like something holding *me*. Squeezing tighter by the second, the sun had just dipped below the treeline when the reception truly came alive. The band played something jazzy and old-fashioned, the kind of song that made older guests tap their feet and younger ones twirl with ironic glee. Long tables lined the garden, glowing with candles and wildflower centerpieces. Laughter rose like music, clinking glasses, old family stories retold for the hundredth time.

And Monica was glowing. Again. Always. She moved effortlessly from table to table, hugging guests, posing for photos, laughing that perfect, easy laugh. The dress fit her like it had been sewn by starlight, and her hair, which had survived ceremony winds and cocktail-hour chaos, still fell in glossy, immaculate waves.

"She looks like her mother did at her wedding," said Grandma Betsie, dabbing her eyes with a cloth napkin. "Maybe even more beautiful. Don't tell her I said that."

"Too late," I murmured with a soft smile.   "She deserves this," Grandma said. "A good man. A strong family. A future. It's what we prayed for." I didn't respond. I couldn't. Not with the secret I am holding. Nearby, a group of Monica's childhood friends from the country had clustered around the dessert table, their dresses more practical, their laughter louder. They were teasing her about how "big city" she'd gone, and Monica, barefoot now and gleeful, threw her head back in mock scandal.

"Y'all are just mad I didn't marry that guy from the bait shop," she said, and the whole group erupted in laughter. I stood on the outskirts of it all, holding a glass of untouched champagne, smiling where I was supposed to smile.

"You must be Melina," said a woman beside me. She was older, elegant, with a hat too large for this kind of event, probably one of the Longhorns' cousins from abroad.

"I am," I said.

"Lovely speech you gave earlier," she lied. I hadn't given one. She just assumed I had. "And such a close bond with your sister, it's rare, you know. Sisters often grow apart."

CHAPTER THIRTY-SIX

I thought about how close Monica and I used to be, really, back when scraped knees and secret handshakes defined our world. But somewhere along the way, as childhood gave way to ambition and expectations, we began drifting in opposite directions. We wanted different things. Spoke different languages, even when using the same words. Our brother Eton, always the peacemaker, more like Dad in that way, tried not to take sides. He'd shrug and say, "You girls are just different," as if that explained the growing silence between us. But in the end, it was always Monica who came out on top. What Monica wanted, Monica got. She moved through life like it owed her something, and somehow, it kept paying up.

And now she was getting exactly what she'd always dreamed of: wealth, influence, the fairytale engagement to a man from a family with an estate so polished it practically breathed power. Monica was stepping into her dream. But I wasn't dreaming. I was awake. Wide awake. And what I'd learned about Sylvester's family was hiding, the cold calculation in the man's voice that night—wouldn't let me rest. I'd even started looking into the family, piecing together whispers and inconsistencies, trying to make sense of what they were covering up. But now that I knew what I knew... did I have the right to destroy everything Monica had worked for? To be the one who shattered her fantasy? How could I do that to her?

How could I *not?*

"Miss Melina?"

The butler's voice jolted me back to the present. He stood at the foot of the grand staircase, holding out a glass of champagne, concern flickering in his eyes.

"You looked miles away."

I took the glass with a faint smile, my fingers cold against the stem. Miles away didn't even begin to cover it. Across the lawn, Reginold Longhorn was giving a toast.

"To family," he said, voice booming over the speakers. "To loyalty. And to love that endures." His wife smiled tightly beside him. Sylvester.   Monica's new husband stood proud, his arm around her waist. Everything looked right. And felt wrong. I glanced around for Sandra. She wasn't near the drinks or with the other bridesmaids. She had disappeared again like a shadow slipping between lights. I hated that part of me still wondered what she was doing. My grandmother clutched my hand as Monica danced with her new father-in-law.

"Promise me, Melina. If you ever find something real, something this good, you won't let it go." I nodded. But I didn't promise. Because maybe what Monica had been good. Maybe it wasn't even real. And the weight of what I knew was beginning to suffocate the silence inside me.

CHAPTER THIRTY-SEVEN

I found Monica alone by the old oak tree, just beyond the glow of the reception lights. Her heels were dangling from one hand, and her veil had been abandoned somewhere hours ago. She was drinking champagne from the bottle and humming an old country song we used to sing in the car as kids. It almost made me want to turn around. But I didn't.

"Hey," I said.

She looked over her shoulder and smiled.

"Look who finally escaped the table of second cousins."

I walked over slowly, the grass soft beneath my shoes. "Needed a break."

"Same." She offered me the bottle. I shook my head. For a moment, we just stood there, listening to the distant sound of laughter and clinking glasses.

"Do you remember the time you made me fake the flu so you could go to that party in high school?" she said suddenly. I laughed, surprised. "You made *me* fake the flu. You promised to do my algebra for two weeks."

"And I never did," she grinned. "God, I was such a"

"You were Monica," I said quietly. "Always knew what you wanted."

She blinked, stunned. "Sandra, of course, she knows. She turned to face me, her brow furrowing in confusion and something close to fear.

"What's going on, Mel?"

I swallowed hard. "She's not your friend, Monica. Not really. But I am." A silence stretched between us, heavy and brittle. Finally, Monica reached out and took the envelope from my outstretched hand. Her fingers trembled as she slid it open, pulling out the single photo tucked inside. Her breath caught the moment her eyes landed on it, on the girl with bruises mottling her skin, eyes hollowed by fear and shame. A flicker of recognition passed over her face before something inside her seemed to crack, as if the truth had knocked the wind out of her. She looked up at me, her voice shaking. "You know this... this isn't real. It can't be." I stepped closer, soft but firm. "What do you mean, not real? Monica, just look at her. Look. You know exactly who that is."

Her eyes dropped back to the photo, and I could see the denial start to crumble. Grief, anger, disbelief, they all washed over her in waves. She wanted to look away, to pretend it was someone else. But she couldn't. Not this time.

"She told me none of it was true," she whispered. "That it was just some stupid rumours…"

"She lied," I said gently. "Because the truth would've destroyed everything, she built with you.

The secret about the family is that they are linked with the cartels, but Monica's fiancé is a promising surgeon and tries to distance himself from that aspect of the family business. The reception was still echoing with laughter when I walked back into the tent like a ghost. People clapped when they saw me. Someone shouted for another dance. I smiled. I waved. I barely felt my own body.

The envelope burned in my hand.

I slipped behind the catering tent and found Sylvester near the back fence, half in shadow. He had his jacket unbuttoned and a phone pressed to his ear, his voice low and urgent. When he saw me approaching, he ended the call mid-sentence and slid the phone into his pocket.

"Hey," he said cautiously, eyes narrowing. "You, okay?"

I didn't answer. I just held up the envelope, the edges crumpled now from being clutched too tightly for too long. "We need to talk." His posture stiffened. I stepped closer, the distance between us now charged with everything I couldn't ignore anymore.

"Is it true?" I asked. My voice was barely above a whisper, but it cut like glass.

He didn't answer immediately, just looked at me. And that was answer enough.

"You were going to let my sister walk straight into this," I said, voice rising. "Into your world, into your family's mess, into whatever the hell the Longhorns have going on with the cartels."

His jaw tightened. "You don't understand,"

"No, you don't get to do that," I snapped. "You don't get to gaslight your way out of this. There's a girl in that photo,"

"She's fake," he said sharply.

I blinked.

"What?"

"The girl," he repeated, more quietly now, she's not real. She's an actress. We paid her. We knew you were snooping around my family. We knew you'd dig until you found something, or thought you did. So, we gave you

322

exactly what we wanted you to find." I took a step back, the weight of the words slowly sinking in.

"We?"

He hesitated.

"Me. Monica. My father. All of us."

It hit me like a slap. "Monica knew?"

"She's known since the beginning," Sylvester said, softer now. "I told her when we first started seeing each other. About the family, the cartel connections, all of it. She kept it to herself because she knew the rumours were worse than the truth. She wanted to protect you, Mel. But then you started listening at doors that weren't yours to open." I shook my head, stunned. "So, this whole thing... the photo, the bruises... that was all to throw me off?"

"Yes," he said. "Because you were getting too close. And we couldn't risk the wedding getting derailed by half-truths and paranoia."

I stared at him, the anger and betrayal surging in waves I could barely hold back. "You think this is just about a wedding? You built a lie to manipulate me. And Monica let you."

"She didn't want to," he said, but even he didn't sound convinced anymore. "She thought it was the only way to keep you out of it. To keep things from spiralling." I looked away, the envelope still in my hand, now just a symbol of how deep the deception ran. "You were all so busy trying to protect your secrets... You forgot to protect her from you. we, Monica and I, she knows about my family connection to the Cartels, but not me, and also her friend Sandra.

"Except you didn't tell me."

"I thought I could protect you from it."

"You thought if I didn't *know*, it wouldn't count."

Silence. Monica found me alone in the garden, just beyond the soft spill of fairy lights and the fading applause of the party behind us. The celebration felt a world away now, muffled by hedges, distance, and betrayal. I stood still under the branches of an old jacaranda, hands folded tightly in front of me, heart thudding in my throat. Her heels clicked sharply across the flagstones, each step like a full stop in a sentence she'd already made up her mind about.

"There you are," she said tightly, her voice cold with fury. "You nearly ruined my big day."

I turned to face her. The garden lights cast a pale gold glow across her face, flawless makeup, perfectly arranged hair, but her eyes were blazing. Beneath all the beauty, she was seething.

"I was trying to protect you," I said, more shaken than I meant to sound. "All this time... I thought you didn't know. I thought,"

"You thought wrong," she snapped, arms folding across her bodice. "You've always been in other people's business, Melina. Especially mine."

I flinched. "Because I care about you." She let out a short, bitter laugh. "No. You like being the one with the truth. The one who *knows*. But this?" She swept her hand behind her toward the house. "This is the life I chose. The life I wanted. The one I *deserve*." I stared at her, stunned.

"You lied to me."

She shrugged as if the word did not weigh at all. "I did what I had to. Sylvester told me about his family weeks after we met. I knew what I was getting into."

"You knew about the cartel connections, the money laundering, everything?"

She glanced away for half a second, then met my gaze head-on. "Some of it. Not all. And honestly? It's better if you don't know everything, Mel." Her voice was lower now, colder. There was a hard edge there I hadn't heard before.

"As for that envelope..." She smoothed down the front of her gown with careful, controlled movements.

"The girl in the photo is an old school friend. She's an actress. We asked her to help. The bruises were makeup. The scared look? She's good at what she does." I stared at her in disbelief. "So, you *set me up*?"

"We knew you were snooping," she said bluntly. "Sylvester and I both did. And we knew your little friends were sniffing around too."

I narrowed my eyes.

"What friends?"

Her lips curved into a smug smirk. "Don't play dumb. The guy in the blue blazer? The girl with the camera pretending to be a wedding planner's assistant? You think we wouldn't notice?" "They are your friends from University," "Isn't it"?

I said nothing.

"Tell them to back off," Monica said simply, stepping closer. "Whatever they're hoping to dig up, it's bigger than all of us. You think you're protecting me, but you're not. You're putting yourself in danger. And them too."

"So now you're threatening me?" I asked, voice sharp.

"No," she said quietly, almost sadly. "I'm warning you."

The wind shifted, and for a moment, neither of us spoke. Somewhere beyond the garden, laughter floated through the air like a reminder of a world that hadn't yet crumbled.

"I can't believe you," I whispered. "You looked me in the eye this morning like everything was real."

"It *is* real," she said. "Just not the way you wanted it to be." Then she turned and walked back toward the lights, the applause, and the perfect illusion she had chosen to defend, leaving me in the shadows, holding the truth like a stone in my hands. I stared at her. "And you still married him?"

"I love him," she said simply. "And he's not like them. He's clean. He told me he wants nothing to do with that part of the family, he's a surgeon, for God's sake, not a drug lord."

"Love doesn't erase what they've done, Monica."

She looked at me, coolly. "No. But it makes it bearable. "I felt like I was seeing her for the first time, truly seeing her, not through the soft focus of sisterhood and nostalgia, but as someone unfamiliar. Yes, I always knew she was self-centred, always gravitating toward the spotlight like a flower chasing sunlight. But not like this. Not this cold, calculated Monica. Not the proud sister I remembered from childhood sleepovers filled with whispered secrets, or our road trip sing-alongs when we made up harmonies and pretended, we were famous. Not the girl who linked arms with me on school trips, or who giggled at family barbecues while balancing three plates like a circus act. That version of her still lived in my memory, wrapped in silk, smooth, shining, untouchable. But this woman standing in front of me had traded her softness for Armor.

"You were going to let me think you were a victim," I said, each word carefully measured, like stepping through glass. "Like I was protecting you from something you didn't even know." She tilted her head and gave a small shrug, just one shoulder, casual as ever. "And I let you," she said, voice even, almost amused. "Because I knew how you'd react. You always think it's your job to save people, Mel. But not everyone wants to save. Not everyone *needs* it." Her words cut more than I expected, not because they were cruel, but because they were true. I had always carried that invisible torch, protector, fixer, emotional paramedic. But standing there, I realized maybe I'd been dragging it through dry grass the whole time, sparking fires where no one asked for warmth. She turned to leave but hesitated, her back still to me. Then, without looking over her shoulder, she spoke, low and firm, like a lock clicking into place.

"And don't tell Mom and Dad," she said. "Or Grandma. They don't need to know."

I blinked, stunned by the casual cruelty of it.

"Are you serious?"

She turned just enough to meet my eyes, her expression sharp, almost brittle. "Yes. Dead serious." Her voice was clipped, the kind of tone that shut down conversation.

"This is *my* life. *My* marriage. I'm not letting you blow it all up just because you feel morally superior for a minute and a half." The words hit harder than I expected. I stood there, frozen in place, as if her anger had cast me in ice. My body felt cold all over, my face, my hands, even my chest, where just moments ago my heart had been pounding with concern. Now it was quiet. Numb. I wanted to say something, anything. To remind her that I wasn't trying to ruin anything, that I loved her, that I was scared for her. But her eyes made it clear: the door was closed, and I wasn't welcome on the other side.

"So, you're okay living a lie?" I asked, my voice brittle with disbelief.

"I'm living in a compromise," she replied evenly. "There's a difference."

The way she looked at me then it wasn't angry or defensive. It was worse. She looked at me like I was a child. Like she'd crossed some invisible threshold in the last few hours, and I was still standing in the doorway, clutching outdated maps. Then, with a final glance, she turned and walked back toward her wedding. Toward the music and the champagne and the smiles that masked everything else. Like nothing had happened. Like I hadn't just watched the foundation of everything I believed about us crumble in real time.

And I stood there, stunned, holding the truth in my hands like it was something fragile and burning all at once. How could I have been so wrong? I thought I knew Monica, her loyalty, her strength, the sister who used to climb into bed with me after nightmares and whisper that we'd always stick together. But this version of her was polished and hardened. This Monica was someone who loved image more than integrity. Wealth. Power. Status. And she had chosen them over truth. What am I supposed to do now? I feel hollowed out by the betrayal, not just of what she said, but of who she's become. And the worst part? I didn't mind the blood. Not really. Because the truth is, I've spent my whole life watching people pretend Monica and I are the same. Two sisters. Two sides of the same coin. But they were wrong. Monica's all ideals and clean lines, symmetrical, elegant, admired. And I'm what happens when you sharpen those clean lines into a blade. She makes things look perfect. I make things bleed.

****

After the heated exchange with Melina, Monica composed herself, smoothing her dress like it could iron out the cracks in her conscience. She rejoined the wedding guests with a smile that didn't quite reach her eyes. Spotting Sylvester across the lawn, she made her way to him.

"There you are," he said, his voice low but teasing. "You shouldn't leave your newlywed husband like that. Had me thinking you'd run off with the best man." He grinned, but there was a flicker of concern behind it.

"Never," Monica said, pressing a kiss to his cheek. "Come with me. I need to talk. Somewhere quiet, it's about Mel."

Sylvester sighed.

"Your sister. What's she up to now?"

Monica led him away from the crowd to the edge of the garden, where the laughter faded and the only sound was the distant clinking of glasses. She hesitated, then spoke. "Melina always believed the truth was something you could chase and catch," she said. "Like it would sit obediently in your hands, not cut you when it turned and looked back."

"She won't find anything solid," I'd told him once. "The Longhorns bury things deeper than that. But she'll find just enough to think she knows something."

Sylvester turned to me now, his expression unreadable. "And when she does?"

"I'll handle it," I said without hesitation. He nodded. He trusted me; he always had. That was one of the reasons I loved him. The other reason was that he wasn't like the rest of them. He wanted out, truly out of the legacy, the corruption, the name that carried too much weight. But walking away from the Longhorn name wasn't like turning in a key or giving back a ring. It was more like trying to claw a tattoo off your skin, painful, slow, permanent. I didn't mind the blood, if I'm honest. Sometimes it looks like silence. Sometimes it looks like a sacrifice.

And sometimes, it looks like letting your sister walk straight into the fire, hoping she burns just enough to stop asking questions. She thinks she's protecting me, from Sylvester, from his family, from a legacy she doesn't fully understand. Melina still sees me as the fragile girl who used to cry in the dark, the one who needed shielding from the sharp edges of our upbringing. She thinks I'm still standing on the edge of the abyss, trembling. But what she doesn't see, what she refuses to believe, is that I've already walked into it. I've mapped the shadows. Named them. Chosen curtains and China for the rooms inside. I've planted roses around the mouth of the pit, lit candles at its edges, and smiled while doing it. I don't need saving. I haven't for a long time. I made a choice when I stayed with Sylvester, not just to love him, but to stand beside him in everything that name carries. I made another choice when I told him, without blinking, that if Melina became a threat, I would deal with her myself. Because love doesn't always look like rescue. Sometimes it looks like silence. the kind you keep in your chest, even when it bruises you from the inside out. Sometimes it looks like sacrifice, cutting off pieces of yourself to keep what matters alive. And sometimes, it looks like letting your sister walk straight into the fire. Not because you want her to burn. But because she won't stop until she's seen the flames for herself.

She'll get too close. She always does. And when she does, she'll finally understand, the truth doesn't save people. It changes them. And it doesn't ask permission. Do not silence her. Do not threaten her. Just remind her of her place, because here's the truth: People like us don't get fairytales unless we're willing to write them in blood, and Melina? She still thinks this story is about right and wrong. But it's always been about power. And I'm not giving mine up.

CHAPTER THIRTY-EIGHT

The wedding was over, the guests long gone, the estate dark and echoing except for the occasional clink of staff clearing crystal glasses from linen-draped tables. I'd been given a guest room in the east wing, far from the newlyweds, far from anyone else. A courtesy that suddenly felt like exile. I couldn't sleep; I paced the room for the third time, then finally reached for my phone and opened my messages. Anna had texted me earlier that night, just checking in. A simple *"You okay?"* followed by a heart. But I couldn't bring myself to answer right away. I was still in shock, my mind replaying everything Monica had said like a scene on loop I couldn't escape. Eventually, I wrote back: *"I'll see you tomorrow."* It was all I could manage. Sleep was impossible.

The walls of my room felt too close, the air too heavy. My thoughts churned in restless circles, and no amount of tossing and turning could quiet them. Finally, sometime after midnight, I threw on a hoodie and slipped outside. The night was cool and still, the kind of quiet that only deep country or long suburban spaces know. A few porch lights glowed in the distance, soft amber halos in the dark. My shoes crunched over gravel as I walked, each step grounding me just enough to keep from unravelling. I didn't know where I was going, only that I had to keep moving. I needed the cold air in my lungs, the emptiness of the road. I needed space to think. To breathe. To try to separate the truth from the damage it had already caused. The silence wasn't comforting, exactly, but it was honest. And right now, I'd take that over polished lies and painted-over secrets. The estate grounds were still. Perfect. Manicured to the inch, like a photograph that had never known chaos. But something about the air felt wrong, too still, too composed. Like the silence was holding its breath. I couldn't shake the feeling I was being watched. And I was right. Monica was already there, lounging beneath the patio on a cushioned chaise, with a scarf wrapped around her, against the gentle night breeze, a coffee cup cradled in her hand. She patted the seat beside her, not unkindly.

"Sit."

I did, against my better judgment. Against every instinct that told me to run. But something deeper kept me rooted. A part of me was still trying to understand who she had become and why. She took a sip of coffee, then glanced at me over the rim. "You think I'd marry into a family if they were still involved in that mess?" I didn't answer. I didn't need to. She smiled, soft, weary. "It's not like that anymore, Mel. Yes, the family had ties. Deep ones. Old ones. There were years, decades, where money moved in ways no one wants to talk about. But that ended before I even met Sylvester."

"And the sealed envelope?" I asked quietly. "The girl with the bruises?" She let out a slow breath. "As I told you, before she said forcefully, we hired her. She was paid to play a role. It's a makeup, a costume. The rest... those are ghosts, Mel. Every powerful family has them if you dig deep enough. Sylvester's not part of that world. His father... maybe, once. But that world is dying. They've buried it. People like Reginold Longhorns don't hand over control; they fade out. Quietly."

I stared at her.

"And you're okay with that?"

She gave a half-shrug; her eyes fixed on something in the distance. "I'm okay with moving forward. By not letting someone else's sins dictate my future."

"Monica, this isn't just ancient history. People got hurt. Maybe they still are."

Her voice sharpened. "And what do you expect me to do? Blow up my marriage? Destroy Sylvester's career? Call the police on a dynasty no one's ever managed to touch?" I looked away, jaw tight. Her tone softened again.

"Mel... you have a real future ahead of you. You're going to finish university. Be a brilliant nurse. You'll climb the ladder, make a life for yourself, you've earned. You don't want to get pulled into this. It's messy. It's political. It's dangerous. Let it go. For your own sake. "She reached out, placed a hand on mine.

"You don't need to be part of this world," she said gently. "I do. But you don't. Focus on what you're building. Let this go." I pulled my hand back.

"I think you believe that," I said. "That burying the truth is noble. Or even necessary. But Monica, you're still standing in it. No matter how much you pretend it's past tense." She didn't respond. Not right away. Her jaw tensed slightly, and for a moment I thought I saw something flicker behind her eyes, doubt, regret, maybe even fear. Then, like a shutter snapping closed, it was gone. The silence between us stretched. The wind rustled the perfectly trimmed hedges, the only sound in a garden that suddenly felt like a stage set for something rotten. I stood, suddenly cold despite the warmth in the night breeze. My skin prickled, not from the air, but from something deeper, something unsettled inside me.

"You're right," I said quietly. "I don't belong in this world."

I let the silence stretch, let it sting. Then I added, "But neither did the girl with the bruises." I scoffed, shaking my head. "Makeup, you said. Hired to play a part. Is that what we do now, turn real pain into a performance?" She said nothing. Maybe she didn't have to. I took a step back, my pulse loud in my ears. And then I turned and walked away, my footsteps deliberate, echoing across the stone path like a verdict. I didn't know if I was leaving my sister behind or finally seeing who she'd been all along. The air shifted as I moved, and I paused near the edge of the terrace, staring out at the distant horizon. The sky was ink-dark, but somewhere out there, dawn would come. Eventually. Was this what freedom looked like? Or was it just another form of surrender, quieter, lonelier? I turned my head slightly, offered Monica a polite, almost mechanical,

"Goodnight."

She didn't reply. I didn't wait for her to. I walked back inside, through halls that now felt colder than the air outside. Back to my room, back to my thoughts, back to a bed I knew I wouldn't sleep in. I lay in the dark, the weight of everything pressing against my chest, and for the first time that night, I stopped trying to outrun the truth.

WALKING IN MY SISTER'S SHADOW

PART FOUR

CHAPTER THIRTY-NINE

The Longhorn estate buzzed softly that morning, like a machine slowly winding down after the spectacle. The air still held the scent of roses and champagne, but the energy had shifted, less celebration, more cleanup. Staff moved with quiet efficiency, clearing empty flutes from the manicured lawn, their footsteps muffled by the dew-damp grass. Inside, the house was unusually still. Not peaceful, just... waiting. Like it was holding its breath, unsure of what came next. Outside the grand front entrance, a sleek black car idled beneath the porte-cochere, its tinted windows catching the morning light. Matching designer luggage stood neatly beside it, monogrammed and honeymoon-bound, as if nothing that happened yesterday could touch today. A soft knock pulled me from the window. Three even taps, and then her voice, careful but light.

"Can we come in?"

I turned toward the door just as it eased open. Monica stepped inside first, flawless as ever in a pale linen jumpsuit that looked effortless and expensive. Her sunglasses were perched on her head like a crown, holding her hair back in waves that had been styled to look like they hadn't been styled at all. I stepped aside. Not because I wanted to, but because I needed to know what game they were playing now. Behind her stood Sylvester, his suit jacket perfectly tailored, his hands casually tucked into his pockets. His expression was unreadable as always, but there was something in his eyes, something wary, or maybe just tired. They looked like a magazine spread: beautiful, composed, untouchable. But I knew better now. Monica perched delicately on the edge of my bed, her posture poised, rehearsed, like she'd sat this way a hundred times in front of a mirror to get it just right. Sylvester stayed by the door, standing stiffly, hands still in his pockets. His weight shifted from one foot to the other, as if he couldn't decide whether to stay or bolt. Everything about him said he was ready to leave, mentally already boarding their honeymoon flight. Still, he managed a polite smile, thin and hollow, like this was just another morning. Monica offered me a small, practiced smile, the kind that didn't quite reach her eyes. "We just wanted to say goodbye before we head out."

"To Italy," she added, as if I didn't already know.

The words hung in the air like perfume, pleasant, distracting, and a little cloying. I nodded, unsure what to say. The silence between us had weight now. Shape. And though everything about her looked perfectly intact, I couldn't stop seeing the fractures underneath, underneath the hairline cracks that no amount of linen or lipstick could cover.

"Before we head out," Monica began, her voice calm and composed, "there's something we need to say. Just… to clear the air."

Sylvester said nothing. He was a presence more than a participant, silent, unreadable, like a statue dressed in expensive fabric. Monica leaned forward slightly, her hands folded in her lap. "I know last night was… intense. And I know we didn't leave things in a great place. But I want you to hear this from me, not from whispers or assumptions. "She paused, searching my face.

"You're my sister, Melina. I love you. I always have. And I know you think you're protecting me or trying to do what's right. But you don't see the whole picture. You're only seeing shadows and assuming they're monsters."

"I understand enough," I said, my voice low but steady. Monica sighed, barely. The kind of sigh you give when someone's just too stubborn to listen, or when you're too tired to keep pretending.

"Look," she said, straightening slightly. "Tell your friends to back off. Whatever digging they're doing, it stops now. Leave things as they are. I'm not in danger. I'm not being coerced. This is my life, and I chose it."

"And what if they find something real?" I asked. "What then? "Her eyes flickered, just for a second. A crack in the veneer.

"They won't," she said softly. "Because there's nothing to find. And even if there was… it wouldn't change anything." Sylvester finally spoke, his voice calm but edged with warning. "As Monica already told you, the girl you saw, the one with the bruises, was an actress. We hired her to throw you and your friends off track. You and your friends were poking around in places you don't belong, asking questions about things that don't concern you." He stepped forward slightly, not aggressive, but deliberate. "And here's the part you need to understand, Melina: this isn't a game. You and your little circle might think you're being brave or righteous, but the deeper you go, the more likely you are to cross the wrong people, people who won't be as patient or… civil as we've been." My jaw tightened, but I said nothing.

He glanced briefly at Monica, then back at me. "And even if you don't care about your own safety, you need to think about hers. Every rumour you stir up, every breadcrumb you chase, it reflects on her now. On her name. On this family, and your family also. The Telfers' name carries a reputation, and I'm sure you are going to keep this all under wraps, not a word to your family, especially that brother of yours. Reputations can crack faster than you think, and some things, once said out loud, can't be taken back." His words hung in the air, sharp as broken glass. That was the most honest thing I'd ever heard him say.

"She chose this life," he added. "You didn't. So do her a favour and stop trying to dismantle it."

There was no anger in his tone, just a quiet certainty, like someone stating a fact, not a threat. But the message was clear: keep digging, and someone gets hurt. And this time, it might not be me. I stood.

"Are you threatening me?"

"No," Monica said quickly. "We're protecting her. And you. Mel... there are people in my new life who aren't as forgiving as I am. We're giving you a chance to walk away from this without any trouble."

I stared at her. "And what happens if I don't?"

Sylvester's eyes didn't flinch. "We make sure no one listens to you. You'll be discredited. Quietly. Professionally. No drama. No noise. Just silence."

Monica stood and took my hand. I tried to pull away, but she held on, her grip tight.

"You're my sister," she said softly. "And I love you. But love doesn't mean letting you ruin everything because you can't accept how the world really works." I didn't say anything. I couldn't. She pulled me into a hug like she used to when we were kids. Only this time, it wasn't warmth I felt. It was a warning. They walked out together, polished, powerful, untouchable. And I stood there with a choice: obey, disappear, and stay safe...Or speak, and risk everything.

****

They stood then, almost in unison. Monica offered one last smile, faint and bittersweet.

"I hope one day you'll understand," she said. "Not everything worth keeping is clean. "And with that, they turned to go, leaving the scent of her perfume and the silence of everything unsaid hanging in the air behind them. The Longhorn estate buzzed softly that morning, like a machine winding down after the spectacle. The wedding is over. As the staff continued to clear champagne flutes from manicured lawns. Flower petals lay crushed beneath expensive heels. The wedding was over. Now it was time for the exit. Monica stood at the top of the grand staircase, dressed in sleek travel whites and oversized sunglasses, arm hooked around Sylvester. They looked like they belonged on the cover of a luxury magazine. Effortless. Untouchable.

The family had gathered in soft-spoken clusters across the marble foyer, their voices weaving a tapestry of goodbyes, congratulations, and half-finished sentiments. Perfumed air hung heavy with the scent of lilies and something more elusive, anticipation, perhaps, or the faintest note of disquiet. Reginold Longhorn kissed Monica's cheek with theatrical gravity, as if bestowing a blessing rather than a farewell. His lips brushed her skin like he was crowning her queen of something unspoken, something inherited and complex. Monica, poised as ever, smiled through it, chin slightly lifted, the way she'd been taught. Berdie clung to her son Sylvester in a long, wordless hug. Her arms wound around him tightly, a maternal coil of love threaded with silent expectation. It was the kind of embrace that said more than any farewell could: *Be careful. Don't forget who you are. Don't forget who we are.*

I stood slightly apart; my hands folded in front of me like a shield. The marble floor reflected everyone's movements but mine. I tried not to notice the eyes that slid toward me and then away just as quickly, furtive, assessing, unsure. I was the odd one out. The quiet sister. The question mark people didn't quite know where to place. Maybe it was the way I dressed, subtler, less polished. Maybe it was because I hadn't said much that day, or most days. Or maybe it was because I'd always been content in the shadows, never angling for the spotlight that Monica wore so effortlessly.

Still, I watched her now, radiant in her pale blue dress, surrounded by people who believed in her story. I wondered what it would be like to be wrapped in that kind of certainty. To belong so completely. Instead, I stood there, an observer of my own family, feeling like a footnote in someone else's grand narrative. And somewhere beneath the hum of conversation and the shuffle of good shoes on polished stone, a quiet voice inside me whispered: *You don't fit because you see things they don't.* Monica caught my gaze. Her expression softened, just enough for the others not to notice. She walked over to me, leaving Sylvester behind.

"You're heading back to campus today?" she asked.

"Yeah," I said. "I've got a meeting with my thesis advisor tomorrow. I'm behind."

She nodded. "That's good. You're good at that. At building your own thing." I didn't answer. She touched my arm. "Take care of yourself, Mel. Really. Don't lose yourself in things that don't belong to you. "I wanted to say something sharp. Something final. But the truth was, I didn't have it in me. Not yet.

"Have a nice trip," I said.

She smiled, then leaned in and kissed my cheek. Whispered just loud enough for me to hear:

"It's all going to be fine. You'll see."

Then she turned, her fingers slipping effortlessly into Sylvester's, like it was the most natural thing in the world. Together, they stepped through the towering front doors, not like newlyweds leaving a party, but like monarchs crossing a threshold into their kingdom. There was no hesitation in her stride, no glance back. Only the gleam of certainty, the kind that made you believe this wasn't just a marriage, it was a coronation. Behind them, the remnants of the wedding party erupted into cheers. Laughter, applause, and the clink of champagne flutes still echoed from the ballroom. People waved, shouted their congratulations into the warm dusk, their voices rising like confetti tossed into the air. I stayed behind for another hour. Milled around the edges. Smiled when expected. Nodded at strangers who knew my name but not my place. When I finally left, it was quiet. No send-off, no spotlight. Just me, my overnight bag, and the echo of everything I hadn't said. The house loomed behind me as I stepped toward the waiting Uber, its grand silhouette framed by the night. Warm light glowed softly in the tall windows, like eyes watching from behind drawn curtains, discreet, deliberate, and unblinking. I didn't look back. There was nothing for me in that place but echoes, and even those didn't belong to me anymore.

Earlier that evening, I'd graciously declined the Longhorns' offer to have one of their chauffeurs take me back to my flat near campus. Mrs. Longhorn had said it with that ever-practiced warmth of hers: *"We're family now, dear. There's no need to be shy."* As if proximity through marriage erased the strangeness between us. I'd smiled politely, as always. Told her my ride was already on the way. No need to worry about me. The truth was, I couldn't stomach another minute in that house. Not after everything I'd seen and heard- I wondered, absently, if Monica or Sylvester had mentioned anything to her. If they'd caught wind of my suspicions. If the

Longhorn matriarch had read it in my eyes, the way I lingered too long in certain rooms, or asked just one too many harmless questions. She was sharp, that one. The kind of woman who could tear you down with a compliment and a smile. I shrugged it off as I settled into the back seat of the cab, but the unease clung to me like smoke. Had I gone too far by digging into the Longhorns' past? Or not far enough? The car pulled away from the estate, its tires whispering against the gravel. The house faded behind me, swallowed by trees and shadows from the sunlight.

But the questions… they came with me.

CHAPTER FORTY

The drive back to campus felt longer than it should have. Every sign, every tree-lined curve of the road, felt like it belonged to a different lifetime, one where things were simple, where my sister was just my sister. My apartment was silent when I stepped inside, the kind of silence that felt like it was waiting for me. The kitchen lights cast a soft glow over the room. My textbooks were still stacked neatly on the counter, untouched since the day before. My thesis notes sat open beside them, mid-sentence, like a conversation I had abandoned. But my thoughts were miles away, back at the garden, back at the party, back in that moment when everything I thought I knew about Monica unravelled.

Then came the noise, the hum of voices, laughter, and shuffling feet. My friends were already there: Anna, Barbara, and the boys, David and Lester. They'd come back from the wedding long before I did. They'd left the reception just after the ceremony. At the time, I barely noticed. Now it felt like a glaring detail.

"Why did you all leave so early?" I asked, trying to keep my voice even.

Anna glanced at Barbara, then shrugged. "We didn't feel like we fit in. Something about that place... it felt off."

David crossed his arms. "Yeah, like everyone was smiling, but no one meant it."

"Did you tell her?" Barbara asked suddenly. "About Sylvester's family? About what we found out?" I stiffened.

"No," I said quickly. "I didn't need to. She already knew." That quieted the room. Even Lester, who usually had something sarcastic to add, said nothing.

"She knew?" Anna echoed.

I nodded slowly, still trying to wrap my head around it myself. "She's known since the beginning. He told her weeks after they met. And she chose to stay. Chose to protect him. And apparently, they knew we were asking questions. They planned that photo, the bruised girl, the envelope. It was all a setup."

"Jesus," David muttered. "That's twisted."

"Okay, guys," I said, holding up a hand, my voice cracking just a little. "Enough. I'm... I'm exhausted. I just need to sleep. Please. "I turned away before they could see the rest, the trembling in my fingers, the tightness in my chest, the ache in my throat. I didn't want them to see how shaken I really was. I'd spent so long trying to protect Monica from a truth I thought would destroy her. And the whole time, she was protecting someone else, not from danger, but from me. As I closed my bedroom door behind me, the walls finally closed in. The silence returned, heavier now, filled with all the things I couldn't say. And for the first time in a long while, I didn't know who I was really protecting, or if I had ever truly known my sister at all. As I lay on my bed, staring up at the ceiling fan tracing slow circles in the dark, the memory came back, uninvited but sharp, like a thorn under skin. It had been weeks since. Maybe longer. The details blurred now, but I remembered the feeling more than anything, the stillness, the chill, the unease. I was at Monica's place, dropping off a box of old photos she wanted for the engagement board. I let myself in, she'd said to me, and was halfway through the hallway when I heard voices. Her parents. Behind the partially closed office door. I wasn't trying to eavesdrop, not at first. But something in their tone made me pause.

"Keep it away from the press," her mother had said, clipped and urgent. "If that shipment gets flagged,"

"We have it covered," her father had interrupted. "The Longhorn name still means something. Especially down there. They'll keep quiet if they know what's good for them." There was a pause. Papers rustled. A low sigh.

"If this ever touches Monica…"

"It won't," her father said firmly. "Sylvester knows what's at stake."

I'd stood frozen for a few seconds longer, heart thudding. Then the floorboard creaked under me, and I slipped back toward the front door like I'd never been there. At the time, I didn't know what they were talking about. I told myself it was business. Something boring. Maybe even harmless. But that name, the Longhorns, lodged itself in my brain like a splinter. I didn't say anything to Monica. Not then. But it stayed with me. And the more I paid attention, the more things didn't add up. Now, lying here in the quiet, I could see it all clearly. That was the moment it began, the first tiny crack in the perfect image Monica had painted of her future. And I had ignored it.

CHAPTER FORTY-ONE

It was amazing how quickly the world forgot. By Monday morning, I was back in a lecture hall with cracked whiteboards and humming fluorescents. My professor droned on about art and ethics, about how intention doesn't erase consequence, and the irony nearly made me laugh out loud. I stared at my open notebook. I wasn't writing. Just pressing the same pen stroke into the paper over and over until it bled. The campus was the same as I'd left it. Crowded bulletin boards. Coffee lines that snaked out of the student union. People are rushing to places they didn't want to be. It should've felt like home. But something had shifted.

Anna met me after class, two lattes in hand, and a tentative smile. "Welcome back to the land of deadlines and caffeine dependency." I smiled. "Thanks. God, I'm so behind, it's criminal."

"You're fine. You needed the break. Wedding stress is legit."

I hesitated. Then, carefully, I said,

"Thanks for backing off… for stepping back from it all." Anna shrugged. "Wasn't worth it. Too many locked doors. Too many quiet threats. You were right to walk." She didn't meet my eyes. And I didn't ask what they'd said to her. I already knew. We sat in the quad and watched the breeze catch leaves in soft spirals. Students moved around us like we were invisible.

"Are you okay?" Anna asked, finally.

I nodded too quickly.

"Yeah. I'm fine. It's over." But it wasn't.

Barbara and the boys: David and Lester, dropped by the next afternoon, unannounced, but not unwelcome. I heard the knock followed by their familiar voices in the hallway, and for the first time in days, something loosened in my chest.

"How's our girl doing?" they all said at once as they stepped inside, grinning like they had a plan. I gave them a faint smile, the kind that doesn't quite reach the eyes but still tries. David clapped his hands together and pointed at me.

"There she is," he said brightly. "That's my girl. That's the smile we've been waiting for."

Lester flopped onto the couch dramatically, kicking his feet up. "We figured if the mountain won't come to Melina, the mountain, meaning us, will bring snacks, sarcasm, and possibly bad jokes." Barbara dropped a paper bag on the kitchen counter. "And samosas. Warm. Straight from the corner place you like."

David grinned.

"After exams, we're kidnapping you. A real night out. Drinks, proper food, none of this microwave nonsense you live on, and a wicked curry that'll make you forget the word 'betrayal.'" He said it with a laugh, but they all went quiet for a beat after that. We were all thinking the same thing: what had happened with Monica, the photo, the lies. The ache I'd been carrying threatened to rise again, but I pushed it down.

"Sounds like a plan," I said, nodding. "But I'm picking the playlist."

"Oh God," Lester groaned, "not another sad-girl acoustic hour."

Barbara threw a cushion at him. "Let her live, Lester." And just like that, the room filled with easy laughter. For a few moments, it almost felt normal again. Not fixed, not forgotten, but lighter. And maybe that was enough for now. Later that evening, after the others had gone home, Anna stayed behind. She lingered by the window, arms folded, eyes scanning the street below like she was still working out what she wanted to say.

"Do you remember that day we went by the Longhorn estate?" she asked after a moment. "You were returning Monica's bridesmaid folder. I didn't even want to go inside, but you insisted."

I nodded slowly.

"Of course I remember."

"We ended up in that ridiculous sunroom with the glass doors," she continued. "And we heard Sylvester and his father talking in the study across the hall, about 'keeping things clean,' and how *the Mexico side was under control now.*"

"Yeah," I said quietly. "You brushed it off. Said they were probably talking about business logistics."

"I did," she admitted, her voice dipping. "Because it was so unreal. Like something out of a movie." She turned to face me then, her expression hardening.

"But hearing everything now… the girl, the staged photo, Monica *knowing* and going along with it: Mel, that's not just messed up. That's cold." I didn't respond right away. The words were sitting heavy in my chest. But Anna wasn't finished.

"You know what's worse?" she said, her voice quieter now. "I'm not surprised."

That caught me off guard. I looked at her.

"She's always been like that," Anna said, a little more gently now. "Monica. It's always been about her. Her plans. Her future. Her image. You were just the little sister, the one expected to follow in her shadow to admire, to stay quiet. But you never did." I swallowed hard. "I didn't think she'd go *this* far. I thought... I thought I still mattered to her. At least enough for the truth." Anna came and sat beside me on the arm of the couch, her hand resting lightly on my shoulder.

"You do matter," she said firmly. "Just not to *her version* of the truth. Monica's always built her world exactly how she wants it, and anything that doesn't fit gets painted over or pushed out." I didn't realize how tightly I'd been holding my breath until I let it go.

"She chose this life," I said softly. "And she chose to lie to protect it."

"And you chose to see her for who she really is," Anna said. "That takes guts, Mel." There was a long pause as we both sat with the weight of it. Outside, the streetlights flickered to life, one by one.

"I don't know what to do next," I finally whispered.

"You don't have to know right now," Anna said. "Just... don't let her rewrite your story to suit hers".

That night, I still saw Monica's face in the dark. Not the radiant bride with the perfect smile and flawless gown, but the other Monica, the one who looked at me like I was a threat. Her eyes weren't soft or grateful. They were hard, calculating. Cold. Sometimes I'd wake up sweating, heart pounding, convinced she was standing at the foot of my bed, still in that shimmering dress, but with that look in her eyes. That quiet warning. *Stay out of this.* And then there was the girl. The one from the photo. The bruises. The hollow stare. She haunted my dreams more than Monica did. I kept replaying the moment I saw her picture, how my heart twisted, how my instincts screamed that something was terribly wrong. But she wasn't real. Just a role. A performance. An actress, Monica, and Sylvester had been hired, coached, and costumed. A perfect illusion designed for one purpose: to scare me into silence.

They had planned it down to the last detail, the bruises, the lighting, the envelope, all of it. And it had worked. For a moment, I really believed I'd uncovered something dangerous. I had. Just not the way I thought. Now, even in my own neighbourhood, I found myself glancing over my shoulder. Waiting. Watching. Not sure what exactly, a shadow, a black car that passed too slowly, a stranger lingering too long by my building. Paranoia was creeping in. Or maybe it wasn't paranoia at all. Maybe it was instinct. Because if Monica and Sylvester were willing to stage something like that... what else were they capable of? And more importantly, what else are they hiding? I assured myself I was safe and that staying silent was wise. But something inside me had changed, and deep down, I knew walking away didn't mean freedom. That night, I called my grandparents. It wasn't planned. I was halfway through reorganizing my sketchbooks when I saw a photo on my desk, the one from last summer at the lake. Me Monica, and Grandma Betsy on the porch, drinking lemonade and laughing like we didn't know the world could turn sharp overnight. I dialled without thinking, needing something, someone, something-something-that still felt real. The phone rang three times before Grandpa picked up.

"Sweetpea!" he said, his voice warm and a little scratchy with age. "Look who remembered us old folks."

I smiled for the first time all day.

"Hey, Grandpa."

"Hang on, I'll put you on speaker. Your grandma's been talking about that wedding since she got back. You'd think royalty had married into the family." A shuffle, then Grandma Betsy's voice joined his. "Melina, honey! You didn't get a single slice of my lemon cake, did you? I knew it went too fast!" I laughed softly. "I think I blinked, and it was gone." We talked for twenty minutes. About the garden. About Grandpa's knee. About how the post office in their tiny town was finally getting digital scales. They asked about school, and I told them I was catching up. They didn't ask about Monica, and I didn't bring her up. Just hearing them made the noise in my head settle a little. No secrets. No power games. Just their voices. Their love. After we hung up, I sat on the floor and hugged my knees to my chest. I used to think family was a fixed thing, like a house. Some rooms are loud, some quiet, but all of them are built from the same wood. Now I know better. Some parts of the house have rot under the wallpaper. Some are beautiful but dangerous.

And some, like the porch swing at my grandparents 'still, creak with the kind of truth that doesn't need to be proven. I wanted to stay in that kind of room. The safe kind. The quiet kind.

The city had started to warm again; the kind of early spring warmth that made you forget how long winter had lasted. Trees outside my apartment window were beginning to bloom, small blossoms pushing through like they'd been holding their breath all season. I watched them from my kitchen table, coffee in hand, sunlight catching on the rim of the mug. For the first time in weeks, the silence wasn't heavy. It was calm. I thought of Monica less now. Or at least, the grip she had on me, that strange mix of admiration and resentment, guilt and longing, was finally beginning to loosen. I still remember the girl she used to be. The one who made her bed with hospital corners even at ten years old. Who won debate competitions, wore perfume to class, and made everyone around her feel just a little bit smaller without ever trying. And I remembered the woman she became polished, ambitious, immovable.

The bride in the garden. The one who looked at me that night was not like a sister, but like someone who needed managing. Silencing. But she didn't win. She got the life she wanted, or maybe the life she *needed* to make herself believe in. But I didn't have to follow her there. I didn't have to stay quiet just to keep the peace. I didn't have to keep measuring myself by the silhouette of her success. No more pretending. No more performing. No more hiding behind someone else's idea of who I was supposed to be. Monica lived in a house of secrets. I chose something different. **_Freedom._** My dreams were still intact, the ones I almost let go of while trying to protect her. The ones with ink-stained notebooks, with night shifts at the hospital, with patients who trusted me to show up as I am, not as someone else's reflection. I used to think the only way to matter was to be like Monica, confident, composed, untouchable. But now I knew better. I didn't want to be untouchable. I wanted to be real. So, I opened my laptop and started typing. Not a thesis. Not a clinical paper. Just a story. My story. No one gets to tell me who I should be anymore. No more standing in her shadow, **_no way. I'm stepping out of her shadow and finding my own light._**

EPILOGUE

ONE YEAR LATER

The ward was quiet that morning, the kind of quiet that settles just before the storm of activity begins. It wasn't silence, exactly, but a gentle hush, like the building itself was holding its breath. I stood by the window in full uniform, hands wrapped around a warm cup of tea, watching the world begin to stir below. In the courtyard garden, staff moved between departments with quiet urgency, nurses, doctors, porters, and support staff in a spectrum of coloured tunics. Their steps were purposeful, practiced. They passed each other with nods, clipped greetings, the occasional laugh, each person a part of the invisible machinery that kept everything turning.

There was something deeply grounding in it all. The rhythm. The routine. The way this place pulsed with intention. It wasn't just about tasks or timetables; it was about people showing up, day after day, to offer care in a world that so often forgets what that means. Here, even the smallest moments could be victories: a patient smiling for the first time in days, a wound healing, a frightened family member reassured. Pinned neatly to my chest was my name badge: **Melina Telfer, RGN Staff Nurse.** It wasn't flashy. It didn't sparkle. But it was mine, and it meant everything. Those letters had been carved from long nights and harder days. They were paid for in sacrifice, in missed birthdays, in exams taken on less than three hours' sleep. In tears shed quietly in toilet cubicles, and in the fierce, stubborn belief that I could make it even when everything screamed otherwise. That title, Staff Nurse, wasn't just a job. It was a hard-won identity. A promise I made and kept to myself, and to the patients I now serve.

As I took a sip of my tea and turned to face the ward, I felt it again, that quiet hum in my chest. Not nerves. Not pride, exactly. Something steadier. A sense of belonging. Of being exactly where I was meant to be. After the wedding and the difficult confrontation with Monica, I threw myself fully into finishing my nursing course. I needed something to focus on, something that felt solid and unshakable. Nursing became that for me. I completed my training, passed my final placements, and graduated with my nursing degree. I am, unapologetically, proud of myself. My parents were there at the graduation, beaming with pride. Gran and Grandad, my aunties and uncles, even a few cousins, made the journey. After the ceremony, we celebrated in the countryside, where Gran hosted a beautiful gathering under the late summer sun. It wasn't extravagant, but it was full of love. We invited old friends, mentors, and neighbours, people who had supported me in big and small ways. It was Gran's idea, and as always, she knew exactly what I needed. Looking out over the hospital grounds that morning, I felt a sense of peace I hadn't known for years. I had made it. Not just to graduation, not just to the title, but to a place where I could breathe, stand tall, and say: this is where I'm meant to be. Outside of work, life had become quieter, simpler in the best kind of way. My friends remained my anchor, steady and unwavering through all the changes. Anna still called almost every night, her voice a familiar comfort in the dark, even when all we did was laugh about our chaotic shifts or vent about difficult patients. David hadn't changed one bit. He still dragged me out for mediocre curries in questionable restaurants, but the conversation was always top-tier. His wit and warmth had a way of grounding me, even when everything else felt uncertain.

Lester, surprisingly, had grown a thoughtful streak. These days, he dabbles in writing poetry, sometimes ridiculous, sometimes beautiful. He'd changed nursing jobs twice already, always chasing something just out of reach. I wasn't sure his heart was ever truly in nursing. One night over drinks, he admitted he still hadn't found his "true calling." I suspect, deep down, he's already made his decision to go back and help with the family business. It wouldn't surprise me if he eventually took the reins entirely. He has the charm and the instinct for it, he just doesn't see it yet. Although we all worked at different hospitals now, we still made time to meet up whenever we could. There was something sacred about those catch-ups, swapping stories, trading gossip, laughing until we couldn't breathe. In a profession where you carry so much of other people's pain, those moments reminded us of who we were outside the scrubs.

And Monica....

She called me on the morning of my graduation. Her name flashing on my screen gave me pause. For a second, I considered not answering; the hurt from the past still lived somewhere deep inside me, but curiosity, or maybe old loyalty, made me pick up.

"Congratulations, Mel," she said. Her voice was soft, lighter than I remembered. "Well done, from both Sylvester and me. I'm sorry we couldn't be there." It was the first time we'd spoken since the wedding. Almost a year of silence, broken by a phone call that felt strangely out of place, both overdue and too sudden. She told me that, although I hadn't reached out, Mom and Dad had spoken to her. They'd told her how well I was doing. How proud they were. I kept my tone polite, but distant. We made small talk about how she was doing, how life abroad was treating her, nothing too personal. I didn't want to open any old doors. Not that day. When she asked if everything was okay between us, I paused. Then I said quietly, "I haven't told anyone anything." There was a long silence on the other end. She didn't press further.

"I should go," I added quickly. "The photo shoot is about to start, before the ceremony." She wished me luck again, and we hung up. There was no argument. No confrontation. Just an oddly careful exchange between sisters, more like strangers, who once knew each other too well — and now, not at all. Before that call, we'd had no contact since the day of the wedding. The silence had stretched uncomfortably long at first a mutual retreat, then a more permanent distance. I'd heard things through the grapevine that she and Sylvester had moved abroad. That he'd taken on more "family responsibilities," though no one ever explained exactly what that entailed. Someone mentioned they'd bought a house, some luxurious property in a gated community with ocean views, private security, and an infinity pool. It sounded like the life Monica had always dreamed of, exclusive, immaculate, untouchable. And that was fine. Truly, it was.

That chapter between us had ended, not with drama, but with quiet disconnection. No apologies or confessions could rewind what had been said or done. And maybe that was for the best. Sometimes people drift so far from who they once were, or who you once were with them, that returning is no longer possible, or necessary. She made her choices. But that chapter, for me, was closed. She'd made her choices. And I'd made mine. There was a time when I would have replayed everything in my head, the conversations we never had, the forgiveness I never asked for, or gave. But not anymore. I've learned that sometimes closure doesn't come from another person. It comes from accepting what is and choosing to move forward with peace in your heart. Now and then, I still saw her face in dreams, or in old family photos I hadn't thrown away yet. But it didn't hurt anymore. It didn't make me feel small. It didn't make me question who I was. Because I knew who I was now.

I was not the second act in someone else's play. I wasn't the understudy. I wasn't the echo of her footsteps. I was walking in my direction.

And my sister's shadow?

I'm not walking in it anymore.

For so long, I lived beneath it, trying to measure up, trying not to disappoint, quietly shrinking so she could shine. But somewhere along the way, I found my own voice. I stepped out, unsure at first, but determined. I made my path. One built on compassion, hard work, and quiet strength. A path that didn't need applause or comparison, just purpose. Her shadow didn't follow me here. It stayed behind, exactly where it belonged, part of the past, no longer part of my present. Because this life, this future, it's mine., I've fought it, sacrificed for it, and earned every single step. I am not living in anyone's shadow anymore. For too long, I measured worth against someone else's light, mistaking reflection for identity. But I've come to understand that my path, though different, is just as worthy- just as powerful,

This is not the end for me.

This is my becoming.

The quiet strength I've carried is no longer silent. The dreams I once put on hold are now within reach. And though I once walked behind, I now walk forward, with purpose, with grace, and with fire in my soul. **This isn't just a new chapter. It's the story I always meant.**

IS THIS THE END?

Books published by Angela Mae Morrison, AKA Darnell

My Weight Loss Journey Throughout Lockdown 2022

Publisher: Olympia Publisher: London 2022

Coming Out Of A Dark Place;

A true-life story about mental endurance through challenging times.

KDP Publishing 2023.

My Diet Log

A journal about maintaining healthy eating and calorie counting.

(KDP Publishing 2023)

Everyday Poetry

Poems about everyday living

(KDP Publishing 2023)

Sunny and Moonie

A children's book about Sunny and the Moonies' adventures

Educational book about the sun and the moon.

(KDP Publishing 2024)

Sunny and Moonie, Part 2 - *Their adventure continued in outer space and beyond.*

(KDP Publishing 2024)

Sunny and Moonie's colouring book

Mother Hen and her twelve chicks - How Mother Hen protects her chicks from predators.